NEW RIVER BLUES

NEW RIVER BLUES

A Sarah Burke Mystery

Elizabeth Gunn

This first world edition published 2009
in Great Britain and in the USA by
SEVERN HOUSE PUBLISHERS LTD of
9–15 High Street, Sutton, Surrey, England, SM1 1DF.
Trade paperback edition published
in Great Britain and the USA 2009 by
SEVERN HOUSE PUBLISHERS LTD

British Library Cataloguing in Publication Data

Gunn, Elizabeth, 1927-
  New river blues. - (The Sarah Burke series)
  1. Police - Arizona - Tucson - Fiction 2. Women detectives
  - Arizona - Tucson - Fiction 3. Murder - Investigation -
  Fiction 4. Construction industry - Arizona - Fiction
  5. Detective and mystery stories
  I. Title
  813.5'4[F]

  ISBN-13: 978-0-7278-6732-2   (cased)
  ISBN-13: 978-1-84751-115-7   (trade paper)

All Severn House titles are printed on acid-free paper.

Typeset by Palimpsest Book Production Ltd.,
Grangemouth, Stirlingshire, Scotland.
Printed and bound in Great Britain by
MPG Books Ltd., Bodmin, Cornwall.

ACKNOWLEDGEMENTS

I have to thank Sergeant Kevin Hall, who currently heads the hard-working Homicide investigations unit of the Tucson Police Department, for a tour of his section that enabled this story to take shape. John Cheek, of Cops 'n' Writers, patiently guided me away from many errors. Greg Shelko, director of Rio Nuevo, and Nina Trasoff, city council member for Ward Six, both gave generously of their time to help me unravel the mysteries of an urban renewal project. Matthew Lottman, of Ttolmann Construction Company, shared his hard-won insights into the plight of the home construction industry caught in the credit meltdown. And without Mike Hayes, author of the *Mad Dog and Englishman* series and passionate car buff, my antique Jaguar could never have roamed the streets.

ONE

The party was big and very noisy at first, two or three groups that didn't mix very well and laughed at everything so they'd know they were having fun. The neighbors huddled in one room, taking careful sips of tall drinks and comparing insurance plans, while a bigger, louder crowd of theater people milled around them, sharing inside jokes and grabbing refreshments with both hands.

A third group, young, clustered in the dining room drinking long-neck beers and wine coolers out of an ice-tub in the bay window. They all talked at once to a beautiful blonde girl who evidently lived there. When the rooms were full of laughing, swilling people the blonde, at a signal from the hostess, took her place under a chandelier hung with balloons and began to open her birthday presents. She showed each gift around, hugged the donor and declared each item to be something she'd always wanted.

Several older guests offered toasts praising her beauty and wit, and a window-rattling cheer went up from the kids when she blew out eighteen candles. Then the birthday girl and her friends ate a lot of cake very fast, kissed the hostess and went out the door in a babbling rush into a red November sunset.

Once the kids' refreshments were cleared away, the drink trays emptied faster and the party warmed up. A hint of high-grade cannabis began to drift through the elegant rooms. The groups that had clung together since they arrived began to break up and drift too, as if the laws of gravity were being gradually repealed. Intense new friendships formed around a sentence or even a glance.

The hostess kept an eye on her guests, joining the singers around the piano for a chorus, making sure the men talking politics in the study had plenty to drink. The high-energy theater people who were clustered around the crinkly smiling man on the stairway didn't need much looking after – they stayed hilarious on their own.

Pauly had only been working parties for a month but already he was a fair judge of what made one fly. This event had plenty of booze and pot, an unusual mix of people in luxurious surroundings and a voluptuous, beaming hostess in the most beautiful beaded green dress he'd ever seen. He thought it was the best party he'd worked yet, probably good for some decent tips and maybe a couple of hours' overtime.

Felicity had found the job for them. She was a waifish actress, too skinny for his taste before he went to Yuma but plenty hot for the sex-starved ex-con he was now. Not that she'd give him the time of day. She had long auburn hair and big eyes that would probably be lovely when her shiners healed up. Right now she was using a lot of makeup to cover her mysterious eye bruises, which along with her oddly swollen nose made her look like a raccoon that had tangled with a trap.

On stage, she covered up her injuries with even more make-up and cagey acting tricks. Felicity was a pro at the regional theater where many of the people at this party were sponsors and board members. Has-been Hollywood stars or TV actors whose series got cancelled would jet into Tucson to pick up some sunshine and easy applause in old Broadway shows – *Brigadoon*, *The Sound of Music* – and locals, sometimes some of the board members, got their grins taking supporting roles. Felicity and one underfed fag understudied all the parts and covered emergencies. Pauly and Nino, this season's staff, moved props and kept the theater clean.

From the theater they had followed Felicity's lead into this part-time job with the catering company that booked parties out of the Spotted Pony, the actors' favorite bar. Not a great job but it beat Dumpster diving and sleeping under bridges, which was what they'd been down to for a while after they got to town.

Pauly and Nino had drifted together in the yard at Yuma during 'exercise,' the time when they stood in corners smoking, saying fuck this and fuck that, bunched for safety with Petey and a couple of other short-timers. Bored dropouts from high schools in small Arizona towns, they'd all made their grab for easy money in the drug trade and been busted almost at once by lawmen who treated them like pathetic jokes. Seething with a toxic mix of resentment and fear after prison had shown them they were not as tough as they thought, they cursed 'the system,' worked half-heartedly on GEDs, and tried to stay out of fights and love affairs while they ran out the clock on their sentences.

Then Petey got jumped in the laundry one day, went in the infirmary and didn't come out. In the yard that afternoon Pauly kicked the wall. 'Fucking guards don't do nothing but supervise the killing, what the fuck?'

Nino pushed him into a corner and stood in front of him muttering, 'Shut *up*,' because one of the yard pigs was looking. When Pauly calmed down he admitted Nino had saved his ass, and before lights out he'd agreed that job one, from now on, was staying alive till tomorrow.

It wasn't much of a plan but it became one. They watched each other's back, thought ahead a little for the first time in their lives. And they began to talk every day about what they wanted to do when they got out.

Most of Pauly's ideas centered on food and sex. Before his arrest he had accepted his limited success with Benson girls because he had nothing to offer but himself and there were plenty of unemployed no-talent yo-yos around. But cut off from society as he was now, he began to fantasize about bedding girls of all shapes and sizes. He wanted to try sex with several girls at once, he told Nino, and then find one slavish female who would cook great meals and put out whenever he wanted it. He masturbated endlessly to one particularly vivid dream of mounting her as she bent to look in the oven.

Nino could read without moving his lips and was open to dreams of the wider world. 'I'm ashamed,' he said one day, 'that I settled for such stupid little crap when there's so much on the outside to choose from.' He had been studying the pictures in dog-eared copies of *Playboy* and *Hustler* the staff left around. He pointed to ads for big cars, good clothes, and glossy living rooms, saying, 'See? *This* is what we should be aiming for.'

'Oh, sure,' Pauly said. 'Just snap my fingers, I can have that stuff anytime.'

'You can if you get in with the right people,' Nino said.

He tilted his head to one side and studied Pauly. 'You know, you'd clean up pretty nice. You oughta think about that.'

'Hell you talking about? I ain't no whore.'

'Didn't say you was. Were. But you want to move up, you gotta consider how to get people to like you. You're a good-looking guy. Learn how to dress and talk, it could change your life.' Pauly stood with his mouth open, not knowing how to respond to the unexpected compliment, till Nino came up on his blind side with, 'Think about it hard enough, you could probably even get yourself to quit saying ain't.'

Pauly said, 'Aw, shee-it,' and turned his back. But he didn't stay mad, he never stayed mad at Nino because Nino was all he had in here and a better friend, come right down to it, than any he'd ever made on the outside. Pauly had seen movies where men at war formed a kind of brotherhood, and he thought that was how it was working for him and Nino in prison.

For the rest of their time in Yuma they talked about how they would 'make it' on the outside. Pauly had always been near flunking out of school and had terrible handwriting, but he was big and strong and as Nino said he cleaned up well. Nino was a skinny little runt but he was canny. If they stuck together, they decided, they could work something out.

'Oh, I got it now,' Nino said one day, grinning in the yard. 'What we need to do, we need to *augment our skill sets.*'

Pauly said, 'Say wha'?'

'Just learned that this morning from that fat counselor with the nose ring.' He crooked his pinkie. 'Ain't it just too, too dee-vine?' Nino was so pleased with himself he forgot about not saying ain't.

They progressed like that, two steps forward and one back, while the relentless sun rolled east to west over their sandy patch of prison yard. Nino turned into a regular suck-up with the counselors as parole time approached, trying to ensure they got everything they were entitled to when they got released. Which wasn't much – a pair of jeans and a gray T-shirt apiece, and a couple of maps Nino begged off one of the guards. Pauly reclaimed his driver's license, his social security card, and the little earring with the dangle he had been afraid to wear in there.

The last thing he put on was his grandfather's turquoise ring. It had one stone missing, but his mother had given it to him for his thirteenth birthday, saying he could get a ruby put in when his ship came in. He'd kept it because it made him feel like he had a goal.

Between the two of them they'd saved just about enough for bus tickets home – the last place, they agreed, that either one of them wanted to go. They pooled their money and bought tickets to Tucson.

The question of skill sets came up again as the bus lumbered past the saguaros on the east side of Yuma. Pauly had grudgingly done a little haying and fence-building for his stepfather, on a ranch south of Benson, before he dropped out of school and ran away. He had just enough ranching experience to know it wasn't for him, and the old man must have agreed because he never came looking for him. He'd washed dishes in a café in town for a few weeks, until he made new friends and learned how to buy and process crack cocaine. He wasn't tempted to try being a drug lord in Benson again, but he thought he might give food service another shot.

In Tucson, they talked to a guy hawking newspapers at a stoplight, found a homeless shelter, got a meal and a free shower. They split up the next morning to look for openings for ex-felons.

Most people didn't want them around at all, Pauly quickly learned, but he used his mother's way of saying 'yes, ma'am,' and 'please,' to persuade an assistant manager at a fast-food stand to give him a trial. Passing out curly fries and Cokes was no fun, but he needed the food and the little bit of money that came with the stupid shirt and hat.

He was able to smuggle out burgers and slaw enough to keep Nino alive, too. Nino didn't get a job right away because, he told Pauly, he was cruising, looking for an edge.

In Yuma, Nino had seemed like the natural leader of the two, but on the outside Pauly began to see that Nino had something in his face, a sneaky, feral look around the mouth and eyes, that put people off. Small-business types looking to hire hamburger flippers or help with yard work looked into Nino's face and said they'd just filled their last opening.

Pauly, on the other hand, given a fresh shave and a clean shirt, projected the kind of clueless muscle that could get him a dead-end job anywhere in half an hour.

Pauly didn't mind being the worker bee, supporting them both for a while. It pleased him that Nino needed him for a change – friendship should be a two-way street, he thought. And when they met after work Nino brought back good stories, never two days the same. He was drawn to fast-talking, tricky types like himself who were always on the prowl, looking for an angle. Sometimes Pauly wondered why they got along so well – everybody else Nino hooked up with seemed to be looking for a soft spot. Or was already in one, like the crinkly smiling man at this party, sitting on the stairs surrounded by young dancers and actors.

Madge, they all called him – Madge baby. He seemed to be kind of a groupie at the theater, had cute nicknames for all the actors. He never acted or directed but he knew all the plays, had wise humorous things to say when people blew their lines or lashed out about not getting a part they wanted. Madge was a patron, Felicity said. He helped people out in small ways, gave lifts around town, and was a big hugger.

Nino and Madge told varying humorous stories about how they met. 'I spotted him copping a feel in the Spotted Pony,' Nino usually said, 'and I knew right away he was my kind of a guy.' Or Madge would say, 'All the waitresses assured me he was not to be trusted, so I asked them to introduce us.'

Pauly couldn't tell if they were a little more than friends. He knew Nino would swing either way – whatever floated the boat was Nino's motto – but he couldn't tell for sure if Madge was a fag. The girl's name seemed to suit him, but he made a big fuss over women, too, usually had his arms around a girl or two.

For whatever reason, he got Nino and Pauly these half-assed jobs as prop guys at the theater, with a room above the stage as part of the deal. Then he and Felicity recommended them to this caterer for part-time jobs, because the theater paid so little, and to get them started Felicity found black pants and white shirts at Good Will. It was all done with a lot of pats and hugs, which Nino said probably wouldn't do any permanent damage if they didn't inhale.

The bossy caterer named Zack let them into the pantry, prep room, whatever these rich people called the great clean space with all the cupboards and coolers behind their shiny kitchen crowded with killer appliances. Leading them under steel overhead racks where shining pots and spoons hung down like icicles, Zack said, 'Your jackets are here, these aprons fasten in back, remember? Why are you standing there, you *have* worked parties for me before, right?'

Nino gave him the ice-cold look out of his colorless eyes and said, 'Sure, Zack,' and you could see Zack go, *Whoa, are you going to give me trouble?* But guests were already arriving in the room on the other side of the kitchen, squealing and doing kissy-kissy with the hostess, so Zack had to launch right into his tray lecture. Pour the wine *this* full in *these* glasses, remember, a dozen only on *this* size tray. And the canapés go on *these* trays with clean doilies *every single* time . . . after that it was just a blur, for hours. A big party, rooms full of people, Zack humping to keep up in the prep room while Pauly, Nino, and Felicity hustled the food and drink out front. Felicity smiled and fawned on the board members who called out to her, 'There's our girl, how's my baby?', the men starting to paw her after a couple of drinks. Felicity whirled around them smiling, making little jokes, doing her cute little winks.

They hauled in platters and baskets of savory, high-cost food and no end of wine and vodka, just keep it coming, nobody keeping track. As soon as they got used to the routine, Nino devised a signal system so they could take turns ducking into the help's bathroom to sample the goodies. They ate their fill of big shrimp, marinated mushrooms, tiny egg rolls with a wonderful sauce. Felicity taught Pauly how to say pâté. He spread that and several cheeses on wonderful buttery crackers, and washed it down with plenty of wine. Before long, Pauly figured, he probably felt as good as any of the guests.

About ten o'clock the party started to wind down. Women began to look for purses, men jingled car keys, a madly giggling group of actors surrounded the sparkly hostess and sang a hilariously obscene ballad of thanks.

By eleven, the front of the house was empty and the hostess

was in the prep room saying, 'Marvelous party, Zack, everybody had fun. Let's have a glass of wine while we clean
up!' Pouring for everybody, turning her gleaming cheeks up
to be kissed by Madge who of course was the last one there.
He wrapped his arms around her, telling her she was still
the best party-giver in Pima County.

She put a big white apron over her satiny-slidy dress and
made little gestures, picked up a few glasses, and poured
some nuts back in a can. Zack and Felicity kept saying, 'No,
no, don't get your dress dirty, we'll handle that.' But Pauly
could see she liked being part of the crew, she wanted to
stay here and share funny anecdotes about the party. Maybe
she didn't want to be alone. Pauly began to wonder if there
wasn't something sad, a touch of uncertainty behind her
gleaming smile.

Madge found some dance music for the CD player and
danced with her, chuckling, then whirled her back to the
wine bottles when she said she needed another sip. He danced
away with Felicity, who moved like a ballet dancer and made
any partner look like Fred Astaire.

The hostess – Easy, was that what they called her? Or
Weezy? – he couldn't tell, if he had to call her anything he'd
call her ma'am. She poured another big glass of wine for
herself and one for Pauly, drank half of hers, treated him to
one of those blissed-out smiles he'd been watching all evening
and held out her arms saying, 'OK, let's dance.' Pauly wasn't
much of a dancer but what were you supposed to do? He
stepped into her arms, moving cautiously at first, hoping his
hand wasn't leaving a mark on the dress. The flesh of her
round arms smelled like flowers, though, and she was
enjoying herself, humming with the music, so he began to
relax. Her hips swayed under his hand and he moved closer.

Madge and Felicity pulled Nino and Zack out to dance,
laughing, Madge whirling Nino around like a debutante.
They danced close to Pauly and his luscious green armful,
Madge looking a question at Weezy but she shook her head.
When the music stopped, the hostess stood beside Pauly at
the counter drinking wine. 'Mmm,' she said, smiling, 'good.'
When the music started again they moved into each other's
arms without a word.

He would never know how the rest of it happened. The lights dimmed gradually, as if by magic. The saxophones seemed to grow creamier as the laughter of the other dancers softened. Somebody passed around a J and after that for Pauly it was all vague and beautiful, there was only the music and the silky slide of her body in his arms.

At the end of one long song he realized the other four people had disappeared, and a bit later he found himself halfway up the stairs kissing his green-clad hostess, who groped him and groaned with pleasure.

In a bedroom that looked better than any dream he'd ever had, this woman who seemed to know no limits wound her arms around his neck and whispered, 'Sweetie, you need some more wine?' Her jeweled hands caressed his back and sides and found his crotch. 'No, I guess not,' she chuckled, and the shiny green dress slid off like magic as they sank on to her silky sheets.

The first time he came in her he was sure he was going to die of pleasure. But he didn't, and she knew exactly how to help him risk his life again.

The second time took longer but finally came to a great shuddering climax that left them both very tired. They lay curled together afterwards, making soft sounds that didn't quite reach the level of speech. Not really intending to but helpless to stop, they fell asleep.

Adrift in dreamless satisfaction, Pauly slept without moving until the lights went on and the world exploded.

TWO

I n Tucson, darkness is more than just the absence of light. It's a highly prized commodity that enjoys environmental protection. Famous observatories cap the mountains around the city, and the discoveries of the world-class astronomers who flock to them add luster to the city's reputation and grants to its university. In pursuit of these benefits the city minimizes street lights, hoods the illumination it can't do without, and supports a Dark Sky Association whose function is to remind suburban dwellers that clear desert air, unsullied by artificial light, has a fat bottom line.

So at 4 a.m. in mid-November, most of El Encanto Estates was black as the inside of a boot. Sarah Burke found the house on Avenida Santa Teresa easily, by heading toward the light pouring out of all its windows.

Big floods were already set up in the yard, too. Yellow crime-scene tape was stretched across the driveway, enclosing a swarm of busy men. Take away a few blue uniforms, Sarah thought, this scene could remind you of an ant farm. She parked her department Impala behind the crime-scene van at the curb. Neat in business casual, she strode at the steady don't-mess-with-me pace of the street cop toward the uniformed officer behind the tape.

I know him, what's his name? They'd worked street patrol in adjacent sections of south Tucson when they were both rookie cops, and backed each other up through many a long night. *Name, name.* Had a wife who sold real estate, twin boys . . . then she got it, Lopez, and stepped up to the tape, smiling. 'Morning, Frankie. How're those twins?'

'Hey, Sarah. They're wrecking my house, you want a couple boys?' He opened his metal posse box and asked her, 'What's your PR?'

She gave him her five-digit payroll number. He wrote it on his sheet after her name, and entered the time, saying, 'You must have really burned rubber, you're the first detective here.'

'I live in Campbell-Grant,' she said, 'just a few blocks north of here.' *A few blocks north in a different world.* She liked her quiet midtown neighborhood, and didn't lust after million-plus mansions like this one. *But maybe just a few square feet of all this space . . .* Her family circle had recently expanded to include a ten-year-old niece and a frequently visiting boyfriend. They were all doing careful minuets around times in the bathroom and her two decent reading lights.

The Field Sergeant was already there, deploying patrolmen at the front and back doors of the house and around the yard. This was going to be an expensive crime scene to secure; there was much more property in back. Directly in front of her, a beautifully tiled fountain stood quiet on its night-time setting. Behind it, the house sat well back on perfectly manicured grounds, a classic Spanish Colonial two-story, buff-colored stucco, red roof tiles and wrought-iron balcony railings. Solid and spacious, it looked like an implicit promise of the good life. But if Delaney's first report was accurate, there would be no contentment at this address any time soon.

She pulled her phone off her belt, remembering the last thing he'd said: 'You'll probably get there first, so go ahead and get the warrant, will you?' *Miserable time to call a judge, but what can you do?*

Judge Peter Geisler answered on the first ring. At sixty-four, he had come to regard his worsening sleep dysfunction as a chance to catch up on his reading. He was halfway through the latest dismal book about Iraq, he said, and was not sorry to be interrupted. She told him she was investigating the double murder of a couple in their own bed and he said that sounded pretty mild compared to what our government was up to in foreign lands. She waited patiently while he ranted about the intellectual disconnect of people in high places.

As soon as he paused for breath she described the house, grounds, garages, and several vehicles that would need to be searched. He endorsed her choices and authorized his signature. Sarah got on well with Judge Geisler, who had a good memory for which detectives turned in complete paperwork.

Delaney was parking behind her car by the time she folded the phone. As she walked over to meet him, she saw Tobin coming half a block away, Menendez just rounding the corner. Delaney, who because he was grossly overworked always felt he was running late, jumped out of his car saying, 'Morning, Sarah,' and walked right past her to begin questioning the officer behind the tape. 'Frankie, you the first responder?'

Lopez nodded. 'Yeah, I just happened to be turning on to Broadway when I heard the tone.' He swallowed when he said, 'tone,' a delayed reaction to the jolt of adrenalin he'd received when the heads-up signal sounded in all the cars. 'Dispatch said three 911 calls in a row from people in this block, saying they heard gunshots and screaming and a lot of dogs barking. Soon as Dispatch said this address I said, "I'm six blocks from there, I'll take it," and then Tommy come on and said he was right behind me.'

'Gil Tompkins? He's your backup?'

'Yeah. He's around there in back somewhere. This is one big mother of a place.'

'For sure. Three 911 calls, that's what they got?'

'Right. Kind of surprising when you see how far apart the houses are here. But the weather's so perfect right now, I guess a lot of people are sleeping with their windows open. The neighbor in that house over there –' he pointed across the street – 'said he was awake when it started so he was pretty positive about what he heard – two gunshots and two screams, coming from this house. Dogs were still barking when I got here, they sounded really freaked. So I got Dispatch to call the house, stood out here and listened to it ring. Nobody answered, but I said, "That's funny though, I can see from here there's a couple of lights on, sure looks like somebody's home." So they sent the night detectives.'

'OK. They still here?'

'Uh . . . just handed it off, I think. No, wait, that's them talking to the Field Sergeant, over there by the front door.'

'Oh, it's Dietz's crew tonight, huh?' Delaney slid a quick glance at Sarah. 'He's doing all right, isn't he?'

'Yes.' Fighting a deep desire to run over and grab him, she stood still and kept her expression bland. Dietz was her new steady. Probably. If she could get herself to believe in this much luck and not do something stupid to wreck it. He had just gone back on full time after a long recovery from a near-fatal shooting, and had taken a night shift gladly in order to get command of a crew again. They were at pains to stay reserved when their paths crossed at work, to show everybody their romance was no distraction.

'OK,' Delaney said, starting toward him. 'Leo, you'll take the scene, OK?'

'You got it,' Tobin said. He pulled his long notebook out of the back of his pants and pulled the fat ballpoint he favored off his pocket protector. All his work utensils showed the wear and patina of long use. He called himself 'the old dog,' and hated change. Ollie Greenaway, smiling and chipper as if it was noon, caught up with them as they walked over, and Menendez was right behind him. So Delaney had an almost full crew by the time he greeted Dietz and the Field Sergeant.

'Well, if you're here already,' Dietz told Delaney, 'I might as well just pass off to you—' The Field Sergeant nodded and took a step back, and Dietz started downloading information at once. Her boyfriend got along very well with Delaney on the job, Sarah noticed with pleasure. Two driven workaholics with hardly a word of small talk between them, why not?

He described the scene he'd found an hour and a half ago, two patrolmen in the yard trying to decide if the neighbors' reports of gunshots and screaming, and the frantic barking of several dogs, constituted enough probable cause to enter a house without a warrant. 'But by that time the neighbors were getting almost as noisy as the dogs. They'd all called each other about the shots and they were all scared. People kept sticking their heads out of doors saying, "Do something!" So I talked to the duty sergeant one more time and we decided to go in.' He made a wry face. 'Deciding was the hard part, going in was no problem. Whole house was unlocked, can you believe it? Back door too.'

They made a standard entry, taking turns covering for each

other, turning on lights and clearing rooms as they came to them. 'The house was fairly clean and neat except some clutter on the stairs and a couple of rugs needed vacuuming. Looked like a big party had been mostly cleaned up. But nothing broken, no signs of a fight. We smelled gunpowder upstairs though, as we went along the hall toward the master bedroom, so we were pretty sure we had a shooting. What we found, though . . . it's quite extreme.'

'What, trashed?'

'No, most of the room is neat like the rest of the second floor. Clothes strewn around the bed is all. But – there's a man and a woman, both naked, close together in this great big king-size bed, both shot at close range. I'm guessing a twelve-gauge shotgun – their faces are damn near blown away. Nothing else touched, looks like.'

'You're saying not a home invasion?'

'Doesn't look like it – no drawers emptied, pictures up on the walls where they belong, nothing tossed. Of course that's cursory, but – just the two bodies in the bed, and a helluva mess of blood and tissue around it. You're going to be working physical evidence for a while. No weapon in sight, though, no ammo we could see.'

'OK,' Delaney said, 'anything else?' He meant out of the ordinary. Delaney and most of his crew had worked night-detectives' shifts at one time or another and knew what they would have done – backed out of the room without touching anything, gone back downstairs, called Dispatch, and said something like, 'We got an 0101 here, two victims, need a U unit and detectives—'

'Time I'd called downtown' – Dietz's face took on a humorous expression that was not quite a smile – 'there were two other cars here, Nye and Bailey near the end of their shifts and looking to blow off an hour. Boy, are they sorry they got curious. Dispatch said keep 'em there, the Field Sergeant's on his way.'

'And now that you're here,' the Field Sergeant said, 'I'll be on my way again. You got four men guarding the perimeter and two in the house, front and back doors. Replacements on the way soon as the shift changes.'

'We'll get out of your way too,' Dietz said, 'we got another scene waiting on us. Oh, there's two crime-scene specialists already up there, working away. Plenty for 'em to do.' He rolled his eyes up.

'You get the name of the neighbors that called it in?'

'Lopez has all that, I told him hang on to it for you.'

'Sarah,' Delaney said, 'would you . . . ?'

Sarah walked back around the fountain to where Lopez still guarded his tape. Dietz, walking past her with his crew, tweaked her elbow and she flashed him a quick, secret smile. He and his night detectives ducked under the tape and piled into their vehicles, their lights raking across the yard as they hurried away toward the next crime scene.

'The first caller was Ortman,' Frankie Lopez said. 'Michael Ortman, lives in that one-story Santa Fe across the street there. He was the only one brave enough to come out in his yard to talk to me.' His quick smile gleamed in the dancing shadows. 'Ortman seems to be kind of the Big Daddy of this block. Everybody kept calling him to find out what was going on. He said, "They all want me to tell them the gunslingers are gone, how am I supposed to know that?" Here's your list.' He tore it off the bottom of a sheet. 'They're all waiting to talk to you, said don't worry, they won't go back to sleep.' His dark eyes roamed ironically over the hand-painted tiles and beautiful wrought iron of the neighborhood. 'They probably don't hear many gunshots in this part of town.' Lopez, Sarah remembered, lived in the livelier streets on the south end, and thought people who lived north of the highway were out of touch with the real Tucson.

Sarah took the sheet of paper and walked back to the bunched knot of detectives – Jason Peete had arrived, adding a dash of street funk to the crew. He had recently shaved off the dreadlocks he'd taken a year to perfect, and now inclined a bald, gleaming dark brown dome toward Menendez. His bold, mocking eyes darted around the yard as he downloaded Ray's information.

Delaney looked up from a clipboard, shrugged and said, 'Well, everybody's here but Cifuentes, hmm? I had him on my list for case detective on this one, but . . . ah, well, let's go up.'

They all put on booties and followed him silently up the

middle of the stairway, careful not to touch anything, pulling on gloves. The deeply carpeted hall was lined with family pictures, identically framed and hung in groups of eight or ten. They featured two tow-haired children who began as toddlers at the top of the stairs and progressed through birthdays, sports and school graduations, often with parents beaming behind them, becoming young adults near the open door at the end.

Inside the room, one crime-scene specialist was taking pictures of the bed and its surroundings while another dusted the furniture and woodwork with black powder. The smell was not bad yet, Sarah thought, and took a deep breath to get adjusted to it early. She hated wearing a mask and would not use Vaporub if she could get along without it. A homicide investigator, she believed, needed all five senses working. After one glance at the horror on the bed, she forced her eyes to go on scanning the room, to set the scene in her mind.

Half my house would fit in this room. It was professionally decorated in soft shades of mauve, gray, and rose, luxuriously comfortable but without ostentation. There was a velvet chaise by a long window, slipper chairs on either side of a low table. A wall of closets was bisected by an open arch leading into a double dressing room with a bath beyond. Everything said, *Stay here and rest.*

But the two people on the bed had not come in here looking for rest, Sarah thought. They were naked and uncovered, the bedspread lay tangled at the foot of the bed. The bodies were close together, their legs intertwined, both on the side of the bed nearest the door. There was plenty of space left on the far side of the king-size bed.

The woman was farthest from the door, turned slightly toward it with her legs curled up a little. Her position would have suggested natural sleep, except that her face was mostly gone. The blood and tissue that had splattered in an elongated oval around what remained of her head made it clear she'd been shot by a very powerful weapon. *I agree with Dietz's guess about the twelve-gauge.* Not that they needed to guess. Identification of weapons and ammo would be up to the lab crew. Her job was to notice, as she did now, that the distribution of pellets and tissue around the woman looked as if she'd been shot from this side of the bed, a couple of steps inside the door. *Not far from where I'm standing.* She scanned the lush carpet, looking for scuff marks or stains to mark the spot. Nothing. *We'll figure it out, though.*

The man's torso was sprawled alongside the woman, face up except that he, too, had hardly any face left. His left leg dangled over the side of the bed, the right lay parallel to the woman, and his hands lay sedately by his sides. *But he must have sat up just before . . .* The overspray of shot that had missed him had left an eerie outline of his head and torso on the headboard and the wall behind it.

Delaney was already talking to the backs of the two crime-scene specialists, who went right on working. The photographer was a new criminologist Sarah had never seen before. Delaney called him, 'Roy,' and told him he wanted pictures of the entire scene from every angle, close-ups and panoramic shots of the whole scene. 'Close-ups of the spatter on the walls, individually.'

Roy answered him in muttered monosyllables, 'Uh-huh, OK, sure,' and went right on shooting.

'The light keeps changing in here,' Roy complained. 'I've got to use flash but I'm worried about glare on the close-ups, I don't know. . . .'

'Just take your time and do the best you can,' Delaney said, trying to be supportive but clearly frustrated about the long wait facing his crew before they could start. He turned to Gloria Jackson, the other crime-scene specialist, and asked, 'How much longer you think you'll be?'

'Better tell the rest of the bad guys in this town to take the day off,' Gloria said, gently spreading black powder over a sill. 'We got all we can do here for quite some time.' Six feet tall, an ex-jock proud of her athlete's body and flaunting glowing copper hair dyed to match her skin, Gloria was usually the antic presence at a crime scene who kept the jokes going. Today's level of violence seemed to have damaged her sense of humor a little.

'Uh-huh.' Delaney was chewing gum and blinking, his default response to heavy thinking. 'OK, let's all –' he turned with his arms spread and herded his crew back out into the hall – 'step back here and talk about what we *can* do.' He had his notebook out, starting a list. 'I'm going to call the ME right now and then the transport vehicle. We need to get the scene sketched and measured before they get here, so Leo, will you go back in there and get started on that? Ollie, you can help him out with measurements, huh? You got a sketch pad, got your tape?' Delaney, who always carried backups for his backups, rummaged in his briefcase till he got them going. 'OK, now . . . I'm gonna have Cifuentes take the lead on this one, if he ever gets here, but Ray?'

The whites of Menendez' dark eyes gleamed in the dim hall when he turned toward his boss. He beamed his abundant cheerfulness at Delaney and said, 'Present!'

'I want you to take the post, because Cifuentes is going to have a lot of other information to correlate. Chances are the doc won't get to it till tomorrow, though, so right now, you and Sarah take that list and start interviewing the neighbors, chop chop, get their first impressions and bring them back here.' He turned away, back toward the bedroom, already speed-dialing his phone.

'Let's go down to that little anteroom at the bottom of the stairs,' Sarah said, 'and find some quiet while we divide up this list.' When she was new in Homicide, trying to learn names fast, Sarah had memorized Raimundo Menendez by dubbing him, in her mind, 'Rye Moon Dough.' It stuck in her mind because it was vaguely noir and suited his beautiful eyes and hair, so reminiscent of old-time Hollywood's Latin lovers. Now she knew him as a good-natured team player, and had forgotten how he looked.

Walking along the hall she noticed something, a glint on the pale rose carpet and then another just beyond. 'What's this, though?' She bent over it, squinting – a hard candy wrapped in bright yellow cellophane. The next glint was an identical candy in hot pink cellophane. 'Funny.' She looked beyond and found a blue one.

'More on the stairs,' Menendez said. 'I'll get Roy.' The photographer planted numbered tags as they went down the broad staircase and along the hall like children on an Easter-egg hunt – seven candies by the time they reached the front step.

'And a pile over by the fountain, look,' Sarah said. 'Oh, and I bet that's the dish they belong in. Isn't that odd?'

'Is it? I don't know much about candy dishes.' Menendez bent over it, a blown-glass bonbon dish with a fluted edge and a handle pulled up out of the middle, all fashioned in one fiery shaping by a skillful hand.

'I don't mean the dish, I mean the candy. A shooter with a sweet tooth?'

'It is a little different,' Menendez said, 'but hey, this is police work.' They followed Roy as he went back and took the pictures, then bagged the bowl and candy and went down to the little room off the foyer to write evidence tags.

They were standing at the little table under the ceiling light, Menendez writing a tag for the candy and Sarah squinting at Lopez' notes about witnesses, when an argument erupted in the hall above them. It cut through the bustle in the house, a young voice, female, talking loud as she thumped along the hall. Aroused but not frightened, she was angrily challenging the male voice telling her she was not allowed in the house.

'Allowed my ass,' the voice insisted, 'I live here! Mother, where are you?'

Ray and Sarah looked at each other, dropped what they were holding, and ran to help.

The commotion reached the far end of the hall as they got to the top of the stairs. A girl shouted again, 'Mother?' and an officer's voice insisted she must not go any further. At the door to the master bedroom she called once more, 'Mo—' and then her voice was quenched like a doused candle as she saw the horror on the bed. She stood transfixed, her back rigid, for two electric seconds before she began to scream.

Delaney was breaking off his phone call, walking toward the door shaking his head, saying, 'I told you not to let anybody—' and the officer behind her, Quarles, fresh on duty for what now promised to be a terrible day, protesting, 'She got in the house somehow, what do you want me to do, shoot her?'

Sarah ran past Quarles and wrapped her arms around the caterwauling girl. The ranch skills of her upbringing came back to her in response to the quivering body hot against her chest. Instinctively, she talked soft nonsense while she patted and stroked, soothing with hands and voice as she would any frightened animal.

'Sshh, sshh, sshh, OK now, over here, that's right, just come with me.' She eased the hysterical girl away from the horror on the bed, walked her back into the hall. Menendez was there, ready to help, looking a question. Sarah met his eyes and pointed one finger. He leaned and opened a door to one of the other bedrooms in the hall, then came and wrapped his bulk around Sarah and the still-screaming girl. Together they eased her into the clean, quiet room and closed the door.

The next half-hour was very hard work – 'One of those times we earn our pay,' Menendez said later. They didn't know her name or anything about her beyond the fact that she seemed to be a daughter who belonged there. Her hysteria lapsed into hiccoughing sobs that transitioned into nausea. Holding her shoulders over the toilet, Sarah muttered, 'Victim's Services,' and Menendez stepped into the hall to call them. As soon as she stopped retching the girl reached some new level of rage and turned it on Sarah, hitting and kicking. Sarah yelled for help. Menendez and Quarles were in the room with them in seconds, wrapping the screaming girl in a sheet. Even so Sarah got a bloody nose and a torn shirt.

When the girl calmed down enough to ask them to take off the restraints, Sarah asked her name. That seemed to shock her again. She must have lived a life in which everybody around her knew who she was. Suddenly apologetic, she pulled a wallet out of the pocket of her shorts and showed them a driver's license made out to Patricia Henderson.

'We've got the whole place staked out,' Quarles said. 'How'd you get in here?'

'Same way I always do, through the hedge and in the side door to the kitchen.' She was a student at the university, she said, she had an eight o'clock class. 'But yesterday was my birthday, I was at a sleepover with my buds.' She'd come home early to shower and change, 'and to ask Mom if I could have . . . ' Then the realization hit her that there was now no one to ask, and she gave way to a fresh burst of weeping. All the fight went out of her, she was going limp even before Victim's Services got there with offers of a quiet place to rest, a counselor to talk to, a mild tranquilizer.

She almost took the whole package. Sarah saw her actually lean toward the pill, longing for some relief from this horror. But at the last second she roused her powerful personality and said, 'No, wait!' Her clear blue eyes met Sarah's, suddenly wide open with a wild hope. 'You're not sure — are you? They might not be . . .' She was standing in an instant, vibrating with energy.

'Patricia,' Sarah said, 'I can't let you go back in that room. We'll have them identified, probably in hours. Certainly by tomorrow.'

'Listen . . . cop lady—'

Sarah pointed to her badge. 'Detective.' But the girl was so young, and that was probably her mother on the bed. 'Sarah.'

'Sarah, if it was your parents would you be willing to wait?'

'No. But see,' Sarah kept her voice calm, 'there's a protocol at crime scenes, we always do the—'

'*Protocol?*' She was going up in smoke again, her voice like brazen trumpets. 'My parents' bedroom is full of dead people and I'm supposed to care about fucking protocol? For Jesus Christ's sake, what kind of a—'

'Hold on, hold on, calm *down* now.' Sarah began stroking and soothing again. 'Just *wait* a minute and I'll see what I can do.' The woman from Victim's Services was shaking her head.

Delaney shook his harder. 'She should never have gotten up here,' he said. 'What are you thinking? We can't have this crime scene mucked up any more than it already is.'

Sarah said, 'Boss, however she got in, she's here now and she needs to know.' He put on his stubborn face, shook his head some more, till Sarah repeated Patricia Henderson's question, 'If it was your parents, would you want to wait?'

'Oh, hell,' Delaney said, 'no, of course not. OK, make it quick, the ME's on his way.'

Sarah found a clean sheet and got Gloria to help her lay it gently over the ruined faces. A daughter would be able to identify chest and arms, surely. They pulled up a sheet to cover the victims' lower nakedness.

Even so she began to doubt herself when it was time to bring the girl in. 'You have to promise not to touch anything and you can stop any time,' she said at the door. 'And listen, if you start screaming again the sergeant will throw us both out.' Delaney stood in the middle of the room with his face like a rock.

But Patricia had herself firmly in hand now. She didn't falter till she got near the bed. Then she focused on her mother's hands and reached out toward them involuntarily, making little mewling sounds. 'Oh, Mummer, look at that, my sweet Mummerdummer, oh no no no—'

Sarah held her on one side, Menendez on the other. Sarah said softly, 'Patricia. You're sure?'

'Of course I'm sure.' She turned impatiently and a few tears flew off her face on to Sarah's, warm little drops that felt shockingly intimate. 'Those are her rings, the way she always wears them, see? All the diamonds on her left hand, the pearl cluster on the right index finger and the emerald on the pinkie . . . and her third finger's crooked, see? She's always had those little freckles on the tops of her arms, doesn't she have pretty arms? Oh my sweet crazy Mother,' she was sobbing again, 'you silly nut, what kind of a mess did you get yourself into this time?'

She wiped tears off her face, sniffling, struggling for self-control. Her voice breaking, she told Sarah, 'She doesn't have a mean bone in her body, you know that? I mean I know she's a space case and lately she's been going looney-tunes over men and parties and so on, but even so . . . who would do a terrible thing like this to a sweet person like my mother?'

Delaney was across the room, shuffling his feet in the carpet, wanting the girl gone. Sarah thought basic decency required letting her have a couple of minutes to grieve. But she was anxiously aware, too, of all the work waiting, the ME probably unloading at the curb right now. So she braced herself to move the girl to the other side of the bed, hoping the lamentations for her father would be shorter.

But Patricia Henderson gave one long, shuddering sigh,

wiped her face again and glanced briefly at the body lying next to her mother. She sniffled indifferently and said, 'Well, and I guess this must be the Flavor of the Week over here, huh? Who is he, do you know?'

Sarah saw Delaney quit punishing the rug and lean forward a little, listening.

'Patricia,' she said, 'this man is not your father?'

'My *fa*-ther?' Patricia hissed softly through her front teeth, a sound somewhere between contempt and amusement. 'This little dweeb with no hair on his arms? Not hardly.' She blew her nose, found a fresh tissue in her pocket, and wiped her face. 'Look, he's wearing a ring with the set missing, how dumb is that?' Her voice was beginning to sound almost like the strong, confident scrapper who'd come raging up the stairs. 'My father . . .' Her voice trailed off into a little choke. She swallowed and came back with an entirely different voice, full of irony and stifled rage. 'My father, if and when he condescends to come home, will be the big guy with arms like a gorilla, and hands . . . ' Her voice changed again, a note of pride mixed in with the anger. 'He's got one short finger that he cut off years ago in a bandsaw. He bandaged it up and went right back to work.' She reached out longingly toward the woman on the bed but dropped her hands before they touched anything. 'Now I've told you my Mom's favorite story about him.'

THREE

Southbound on I-10 at sunrise, Roger Henderson gripped the wheel and got ready to change lanes. Then traffic closed in ahead of him and he saw he had no choice but to stay with the flow in the packed lanes under the 202 Interchange south of Phoenix. *Damn, you can't get up early enough to beat rush hour on this road anymore.*

Even as he groused to himself he knew he was blowing a little smoke, to cover the guilt he felt over the whole weekend. He felt wretched about missing yesterday's party at home, and about the too-late phone call that didn't appease his wife. But he couldn't explain – there would be bloody hell if Eloise ever learned the truth about where he'd been.

And now he'd even have to calm down his secretary, who by the time he reached his office would be jumpy from fielding a dozen irritable queries about where her boss was. He dreaded the half-truths he'd have to try to keep track of all morning – damn! Tell one necessary lie and all the truth around it begins to sound fishy.

To take his mind off the demeaning need to make excuses, he rehearsed today's first phone calls. Get Ruth to move the Dahlberg meeting to the afternoon. Ask her to find Dan, remind him the big earth-mover had to be at Quail Run by eleven. Call the railroad to find out what in hell had happened to the last shipment of rebar – shunted off on some siding in New Mexico, probably, but whose computer keystroke was going to locate it?

Call Jennings at the bank, nail down the extension on the Hen-Trax line of credit that he'd seemed so tentative about last Thursday. Maybe call the Rio Nuevo office first, find out if there was any movement at all on Gray Hawk Terrace. His bankers had quit laughing, some months back, at jokes about how long it took to move urban-renewal projects out of committee. The subprime-mortgage crisis had virtually stalled his home-construction projects, so they wanted to see some other revenue streams flowing. Well, who didn't? Damn! They had loved his rapidly growing cash flow during the great years just past. Now they wanted to take a pass on the lean years that always follow booms, but he was trying to hold their feet to the fire, to keep his credit line open till he got something new started up.

It certainly wasn't his fault that plans for Rio Nuevo kept changing. The whole 'New River' concept had become an ironic joke early on, when it was determined that there wasn't enough water to rehydrate the dry Santa Cruz channel through town. And since the downtown renewal project had been wrongly named to begin with, it probably should have come as no surprise that it went through agonizing bouts of committee meltdown and political grandstanding. Not to mention time-consuming protests from citizen groups alarmed at the passing of the traditional Desert Southwest values everybody agreed were so intrinsic to the Tucson way of life. Roger shared that concern, actually, but felt some ambiguity about whose values they were all talking about – the pioneers who settled the place, or the Spanish who were there before them? How about the tribes that had occupied the valley for unknown centuries before? And the hordes of seniors from up north who were invading the valley now, armed with good green retirement money? It was an interesting debate, but it all took time, and the project was running out of that.

But the planning was done now, the first few projects built had turned out to be very attractive, and if he could just get the committee to confirm that he'd been picked for the Gray Hawk Terrace job, he knew everything else would fall into place. It was down to two of them, everybody else had been eliminated or dropped out during this long design phase. But Ames & Proctor had the resources to hang on, and the big Las Vegas firm had made all the modifications and posted the bond. He still liked his own design better and hoped his being local would tilt the committee his way.

He was brought back to the moment abruptly by the sight of a tarp tearing loose on a flatbed in the oncoming lane. As he watched, the last cord frayed through. The canvas flew over the minivan behind it, fluttered aloft for an improbable couple of seconds before it lost its lift and slammed into the windshield of the Durango that was following the minivan.

The Durango's driver, his world gone suddenly dark, hit the brake and pulled off the highway to his left. But his panicked swerve was a little too fast, maybe, or the pitch on the shoulder steeper than he thought. At seventy miles an hour, terrible luck met less than perfect reflexes, and the Durango flipped and rolled across the median.

Roger had one gut-wrenching second to decide, brakes or gas? The convertible ahead of him laid on extra speed and got out of his way, and as space opened up he decided it would be better to try to outrun the thing than dodge it. He gave it everything he had, and his speed was close to ninety when the Durango, rolling, hooked his back bumper with its own and spun him in a perfect one-eighty. The two behemoths of the highway slammed together and whirled again, grinding each other into a pricey mass of flying shrapnel.

Even so it could have been worse. The Wal-Mart eighteen-wheeler following Roger came within inches of crashing into the newly formed pile of rubble, but preempted the lane to its right, and the drivers around it managed somehow to stay out of its mudguards.

And the Yukon's systems all worked to perfection. Roger's seat belt kept him from impaling himself on the steering column and triggered the airbags. He was sitting a notch too far forward, so when his front airbag inflated it broke his nose. Horns brayed and brakes squealed all around him for a blurry terrifying minute, and then the world went bright and still. His inflated cocoon began gently losing air, and white powder settled slowly around him. He was pretty sure he was still alive because he was hurting all over. He wanted to yell but couldn't get his breath. He never knew how long that interval lasted before he quit feeling anything.

He woke up lying on the edge of the road. A voice said, 'This one's coming around.' He opened his eyes to blinding light, closed them back to slits, and saw the outline of a figure bending over him. It said, 'You OK, buddy? You with me here?'

He sat up, embarrassed to find himself lying on the ground in a public place. He was not accustomed to needing help, especially from strangers – he hired the help he needed, paid them well, and worked them hard. 'I'm all right,' he said quickly. 'Don't worry about me.' Then he fainted and fell back.

'Patricia.' Sarah kept her voice as matter-of-fact as if she were asking directions to the bathroom. 'Do you know where your father is now?'

'Uh . . . not exactly.' She glanced at her watch. 'You could try his office pretty soon. He usually goes to work early.'

'Doesn't he live here?'

'Of course. But this weekend he's been out of town.'

'Did your mother know where he was?'

'Oh, sure. I asked her during the party why he wasn't there and she said he's in Phoenix running late again at another damn meeting.'

'Your parents have been fighting?'

'Oh, not fighting.' She seemed shocked by that sugges-tion. 'My father would never . . . But they haven't been . . . communicating very well, either.'

'Do you know what they're not communicating about?'

'Not exactly. I'm not here all the time, you know, I'm in school. But I know Mom's been on one of her talking streaks, full of plans . . . all kinds of ideas. And Dad's been rushing around not listening to her, looking kind of . . . desperate. But he was supposed to be here for my birthday party yesterday. I heard her tell him, be sure you get back by three on Sunday for Patsy's party, and he promised he would. But he never showed.'

Delaney cleared his throat behind them. Patricia looked around and asked him, 'What?' When he didn't respond she turned to Sarah and said, 'I guess the other policeman wants me to leave.'

'Yeah, but wait a minute,' Sarah said. 'I need a number for your father – and one for you.' She glanced quickly at Delaney, who was puffing up, turning pink. 'Let's step into the next room there and you give me some numbers.'

They went into the small bedroom where Patricia had so recently thrown a fit of hysterics. She seemed to have put all that behind her now. Ignoring the woman from Victim's

Services who still sat there waiting in her plain blue suit, she
stood by Sarah's shoulder and reeled off letters and numbers.
Her own cell phone and email address, first, and then a whole
row of ways to reach her father. Roger Henderson had two
companies, each with an office number, secretary, fax, and
had his own cell phone and pager besides.

'But all you really need for Dad during business hours is that
first number, the Hen-Trax phone. You'll get Ruth, his faithful
slave, and she'll find him if he's alive on this planet. She can
find him on any job site, or on the road . . . get Ruth on the job,
if she decides your reason's good enough pretty soon you'll be
talking to Daddy.' A testament to teenage resilience, she tossed
off this easy-going irony while the tears of her horrified meltdown were still damp in the rug where she stood.

When she finished the numbers recital she pushed her hair
back, took a deep breath and said, 'Look, don't be misled
by that . . . sordid scene in there.' Her voice wobbled again
on the last few words and Sarah watched her carefully, afraid
she was losing it again. But she seemed determined to make
this difficult statement. 'My mother's been orbiting the moon
more than usual lately –' she was looking into the corner
now and her voice had gone up a notch – 'but this is the
first time I've ever known her to bring one of her toy boys
home. My parents have some . . . problems in their marriage,
naturally, due to her . . . the way she is. But they're – we're
all very solid citizens and we're a family.'

'I see,' Sarah said, although she didn't. 'Thank you,
Patricia. I know that wasn't easy to say. And now that you've
helped us so much I'm going to turn you over to Victim's
Services, and get you some help. This is Ellen.'

Ellen put out her hand and murmured, 'I'm sorry for your
loss.'

'Ellen will take you wherever you want to go. Do you
have relatives in Tucson?'

'I don't need a ride.' Patricia looked surprised. 'I have my
own car.'

'Well, but you've had such a bad shock,' Ellen said. She
had all the requisite skills, the kindly face and voice her job
description promised. 'Do you think it's wise for you to
drive?'

'Of course I can drive.' Patricia Henderson's expression made it plain that being too overwhelmed to operate heavy equipment was for craven wimps, a group in which she never expected to find herself. 'And I think I'll go to Aunt Bella's house, I don't want her to hear about this on the radio. I'll keep trying to find my father too,' she told Sarah, her voice steady again, 'but if you see him first will you tell him to call me?'

'Of course,' Sarah said. 'And here, take my card, it's got all my numbers. Call me if there's anything else I can do.' Thinking again that this girl was only a few years older than her niece, she said, 'Can you stay with your aunt for a few days?'

'Sure. Her or Aunt Louise, they both live close to here.'

'Do you need help locating other family members?' Ellen asked her.

'No. My brother Adam's at a prep school in Boston . . . I hope,' she added, half to herself. 'I'll call him as soon as I decide how to say it.' She looked momentarily white and forlorn, then made one of the supreme efforts of will that seemed to be her specialty. 'I'll do it soon.'

'Very good,' Sarah said. She felt surrounded by rocks she didn't have time to turn over. 'Patricia, won't you at least talk to Ellen about counseling? It's a free service offered to everyone, you're entitled to—'

Looking at Sarah as if she had made an obscene suggestion involving body parts, Patricia said, *Counseling?'* She took the card Ellen pressed into her hand and bolted down the stairs without another word.

Sarah heard Ray Menendez, at the foot of the stairs, say, 'Ms Henderson? There's a nice lady out at the tapeline in front, says her name is Maria and she works for your mother. Could you speak to her?' There was a murmured response from Patricia and then Ray's voice again, nearer the front door, said, 'Here, I'll walk out with you. Why don't I give you my card now too, so in case you think of anything you want to tell us or ask us later you can call me?'

Well, for what it's worth she's got plenty of cards now. A young girl who just found her mother cruelly murdered should have people around her for comfort, not cards. And then another unwelcome thought: *Menendez, are you putting the moves on that girl?*

He wouldn't. She'd worked cases with him for two years, he was as straight as anybody she knew. A beautiful young girl surrounded by riches, though, and in distress now, it had a kind of dark glitter about it. The best thing for all of them, Sarah thought urgently, was to find Patricia's father.

Looking down the list of numbers Patricia had given her, she shrugged and dialed the cell phone, let it ring five times, and punched END. *What kind of busy executive keeps his cell phone turned on but doesn't answer it?*

She went back in the master bedroom and told Delaney, 'Roger Henderson's cell doesn't answer. It kind of creeps me out that he hasn't turned up.'

'Me too,' Delaney said, 'I want to see him *and* his guns.'

'Is somebody checking the house for weapons?'

'I sent Peete to go through all the cupboards. Next I'd like to ID the stranger in the bed.' He looked around. 'Where's Gloria?'

'Here in the closet,' Gloria said, not coming out.

'You didn't fingerprint the victims, did you?'

'Well, no, won't they do that in the autopsy?'

'Sure, but now that we know the second victim's not the husband, we'd like to find out who he is. Was.'

'Come on, he'll still be dead tomorrow.' Gloria had been in the lab long enough to pick up some very bad jokes.

Delaney was not amused. 'Come out of there right now, Gloria.' He watched her coldly as she emerged, sulky-faced. But his anger crumbled when he saw the bright silk belt that had tangled in her tousled curls. He plucked it off her head grinning and said, 'Get your butt over there and print that male victim *right now* before the ME and the transport people get here. And then I want,' he swiveled away from her, looking around, 'let's see, where's Greenaway?'

'On the street, talking to the neighbors,' Ray Menendez said, walking in.

'OK. Why aren't you?'

'I was helping Sarah with that distressed young woman,' Menendez said. 'And then I – what do you want?'

'Help Gloria print this male victim,' Delaney said, frowning to let Menendez know his answer wasn't good enough. 'And then run the prints down to the lab. At once! No time to fool around here!'

'Who's fooling around?' Menendez said, frowning back. 'Not me.'

The ME walked in with his bag and began harassing Gloria. Why was she fingerprinting this body here, getting in his way? She rolled her eyes silently toward Delaney, who said, 'I told her to do it, she'll be done in just a sec,' and stared down the doc, refusing to explain further. The transport people were waiting in the hall with their gear, and a public-information officer was downstairs, demanding facts for the early news cycle. Annoyed by how chaotic and noisy the scene was getting, Delaney asked Tobin, who was still measuring and muttering over his drawing pad, 'How about it, you just about done with that sketch?'

'Pretty close,' Tobin said, without looking up. He had more than twenty years of overstressed sergeants behind him; his calm was unshakeable.

'Well, soon as you can,' Delaney said, softening his tone, 'go on down and give that info guy just enough to get him out of here, will you? And Sarah, hook up with Ollie out there and help him canvass those neighbors before they talk to each other any more. I'll keep after the husband and then – where in the hell is Cifuentes, does anybody know?'

Sarah walked down the stairs and out into a pink dawn in a busy yard. On the steps behind her, she heard Leo Tobin say, 'All we can say so far is two victims of traumatic death here. No ID pending notification of family members, no other details as yet.' And then, coldly, taking his irritation at Delaney out on the hapless reporter, 'What part of no don't you understand?'

The reporter would get something on the air, though, a picture of the house from the street, the reporter standing in front repeating the nothing she knew in three or four different ways. Secretaries in both Roger Henderson's offices, probably, bankers and business associates and friends would turn on their TV sets, and soon the whole town would know, maybe before Roger Henderson did, that there was trouble at his house.

She heard the click of a timer and the fountain came on as she passed it. Water bubbled up gaily and fell into its elegant brick-and-tile basin, striking a discordant note in this grim scene.

At the tape, Frankie Lopez was telling the photographer from the TV truck in front of him that they could not park their van there, the street had to be kept clear for police business and no, media was absolutely not allowed across this line. As Sarah navigated the busy street she saw Cifuentes, far down the block, nosing his department vehicle into a mini-space at the corner.

'You take the one on the corner,' Ollie said, when she found him. 'I'm just about to start on the one next door.'

The Ortman house stood well back on freshly raked gravel around neat brick walks and patio. The front door opened as she walked up to it. A large, florid-faced man stood inside, wearing a robe over pants and an undershirt. He held on to the latch, blocking her way. Sarah, who because of her careful grooming sometimes got mistaken for a Mary Kay rep, held up her shield as she said good morning.

'You're the detective?' He looked dubious, but he put out his hand. 'Mike Ortman. My wife, Yvonne.' She was behind him, tense, wearing what Sarah guessed was her best robe. She'd had time to put on light make-up, but her hair still hung tousled to her shoulders.

They both wanted details. Sarah convinced them quickly that there were none she could share yet. 'But I need to hear from you,' she told Ortman, 'exactly what you saw and heard.'

They both began talking at once, finishing each other's sentences and arguing over tiny details. One convenient fact soon emerged out of the tangle of half-sentences: Mrs Ortman had slept right through the gunshots and screaming.

'He snores, so I have to wear earplugs. I didn't hear a thing until Mike woke me up,' she pushed her limp hair behind her ears, taking her anxiety out on her hair and her husband, 'slamming doors and making phone calls.'

'One lousy 911 call, Yvonne,' her husband protested, 'how else do you call the cops?'

'And all your golfing buddies, talking on and on—'

'Just Mel to tell him we might have to delay the game. Then everybody from a block around here called *me*. Nothing I can do about that. People are curious,' he explained to Sarah. 'They want to hear the details.'

Tell me about it. Sarah opened her notebook and said, 'I need to talk to you one at a time so we don't mix up the two stories. Mrs Ortman, will you wait upstairs till I call you?'

Yvonne didn't want to go. She tried pleading and then outrage. The story of the year was unfolding in her living room and she didn't want to miss a word. Sarah shook her head dolefully and mentioned the possibility of going downtown. When Yvonne's pink mules had finally clumped up the stairway, Sarah asked her husband, 'The first thing you heard was a shot?'

One shot, very loud, and then a terrified scream.

'Man or woman screaming?'

'Woman. I think. Although, screaming, it's harder – but I think a woman.'

So the woman was shot last? Her mind said that was wrong but she didn't want to distract the witness with an argument. *Press on, get it while it's fresh.*

By the time the second shot sounded, Mike Ortman said, he had rolled out of bed and was across the room, peering out the window, with his phone in his hand.

'Any idea what time that was?'

'Yeah, I looked before I dialed 911. It was one forty-five.'

The Ortman house, on a corner lot, was turned about sixty degrees from the Henderson house. From his master bedroom, Ortman's side window looked almost directly across the street at the Henderson house.

'I opened the window,' he said, 'and watched and listened while I talked to the police. The man who answered asked a lot of questions, and I watched the house the whole time I answered them. After I hung up I stayed there, by the open window. It was a nice night, I wasn't cold, so I stayed there and watched, but nothing moved. I finally turned away to go to the bathroom, and then I heard the second scream.'

'This was how long after the second shot?'

'Ten minutes . . . maybe closer to fifteen. I never thought

to look at my watch that time. Because . . . maybe it was just because I was fully awake, but something about that second scream almost stopped my heart. Just talking about it . . . shall we sit down?' He led her to a pair of sofas in the middle of the room. 'The first scream was just a loud noise, you know, the sound you make when you're startled. But that second one . . . I thought it sounded like a word.'

'What word?'

'Something like . . . Molly? Or Polly. But none of the Hendersons have those names, so maybe not. Anyway it started the dogs barking louder than ever, and I guess about then Yvonne started to wake up. I had to tell her what was going on and of course she was very upset. The dogs were still barking like crazy and the phone was ringing off the hook by then, Yvonne answered one of the calls and I walked over to look at the house again. I heard a motor start up somewhere nearby, I was scanning the area and I saw a large, light-colored vehicle pull away from the back of the house. It went out the back driveway and I saw the lights go on west.

'My first thought was it was Roger's car. He drives a light-tan Yukon and I thought . . . but the more I think about it I believe it was more like a minivan than an SUV. Anyway I guess it couldn't have been him, could it? If they're both . . .' He rolled unhappy eyes away, not wanting to say 'dead.'

Sarah didn't confirm or deny. She knew that her question about the gender of the screamer gave away one important fact about the crime. Two bodies, one of each sex. Soon enough they'd identify the second victim's prints and then everyone on the street would know the most titillating fact about the killings on Avenida Santa Teresa, that the man in bed with Eloise Henderson was not her husband. Soon enough, Patricia would be jumping to turn off the TV set when that story came on.

'Then two police cars stopped in front of the Henderson house, I stepped out to talk to them, and by the time I got back inside my phone was ringing. I've been on the phone most of the time ever since, it's crazy.'

'Listen, I just can't stay upstairs by myself, I'm too *nervous*.' Yvonne Ortman came back down the stairs, talking fast. 'I'll wait in the kitchen and I won't say a word, I promise. I don't really have anything useful to add anyway. But I need to hear voices near me or I'm going to jump out of my skin. Honestly,' she turned on Sarah, indignantly, immediately breaking her promise not to talk, 'what on earth is happening to this town, anyway? I mean, right here on our own street, who'd ever expect . . .'

'Always hard to believe when it's close to home.' The usual bromide only made Yvonne more indignant.

'Well, but for Heaven's sake, this isn't just any street, this is El Encanto!' Vaguely aware she sounded elitist, she added lamely, 'Most of these people have lived here for years!'

'I know.' Sarah held the woman's own kitchen door open and waved her through it. Half expecting a reprimand she asked Mike Ortman quickly, 'Have you lived here a long time too?'

He shrugged. 'Eight years. Always wanted to live here. Moved in as soon as I could afford it.' She took a fresh look at him, liking his blunt, straightforward answer.

'Do you know the Hendersons well?'

'Roger and I play golf occasionally. Our wives have never mixed much. Eloise is kind of a . . . *social butterfly* . . . I guess you'd call it. Gives a lot of parties. Serves on boards, does all those charity and theater things that get your name in the paper.' Having made social prominence sound vaguely disreputable he tried to take it back. 'Don't get me wrong, they're, you know, *nice*. Like everybody here.' He jingled the coins in his pockets and added, 'This is the first time we've ever had any . . . rough stuff.' Like his wife, he seemed anxious to defend the neighborhood.

Sarah's phone rang. Delaney said, in an ominously calm voice, 'Sarah, can you leave what you're doing there and come back over here, please?'

'Sure.' She closed the phone and told Ortman, 'I'm sorry, I'll have to finish this later – or somebody else will. My boss needs me back at the house.'

'Well, I can't sit here all day,' Ortman said.

'Of course not. But will you wait just a few minutes till I find out what's going on? Then I'll either come back or send someone.' She took his phone numbers and hurried next door, found the owner talking to Greenaway in front of his half-open door. Greenaway gave her a little ironic nod that said plainly, *Not going to get much out of this one.*

'When you're done here,' she said, 'will you finish up next door there? Delaney just called me back.'

'On it,' Greenaway said, and turned back toward his rock-faced witness as Sarah walked away.

On her way back through the Henderson house, she ducked through the kitchen and looked in the garage. One white Mercedes convertible stood alone in the stall nearest the kitchen door. *Looks like the wife's car.* Jason Peete was in the kitchen, poking his bald head into cupboards. She hurried upstairs.

Delaney stood facing Oscar Cifuentes in the dressing room. Both men were red in the face and looked ruffled, like fighting birds.

Cifuentes was the new man in Homicide, a replacement for Eisenstaat, the over-the-hill detective who had retired a couple of years too late to ever be missed. In his place they got Cifuentes, who came so highly recommended by his new female supervisor in Auto Theft that Sarah suspected she was trying to offload him.

There had been no complaints in Homicide about his work, he did his share and got his reports in on time. But the man was so sure of himself, so macho and serenely condescending to women, that she knew from the first week she'd guessed right about his transfer.

Oscar Cifuentes, it turned out, could make her angry by saying, 'Good morning.' Or by not saying it. Recognizing the unreasonable nature of her reaction to him and ever vigilant about her performance evaluations, she was careful not to get overtly hostile toward him. She just found ways to stay away from him as much as she could, and treated him, when they worked together, with strictly controlled civility.

Right now, it amused her to see, he looked about ready to jump off this bedroom's elegant balcony.

'I've just finished talking to Mertz,' Delaney said. 'I'm waiting for him to call me back with his opinion.'

'I'm sorry, remind me,' Sarah said. 'Mertz?'

'Our legal advisor.' Looking about as grim as a man could

without bleeding, Delaney closed the door between the dressing room and the bedroom. *Doesn't want the crime-scene specialists to hear this, oh my.* 'It seems that Oscar here is going to have to recuse himself from this case because of a previous intimate acquaintance with the female victim. He didn't tell me about it before he came over here and poked his face into the crime scene, so now I'm trying to find out if prompt and full disclosure of the problem will be sufficient, or if he's tainted the case so badly we might have to surrender it to County.'

Sarah didn't need to ask what the prospect of passing off a high-profile homicide case to the Pima County sheriff was doing to Delaney's digestive system. Reluctant to meet Cifuentes' eyes for fear her own might show how pleasant it was to see him in the weeds, she stood vacantly inspecting the shower curtain for the longest ten minutes in world history. Finally Delaney's phone rang, and she continued her scrutiny of the shower curtain through a long dry crackle of lawyer's terms, broken by Delaney's occasional monosyllable.

'Yes. No. Mmff. Right.' Finally he closed the phone and told Cifuentes, 'Go back to the station and wait till I tell you what comes next.' He added, as the hapless detective turned to go, 'Do not speak to anyone on the way out, do you understand? Do not discuss this case with anyone, at work or anywhere else, today or ever.'

Despite the obvious unenforceability of Delaney's last order, Cifuentes said only, 'Yes, sir,' and walked stiffly away.

Sarah waited again while Delaney consulted his watch for several seconds, chewing gum ferociously and blinking as if the time was too incredible to be believed. Apparently satisfied at last that it was in fact 7:42.19, he raised his head and calmly started over.

'Mertz thinks we can salvage this case if we build a firewall and keep Cifuentes on the other side of it. So let's figure out what we have to do. You've got, what, two other cases where you're primary?'

'Yes,' Sarah said, 'but the drive-by, you know, we're probably never going to get much on that. None of the eyewitnesses will talk. The other one, though, the domestic that we think's a murder-suicide? That's going to take some work.'

'Mostly lab work, though. I'll get you all the help I can with that one if you'll take the lead on this case, Sarah. It's going to need very careful handling. All the physical evidence I see here is the kind that gets questioned endlessly by busy-body jurists who know zilch about the subject but they've seen this thing on TV . . . blood evidence and gunshots with no casings, could you design a deeper swamp?

'And what's worse,' he said, scratching his sun-ravaged cheeks, 'the victims are upper-crusties and so are their neighbors. All these witnesses are used to being in charge. They're not going to like it one bit, us all over the place asking questions. They're going to want it handled *their way*. But you're good at dealing with people like that, Sarah. You grew up here and you understand them.'

No need to slather it on, boss. You know perfectly well I'll bust my butt for one good word from you. When the time came for her to be considered for his job, Sarah was going to need Delaney's endorsement. He knew that and took advantage, piling work on her so he could build a reputation as the Homicide boss who closed more cases than his predecessor with the same number of detectives – as good a way as any to get your name shortlisted for Chief.

They had built a nearly perfect symbiosis, she reflected as she watched him walk away. She accepted, without complaint, his unreasonable demands on her time and energy. He pretended not to know she was making a list of things she thought she could do better when she got his job.

She looked at her watch. Almost eight. If Roger Henderson went to work early, maybe Ruth, the wonder secretary, did too.

Before the first ring ended, a professionally cordial voice said, 'Hen-Trax.'

'I'm hoping you're Ruth,' Sarah said.

'I am indeed,' the voice said, warming up still more. 'What can I do for you?'

Sarah identified herself and then, picking her words carefully, told Ruth there was a problem at the Henderson house. 'I can't share any details until I've spoken to Mr Henderson, of course. Do you know where I might find him?'

Deeply curious at once but flawlessly polite, Ruth said

her boss had been at a meeting in Phoenix all weekend, but 'I really expected him back by now. I'm waiting to hear from him.' She probed all around the problem. Was there something she could help with? What message did Sarah want to leave for Mr Henderson?

Sarah left her cell number, already rehearsing what she would say when he called.

The second time Roger regained consciousness, he was on a gurney being wheeled down a hall. There were people around him, busy but calm, all talking to each other but not about him. The young man in blue scrubs who was pushing the gurney had been to a baseball game recently and was sharing his enthusiasm about a Diamondbacks pitcher. 'That Brandon Webb, I tell you,' he said, 'he's just a throwing animal.'

Roger tried to sit up but his arms seemed to be fastened to the narrow cot. There was a needle in his left arm, too, he noticed now, and a tube running up to a nearly full bag that hung from a shiny stand like a coat rack. Another young man beside him was pushing the rack, keeping pace with the gurney so the IV stayed in Roger's arm.

He had not been in a hospital as a patient since he sprained an ankle in high school, and his first thought was that he didn't want to be in this one now. But most of his waking hours were spent thinking about how systems worked, and in spite of himself his attention was caught by the clever coupling that fastened the IV tube to the needle in his arm. He admired it for a few seconds, thinking, *Wouldn't I like to hire the guy who thought of that.* Then the here and now he had been hurrying toward came back into his mind, and he said, 'Where am I?'

The young man pushing the rack told him he was in Chandler Medical, and congratulated him for having his accident so near a big emergency medical center. 'I mean, if you gotta mess up you did it just right,' he said. 'We zipped you over here in nothing flat, the triage doc's already seen you and you're on your way to a scan. You're doing great, buddy. Just relax.'

The world was suddenly full of young men who thought

he would like to be their buddy. *Fat chance of that.* He opened his mouth to ask what time it was, but the lights blurred and he lost focus for a few seconds. Or hours? He wasn't sure.

He came fully awake again in a curtained space surrounded by a different set of people, older and quieter, all watching him.

'What's going on?' he asked them. He expected to sound the way he usually did, like somebody to be reckoned with, but his voice wasn't working right. The plaintive whisper that came out of him wouldn't get respect from a child. *Damn.* He shook his head in disgust. That was a mistake too. The world rocked alarmingly, and for a minute he thought he was going to be sick.

He held his breath, got his equilibrium back and boot-strapped mentally back up toward his usual self, a person with a lot on his mind. *Got to get off this bed.*

The people around him had other ideas. They wanted him to raise his arms, for some reason, and then to smile. Smile? His arms both worked all right, why wouldn't they? He smiled reluctantly, feeling silly, at a fat nurse who seemed satisfied, though she didn't smile back.

A gray-haired physician in a white coat pressed a stethoscope to Roger's chest, asking, 'What's your name?'

'Roger Henderson. My wallet's in my clothes, didn't you find that?' The doctor didn't answer. He wanted Roger to tell him how many fingers he was holding up. Why were they playing children's games? Now he wanted Roger to say his mother's maiden name. For a minute he couldn't remember it.

'Why . . . same as her married name. Antrim,' Roger said. 'I guess she was one of the early feminists.' He went on, at the doctor's request but with mounting annoyance, to counting backward from twenty. Finally the doctor muttered something to his two serious aides, who scurried away to do his bidding while the doctor sat down on a little stool by Roger's narrow bed.

'OK,' the doctor said, 'you remember being in a car accident?'

'It wasn't my fault. I tried to get out of the way but—'

'Yes. Well, you were very lucky. You've got a broken nose and some bruises on your chest. We taped that up a little and set your nose, but you're going to have some beautiful shiners, probably. What's really got us concerned is that your blood pressure was critically high when you were brought in. We've brought it down about a hundred points since you've been here, we're giving you –' he said something Roger didn't understand – 'but you were way up in stroke territory there for a while. Are you on medication for high blood pressure, Roger?'

'Oh . . . I got some pills a while back. I guess I left them at home.' *I forget them half the time anyway.* 'I've been at a meeting in Phoenix and I didn't think—' He watched the doctor's mournful little headshake. 'Wrong, huh?'

'They aren't doing you much good in the closet, are they? Skipping your blood-pressure meds is a very bad idea, Roger. Also . . . you're a big guy, but even so, you're carrying a few extra pounds.'

'Been too busy to get much exercise.'

'Uh-huh. Have you been under a lot of stress lately?'

'Some. I'm a builder.' He had learned not to say 'developer.' Suspicion of large-scale builders, always simmering on a back burner somewhere, was approaching full boil. The damn developers had built too many houses, people were saying. Oughta shoot the whole bunch of crooks, and their bankers too while we're at it.

'I'm going to be a lot more stressed if I don't check in with my office pretty soon,' Roger said, 'I think I've missed a couple of meetings already. Is there a phone I can use?'

'In a minute. Is your office in Phoenix?'

'Tucson. Why?'

'You shouldn't drive yet. Well, but you don't have a car anyway, do you?' The doctor smiled cheerfully as if that was a good thing. 'Tell you what, we did a CT scan and an ultrasound, the results should be ready by now. You just rest a few minutes while I look at those, and I'll be back.'

He was gone before Roger could ask again for a phone. Every time a uniformed person came within hailing distance Roger asked for his clothes. He had remembered his cell phone was in his jacket. If he could get his hands on his phone he could start making calls, find out where his car was, put the spurs to his staff and fix whatever he'd missed . . . What in hell was wrong with these people? Nobody seemed to be paying any attention to him.

Part of his mind had begun to compose a story about the mounting frustration of this hospital experience, something he could tell his secretary to keep her from enquiring too closely into his whereabouts during the twenty-four hours before his accident. She was a plump divorcée named Ruth, very smart and serious, but she liked to be jollied along a little, it helped her put up with being worked like a donkey.

So there I was begging for my pants . . . beginning to think about tearing up a sheet and making a rope to jump out a window . . . She would laugh with her hand over her mouth, saying 'Oh, isn't that just priceless?' Then the builder in him noticed that the double-glazed windows in his room would never open to let anyone jump out, and he was thinking about fire and scrutinizing the sprinkler system when finally the doctor came back.

'Well, you don't show any sign of having had a stroke. So . . . you were lucky twice this morning, Roger. But if I were you I wouldn't count on being lucky with blood pressure that high again. They don't call it the silent killer for nothing. Take your meds regularly and talk to your doctor about making some changes in your lifestyle, hmm? The hellish aspect of strokes these days is that we usually keep people alive after they have them so they can spend years in rehab, learning to walk and talk again.' He looked at Roger sternly over his glasses and said, 'Trust me, you'd hate it.' He jumped up off his little stool and said, 'There now, I've delivered my jeremiad about following doctor's orders, now you can have your clothes.'

The cell phone was right where it belonged, in his jacket. He could not get his Monday morning back, but he could get his foremen on the phone and check on the jobs. First, though, he called a limousine service to take him to his Tucson office. The cell showed one missed call from a number he didn't recognize, that could wait. He knew he should call home next – a man who'd been in an accident would normally do that. But he didn't know what kind of a mood his wife might be in by now and he didn't feel up to dealing with her if she were angry. He stared out at the unloading zone where the limo would come, collected his thoughts for a minute, and dialed his secretary.

He hardly recognized Ruth's familiar voice. 'Oh, Mr Henderson,' she said, and he realized she was crying. 'I am so very sorry. What can I do to help?'

FOUR

Ollie Greenaway walked out of the Ortmans' front door as Sarah approached it.

'Oh, good, you finished my interview,' she said. 'How'd it go?' A twenty-year man who'd seen everything twice without ever finding his hard side, Ollie had a reputation for getting good interviews. His sunny nature put people at ease.

'More of the same. Gunshots, barking dogs,' Ollie said. 'Golf, a lot about golf. Ortman shoots in the mid-eighties and favors a center shaft putter. His is a Nike.'

'Good to know. Where you headed now?'

'People named Worthington live in that split-level at the end of the block. According to the Ortmans they see a lot of the Hendersons.'

'OK. You hear I'm the case officer now?'

'What, Cifuentes never made it? I thought I saw his car.'

'He was here. He admitted to knowing the female victim.'

'So?'

'Knowing in the biblical sense.'

'Oh?' He perked up, pleased. 'I'll be damned. Cifuentes? I thought he was all flash and no fire. Shows you what I know about sexy, huh? Well, c'mon, dish!'

'Didn't get any details. He was gone before I could blink. Delaney canned him off the case. We're not supposed to talk to him about it ever.'

'Oh, yeah, that'll work.'

'Be careful when you do. Delaney's got his bloomers in a twist about this case.'

'I suppose. This one's gonna get some ink, huh? High-toned lady gets offed while she's getting it on? Delaney won't let that one get out of his meat-hooks if he can help it.' Content with his own station in life, Greenaway enjoyed watching people sweat the promotion ladder. He gave her a sneaky sideways grin. 'So, you grabbed the case away from the hot new boy, huh? Way to go, kid!'

'Delaney called me over. I didn't do any grabbing.'

'Sure.' He nudged her elbow. 'Listen, I'm all for gender equality. Ask my wife, I'll let her haul out the garbage any time.' Thoughtfully checking house numbers, he asked her, 'So . . . you're saying if I do talk to Cifuentes about his roll in the hay with the victim, you don't want to hear a word about it, huh?'

'You kidding? Bring me every juicy morsel as fast as you get it.'

Greenaway cackled happily and said, 'OK, then!' Tucking his notebook into the back of his pants, letting his pale eyes wander over the well-tended yards around him, he mused, 'Jeez, you know, Sarah, if you were inclined towards rebellion this neighborhood could almost make you tip over a bus, couldn't it? I mean, look at that Porsche.' Sleek and glowing as a crown jewel, it was backing out of a three-car garage thickly hung with high-end sports equipment.

'Mmm. I can't decide if I want the car or the garage.'

'Go for both, why not? Envy's only a venial sin. Few Hail Marys, couple Our Fathers, and you're good to go again.'

'Ah, it's so handy to have an altar boy along when you're working the tempting parts of town. Listen, Ollie, you OK to go on with these interviews by yourself? I need to get back in there and ride herd on the physical evidence.'

'Sure, don't worry about me. I'm getting my jollies out here, talking to rich people in their jammies.'

She hustled back into the house, where Peete, gloved and silent, was still poking through closets, making careful notes in some personal code that helped him keep track of where he'd been. Way to go, she thought, watching him – this house, with whole walls of built-ins, almost guaranteed confusion. But Peete had it organized.

Upstairs, Gloria was still dusting doors on the wall of closets. When Sarah paused by her side she straightened, rubbed her back, and said, 'Now what do *you* want?'

'I was just going to ask how it was going. You did the front door first, I hope. Didn't you?'

'Front, back, side. You bet. Still got all them surfaces in the kitchen and prep room, though.'

'OK. Where's Delaney?'

'Gone downtown. And Roy went out to meet Jenny Skidmore. She's bringing in the lasers.' Sarah heard them huffing up the stairway, carrying boxes that they stacked in a corner by the dressing-room door and began to unpack.

'OK, looking for an angle,' Roy said, peering into the tiny birdshot holes that peppered the walls and headboard. He sang it softly, 'Now show me an angle, an angle,' to the tune of an old song that started 'I'll give you a daisy, a daisy.'

'Man, these things are just so damn small, though – oh, looky here.' He beamed at an ugly scratch a metal pellet had made across the front of a nightstand. 'More like it! Pass me the little square laser that figures angles.' He held the black plastic device next to the scrape and turned it on. A red tunnel of light cut through the dim haze in the room. He fiddled till he was sure he had the beam lined up with the scrape, then read the angle. 'Seventy-eight degrees. Beautiful. Sarah, bring that artist's tablet over here, will you? Good, now stand about where you think the shot came from. There you go.' A red dot appeared on the tablet. 'Jenny, bring over the other laser, please.'

He lined up his beams with scrapes and nicks, and measured the angles. When most of the dots lined up on the tablet Sarah was holding, they took that for the shoulder height of the shooter, and measured the distance from the dot to the floor. Roy consulted a chart and told Sarah, 'If your shooter aims from the shoulder like most shotgun users he's shorter than average, not over five feet eight.'

'But if he shoots from the hip he's a giant, right?'

'Way over six feet. Which do you like?'

'Don't know yet. Haven't seen the husband.'

Her phone rang and Lopez said, 'Gentleman just drove up, says he owns this house and he wants to talk to whoever's in charge.'

She put the phone against her chest and asked Roy, 'Is this weird or what? I say "husband" and he appears in the yard.'

'Awesome. Could you conjure up another lab tech? I could use some help here.'

Sarah put the phone back on her ear and said, 'Hold him right there, I'll come down.'

Holding Roger Henderson anywhere might be quite a job if he'd decided to put up a fight, she thought as she walked toward him. He was a big, solid man, looming over Lopez. Muscled up in the chest and shoulders, too, and Patricia hadn't exaggerated about his arms and hands.

Her watch said one-fifteen. *Where the devil has he been?*

Frankie Lopez was squinting and shrugging and waving his hands, using body language to emphasize his deep regret at keeping Henderson out of his own house. Lopez had learned to compensate for his small stature by defusing tense situations with good nature and guile. Just now the tactic didn't seem to be working very well. As Sarah walked up to them, Henderson turned toward his house and snapped, 'Oh, bullshit!'

She ducked under the tape and stood erect in front of him, holding up her shield. 'Hello, Mr Henderson. I'm Detective Sarah Burke.'

'I asked to speak to the person in charge.' His voice was hoarse. He had a wide face with a bad scrape on one cheekbone. His nose had a neat flesh-colored bandage that she hadn't noticed before, and his eyes were bloodshot. In puzzling contrast to his commanding manner, his head looked as if it might have been in a bar fight.

'I'm the case officer, Mr Henderson. I'm very sorry for your loss.' Her quiet courtesy pricked his bubble of outrage; he opened his mouth and closed it again.

While the quiet lasted she looked him over. He wore neatly pressed khaki pants and a blue button-down shirt with the sleeves rolled twice. Two pens were clipped in his shirt pocket. The cell phone that hadn't answered earlier was in a carrier on his belt, along with a measuring tape, hand-held GPS, and a beeper – his belt was almost as busy as a patrolman's, she thought, all he lacked was a gun. Or did he? She considered patting him down but decided, *Not in front of his house.*

'I called my office,' he said, 'and my secretary said trouble here at the house – so I called the County Attorney . . . he's a friend of mine.' *Of course he is.* 'He kindly sent one of

his assistants to meet me at the morgue so I could see the—'
His big jaw clamped shut and a muscle in his face flexed.
He swallowed. 'It's my wife . . . and another person. Is my
daughter . . . ?'

'Daddy, I'm here,' Patricia said, suddenly behind him on
the sidewalk.

Shit. Here we go again. Sarah braced for a new emotional
storm.

Instead, what followed was an awkward short ballet of
painful body language between father and daughter. Roger
Henderson said, 'Oh, Patsy,' with what sounded like relief,
and reached out for her. She leaned toward his arms for a
nanosecond, then pulled back and blurted, 'Mom's dead!'

He took back his unused embrace quickly and put his
hands in his pockets. 'I know. I saw . . . somebody shot her.'
They stared at each other, breathing hard, for two or three
seconds before he said, 'Well, I guess we have to . . .' inclining
his head sideways toward Sarah.

Patricia nodded curtly, the way you'd confirm a drink
choice or an order for pork rinds, and the two faces turned
toward Sarah as if it was her job to figure out how this
complicated pair should deal with each other.

Sarah gestured toward the busy yard behind her. 'I'm sorry
to say that your house has become a crime scene. Do you
understand why I can't let you in there till we're done? We
have to protect the chain of evidence.' Patricia looked at her
shoes and said nothing about getting in there by accident.

'But we need to talk,' Sarah said. The two Hendersons
nodded again, identical businesslike nods. Patricia
Henderson's features were a near-perfect copy of her
mother's in the younger pictures back there in the house,
but all her body language seemed to echo her father. 'We
could sit in my car but it isn't very convenient. Why don't
we go downtown?'

'The police station?' Henderson's guard came up. 'I don't
want to—'

'We can talk in a private room there,' Sarah said, 'and –
would you like to come too?' she asked Patricia.

'OK.' Patricia looked more than willing to go hear what
her father had to say. He muttered something about needing

to make some phone calls first. Patricia asked him coldly, 'Are they more important than finding out who killed Mom?'

'No, of course not,' he said, 'but it's already one o'clock and . . . all right.' He clamped his jaw shut around the rest of his objections and told Sarah, 'Shall we go in my car? It's over there in Ortman's driveway.'

'It is?' Patricia stared across the street. 'I thought Ruth said you wrecked it.'

'I picked up another car at the office.'

'It looks exactly like the one you had.'

'It is. We lease a whole fleet, you know that.'

'Mr Henderson,' Sarah said, 'you had an accident?'

'This morning, a few miles south of Phoenix. That's why I'm so late getting home.'

'Are you OK?' Patricia asked him. 'Did you get hurt?'

'I got a bump on the head and spent a couple of hours in an emergency room. Got these fancy bandages and they say I have a bruise on my cheek, can you see it?' He gave Patricia an ironic little insider nod. 'You know how I always nag you to wear your seat belt? Well, my seat belt saved my life this morning.' They stared at each other, rendered speechless by so many calamities back to back. Finally Henderson took a deep breath, dug out his keys and said, 'Well . . . you coming with me?'

'I guess.' She asked Sarah, 'Can I put my car in the garage?'

'Give me the keys, will you? I'll get an officer to take care of it. And then,' to both of them, 'I guess Patricia better ride with me.' She had to try to keep them separated until they'd been interviewed, but she expected an argument, and was surprised when they both gave her another businesslike nod. This pair had similar instincts when it came to picking their battles. To Henderson she said, 'That's my Impala behind the van. Will you follow me, please?'

She rolled away from the curb quickly, relieved that Roger Henderson hadn't staged a fight with photographers nearby. She was wary of complaints about overzealous police work from his friends at City Hall. On the other hand, Roger Henderson was such an obvious person of interest, she really shouldn't let him out of her sight till he'd answered some questions.

Also, she needed to talk to Henderson alone. So now, what
to do with Patricia? She called Delaney as soon as she put
the car in gear and told him Roger Henderson was coming
in with her.

'Nice work.'

'Yes. His daughter Patricia is coming along as well. She's
here with me.'

'Ah.' His voice changed at once as he realized she couldn't
speak freely. 'Let's see, we'll need somebody to talk to her
while we interview her father, hmm?'

'Right.'

'I'll see if Menendez is still here, I saw him a minute ago.'

'Well . . . I'd really rather have Ollie. But . . . I guess he's
still working on the crime scene, isn't he?'

'Yes. You want me to interrupt him?' It was her case now,
her call.

'No . . .' She tapped the steering wheel, thinking. 'If
Menendez is still there he'll be fine. Tell him we'll be there
in about five.'

She parked quickly at the station, jumped out, and watched
as Henderson maneuvered his big shiny car into the parking
space she indicated. He had every gadget on board that
anyone could want, hands-free telephone system, GPS navi-
gation . . . A sticker on the driver's-side door read, 'This
vehicle protected by Accu-Trak.' *A tracker? Makes sense. If
he's got a fleet of these out on the road he needs to know
where his crew is* . . . 'I'll get the door,' she said, pulling out
her card.

Her little group moved into the station like a slinky toy
with a kink in it. Henderson's natural tendency was to open
all doors and gesture women through them with elbow
support and back touches. Sarah lengthened her stride
enough to get ahead of him, and since she was the only one
who knew where they were going she managed to direct
the line of march. But following was plainly not a word in
Henderson's lexicon. He moved in stiff-legged lurches,
distraught at not being in charge of the group, and compen-
sated by dominating his daughter at every turn and doorway
as if she was too retarded to navigate a hall. Patricia gave
him neither resistance nor gratitude, sailing through the

spaces he indicated with an expression that said she had no idea who this pesky doorman was.

Delaney was waiting for them at the elevator. He shook hands with Henderson, repeated the department's sympathy, and acknowledged Patricia with a grave nod. He ushered them courteously into his office and said, 'Sarah, could you just step out here a second and look at . . . uh . . .' and to Henderson, 'If you'll excuse us for a minute . . .'

In the hall he said, 'I've set up two rooms. What's your take on Henderson so far? You like him for the crime?'

'Well . . . he's the natural first choice, isn't he? The husband?'

'Always.'

'But you know, he's already contacted the CA, who sent one of his aides along to take him to the morgue.'

'I know. I told you, it's going to be that kind of a case. Did he say what happened to his face?'

'He was in a wreck this morning. On I-10 just south of Phoenix. While I'm talking to him . . . you must have a friend at DPS in Phoenix, don't you?'

'Several. Sure.'

'Will you ask one of them to find out where his car was taken, and get it towed to the DPS lab down here? They'll do that for us, won't they?'

'Sure, if I ask them.' He blinked rapidly. 'You fishing?'

'Yes. Who knows what's in it? And I'm saying, let's move on it right away, get it in our custody while he's still distracted, before he starts throwing up road blocks. This man has good attorneys, I'm guessing.'

'For sure. And friends in high places. What else?'

'Anything on the other victim's prints yet?'

'No, but we should get that soon. Here comes Menendez.'

Sarah hunkered with him in his crowded workspace while they pooled what little they knew.

'That screaming Patricia did at the house, I think that's atypical behavior for her,' Sarah said. 'She was shocked then. But she's no hysteric. Kind of a powerhouse, actually. She seems to have been very fond of her mother – well, you saw that – but she moves and talks like her father, almost a carbon copy at times. You might probe around that a little.'

'You think she suspects he did it?'

'She never suggested that. But she wasn't surprised by her mother's infidelity, or even very concerned about it – that seems odd, doesn't it? I asked if there was a lot of fighting between the parents, and she got kind of indignant, like, "Who ever heard of parents fighting?" But they weren't *communicating* very well, she said.' Sarah turned her hands up. 'Nothing about her attitude toward her parents makes sense to me yet. She doesn't want to touch him.'

'You think she's afraid of him?'

'Not afraid. More like seriously pissed off.'

'OK, so besides why she's mad at Daddy, what else do you want to know about Patricia?'

'Ask her to think again about the man in the bed. Is she sure she never saw him at the party? Did she stay to the end? Maybe there was a guest list, could she get that for us? Which parent does she ask for advice? Or money? Come to think of it, how come her brother went east to school but she's getting her degree in Tucson? If you get some rapport going, see if you can get a clue as to why it doesn't bother her that her mother sleeps around. Maybe find out, how upset is Daddy?'

'Why don't you ask him that?'

'Oh, I will. But – get all you can from Patricia, will you? Make friends, so she can spill the beans about the Henderson family circus. She must need somebody to talk to about now.'

Menendez looked up from his notebook. 'Hey, you want me to ask her about the candy?'

'The what? Omigod, Ray, with all that screaming I completely forgot about the candy! Do you think it's lost or—'

'Take a breath,' Menendez said. 'I turned it in to the DNA dollies when I brought the prints down.' By coincidence, all the DNA specialists in the Tucson crime lab were female, so male detectives called them 'DNA dollies,' and pretended to think their specialty was slightly bogus. It helped salve their egos, which were bruised by not understanding what the hell those bright-eyed women were talking about. 'So, shall I find out if Patricia knows where the dish belongs?'

'Absolutely. Oh, Ray, you were brilliant to remember the candy.'

'It's nothing,' he said. 'Standard police procedure, plus great genes and once in a while I pop a few steroids.'

'This ain't gonna cut it,' Nino told the overhead light. His earlier resolutions about grammar had evaporated and he was going downhill in other ways as well, lying in his unmade bed in his shorts at three in the afternoon, staring at the ceiling with bloodshot eyes. His room smelled like a winey swamp.

He needed to get up, take a shower, and get the hell out of town. But his head hurt so much he couldn't move without moaning. His stomach felt like it had been kicked by an elephant. He was sure the remedy was water, but every time he drank some he threw up again.

The most dismal part of this hangover was that beyond it lay something worse. As soon as he quit being actively sick and got up, he would have to face the old Yuma feeling – the fear, rage, and self-hatred that came from knowing he'd screwed up again and was going to have to pay for it with more hard time. Because caught or running, locked up inside or living under bridges, what difference did it make, really? Same old same old, Nino the dipshit running again. Fuck, he wanted to stop!

Some day maybe but not today. Today he had to run again, and he didn't know where to go.

Before the Yuma feeling there'd been the Sierra Vista feeling, the sick terror he'd carried around for months after a knife fight in a hotel kitchen there. That time he had to bite down on a toothbrush handle to keep from crying while he wrapped a towel around his arm, so the bandages would quit leaking blood while he bought a ticket on the bus.

And before Sierra Vista there'd been Willcox, the time he slammed a ladder into the face of the head picker in the pecan grove and ran.

If he thought long enough he'd work his way back to Bisbee where it all started, the day his grandmother yelled at him once too often. Big fucking deal over one broken egg on the floor. Why couldn't she cook it herself like he asked?

But no, she had to sit there, humped up at the kitchen table sucking on a cigarette, saying, 'Get home at meal times or go hungry.' Then when he dropped the egg he was trying to cook she snapped him with her dish towel and yelled, 'Fool, you're just like your worthless mother!'

It felt good to throw the heavy iron pan at her head, yelling, 'Whose worthless mother do you want me to be like, bitch?' His aim had been so much better than his judgment that day. But he had never believed she would actually do what she was always threatening, dial 911 with the blood running out of her cut lip and tell the sheriff to come take him away. When he heard the sirens coming he ran into the wash behind the house and hid in the mesquite, no jacket or nothing and it got cold out there when the sun went down. Shivering with cold, hungrier every minute, and thinking he was the worst age of all, fourteen, too young to hire and too tall to attract any sympathy. That was the first time he got that oops-too-late, hopelessly-screwed-up jolt of adrenalin and bile that he would later call the Bisbee feeling, the Yuma feeling. Over and over again, the same old feeling, *How did I get into this fucked-up mess?*

That time in Bisbee, the HHS agent was way too over-loaded to come looking for him. But by the time he realized that, he was gone. Just like he always was from then on, whenever trouble found him, gone down the road to try some-place new.

The DEA had not been too busy to look for him, later, and when he first got sent to Yuma he told himself that this hell-hole on the Mexican border was the worst mess yet. But later, coming out of prison with Pauly, for a while he felt like his luck had changed. Maybe he could get a fresh start in Tucson with somebody to watch his back for a change. And it worked out that way, at first – hell, Pauly even fed him, till he found Madge and this harmlessly crazy bunch of artsy-crafties at the theater.

Safe upstairs in the dusty attic room that went with the job, they had laughed till they choked at these clueless actors who talked endlessly and posed and took them at face value. For a few weeks they'd both been pretty contented here. They got hilarious again the day Nino reported how Madge said, 'I think the theater might turn out to be just the right *lifestyle* for you, Nino.'

Madge was so full of shit it was a wonder he could move without sloshing over, but at the same time, the man undeniably had some kind of an edge, he knew *something*. Because look at him, way too young to be retired and yet he did nothing for a living. 'Nada nada nada, my dear,' he said. 'Work? Surely you jest.' And all the little actresses giggled and rolled their eyes. But Madge drove a very nice vintage sports car and hung with the people who seemed to run everything, people who lived in beautiful houses like that one last night. Thinking about that house and last night, Nino turned over and groaned.

He drifted into a doze for a few minutes, till Felicity walked in and touched his forehead with her dry, cold hand. He sat up and yelled, 'What?'

Felicity made that tinkling sound that was her version of a laugh and said, 'My goodness, did I scare you?' Which, since she weighed maybe eighty-seven pounds with her shoes on, made him feel like a hopeless dork. But at the same time she did her cute eye-squinch thing – that was Felicity's special trick, to make it clear you were a jerk but then sweeten it up some way so you'd be an even bigger idiot if you took offense. She could do all that with just two or three words and a nose wrinkle.

Nino asked Madge once, 'What is it with Felicity? Even when she's doing me a favor she makes me want to break her face.'

'Oh, well, sweetie,' – Madge called everybody sweetie, men and women, young and old – 'don't take it personally, she does that to everyone.' He gave one of his forget-it waves, like shooing away chickens. 'Felicity can't help it, she's passive-aggressive.' He liked to sum people up like that, in one or two words, boom. The theater director was an insecure bully, boom. The dance instructor was a fraud, bam. The celebrity-worshipping CPA volunteer who did the theater's books for free? Anal-retentive. And now Felicity was passive-aggressive, whatever the fuck that meant.

Nino repeated it to Pauly, asking, 'You ever hear that expression?'

'No, but if it means uppity snot,' Pauly said, 'the silly old
fag called one right for a change.' Pauly was pretty good at
summing people up, too. Felicity, like every other female in
Tucson under fifty, Pauly wanted to fuck all day. But since
he knew he had no chance with her he just sneered past her
and waited for the noise to stop.

Now she stood over Nino, vibrating with her strange mix
of neediness and contempt, saying, 'Don't worry, I only
touched you to see if you were dead.' She handed him the
glass she was carrying. 'Drink this.'

'Why?'

'Because I have to get you going. Dress rehearsal in four
hours and the stage is still set up for Sunday's matinee. And
Pauly's not here to help us, remember?'

That made him sit up and drink the antacid. He had not
dreamed that part, then – Felicity had been there. So why
hadn't she called the police? And why would she expect him
to fool around setting up the theater if she knew he . . . A
dozen questions fought for attention and his brain felt like
it was on fire.

When did the party get so out of hand? He remembered
the fun, after the guests left and they started cleaning up –
the music going and some silly dancing between chores.
Then Madge passed around this big ballsy toke that had such
a kick . . . but maybe it didn't mix very well with that last
glass of wine. He'd been dancing with Felicity when he
began to feel like his eyeballs had come loose and were
rolling around in their sockets, getting a glance now and then
but no longer able to focus.

But he couldn't connect that memory to whatever happened
next. There was a blank space of nothing, and then Zack
was shaking him awake on the floor somewhere upstairs in
the dark, saying, 'Nino, what the Christ have you done, man?'

Nino didn't know. He kept saying, 'What? What?'

'We were in the kitchen and we heard the gun,' Zack said.
'Felicity, get the light, will you?' The light came on and
Nino found that he was holding this big monster of a weapon,
what was it? He let go of it but Zack said, 'Oh, God, don't
drop it,' and pressed it back into his arms. 'Be careful,' Zack
said, 'it might go off . . . oh.'

Zack had turned a little, toward the bed, and stood with his mouth open, staring. 'Omigod,' he whispered.

Nino saw the blood then, the two naked bodies on the bed. He started to gag, but he never finished that because he saw the funny little earring with the dangle, and that stupid ring with the missing stone, and his heart stopped. He felt his chest tighten, he couldn't breathe, the room whirled. He sucked air desperately and yelled, 'Pauly!'

Zack clapped a hand over his mouth and the two of them, Felicity and Zack, grabbed an armpit apiece and got him out of there. He remembered getting dragged downstairs, but he must have blacked out again when they got outside. Some time later he was getting out of the catering van at the side door to the theater, and Zack was telling him to sleep it off, whispering, 'I'll get rid of the gun.'

That part must have been a dream, wasn't it? He sat up on the hard little bed above the stage, drinking Felicity's hangover remedy and wishing he knew for sure. Alcohol sometimes made him hostile, he knew that, but then, face it, almost everything made him hostile sooner or later.

Not Pauly, though. He'd hardly ever been even seriously annoyed by Pauly, who was a dork but a good-hearted dork and somehow comforting to have around. *So why did I go get that gun?* Zack had showed him the gun rack earlier, coming back from the help's can. He'd said, 'You want to see something fancy, look at this,' and turned on the light in the den.

But why would he go back out there and take that big gun off the rack, carry it upstairs, and shoot old Pauly and their fancy hostess . . . *They were just having a nice hump on that big expensive bed. Why would I shoot them for that?* He shook his head and the room whirled. He closed his eyes and whispered, 'Before when I hurt people, there was always a reason.'

'I'll come back tomorrow,' Zack had told him as he helped him up the stairs to his room, 'and we'll figure out what to do.' But what was there to figure out? Nino just had to run. If he could get up the nerve to go outside.

What he needed right now was the kind of courage he would get from a cold beer and a joint, and then another cold beer and a lift out of town. All of which he might have been able to find, he thought, even with a crippling hangover, if his old buddy had been here to help. But Pauly was up there in bed in that elegant house with his face blown away.

Why, though? *Why did I go and kill that silly little turd?*

FIVE

Sarah's cell phone rang as she walked away from Menendez' cubicle. Jason Peete, talking from some noisy space with voices all around him, said, 'Sarah, you downtown?'

'Yes. What's up?'

'Well . . . you know Delaney told me to look around for the gun.'

'And you found it?'

'No, but I think I found the cupboard where it belongs. There's a paneled den at the back of the house on the first floor, has a gun rack full of hunting rifles and skeet-shooting guns and ammo, and a space at the top for a bigger weapon. Double-ought shells for a shotgun but the gun is missing.'

'Really?'

'Yes, indeed. Gone gone gone.'

'Well, that is very interesting. Nice timing, Jason, I'm just about to start talking to the husband, I'll ask him where it is. Call me if you find it, huh?'

'Without even pausing to scratch,' Peete said

She went on down the hall to the 'good' interview room, where Henderson waited, stolid in an overstuffed chair. She'd hoped he might feel a little nervous by now, but instead he was beginning to look numb.

'Let's start with your whereabouts for the last couple of days,' Sarah said, turning a page on her legal tablet. 'And nights,' she added, watching sideways to see if he took offense. He showed no reaction, staring blankly into the corner of the room. 'When exactly did you leave Tucson?'

'Uh . . . Friday afternoon. Late, maybe five o'clock.'

'And you went directly to Phoenix?'

'What? Oh, yeah, to Phoenix. To a . . .' He paused so long Sarah considered checking the pulse behind his ear. Finally he roused, took a deep breath, and said, 'conference.'

Finishing the sentence seemed to get his gears unstuck. He sat up, shuffled his feet, sipped his coffee.

'At a hotel?'

'Yes.'

'Which one?'

'Um . . . let's see, which one was it?' Another sip. 'Wait, I've got my checkout slip here someplace.' He dug through his briefcase till he found a crumpled receipt.

'Good.' She smoothed the paper in front of her like some praiseworthy piece of homework. 'This was a work-related meeting?'

'Well . . . sure. It was hosted by a company that makes . . . wait.' He groped through his pockets till he found a brochure that touted the advantages of a brand of metal framing that was lighter, stronger, went up faster and easier . . . the brochure didn't specify which products suffered by these comparisons.

'Thank you. And were you . . . at this hotel at the meeting the whole time, or did you visit friends while you were there?'

'Friends?' His expression suggested that no reasonable person would have friends in Phoenix. 'I got in late Friday night. Saturday I had a breakfast meeting and listened to a panel of builders and company reps until noon. I met with some bankers in the afternoon and then we had one of those terrible dinners with speeches. I snuck out and went to bed early.'

She stared down at the lines on her empty legal pad. 'And Sunday?' She sounded ridiculous to herself, naming off the days of a weekend to a grown man. But she had the feeling if she stopped he might run himself mentally into some corner and sit there spinning his wheels. 'After all the speeches, were there still more meetings?'

'Sunday.' He cleared his throat, shuffled his feet some more. Sunday was going to be a slog, evidently. 'I was supposed to be here at home for Pat's birthday party. She's mad at me because I didn't make it. She's eighteen, I guess that's kind of a milestone. But I got to thinking . . .' the dead-air pause again . . . 'about a piece of property I've been interested in for some time. I decided I'd like to have another look at it by myself before I contacted the brokers. So I drove out Sunday and walked around it.' He shrugged ironically and said, 'Bad old Dad.'

'Anybody with you while you walked?'

'What? No, I just told you,' he frowned impatiently, 'I wanted to see it by myself.'

'I see. May I have the address?'

'It doesn't exactly have one. It's just a piece of land, out in the middle of the desert. It was only about fifty miles out of my way, so—'

'You could show me on a map?'

'Sure. Got it marked up on a topo map, right here, just a minute.' He dug in the briefcase a few seconds before he sat back and said, 'I forgot. It's in the door pocket in the other car.'

'The one that got wrecked?'

'Yes.' He looked at her over the half-rims he'd put on to look through his briefcase, as if he'd just realized she might not believe him. *Roger Henderson, you are either pretty dense or very clever.* Either way, she had his full attention now. 'Soon as I get back to my office,' he said, 'I can find another map and show you where I was. It's an interesting location, right in the middle of an area that's predicted to see explosive growth in the next – oh, well, I guess you're not interested in that.'

'Oh, I'd be interested, sure.' She looked down at her notes, sat back in her chair and said, 'Where's your shotgun?'

'What?'

'The shotgun that fits in the rack in your den, where is it?'

His whole face got darker. 'You saying it's missing?'

'You saying you didn't know that?'

'Well, no, goddamn it, of course I didn't know that. Is that what – you mean somebody used my own gun to kill Eloise? Is that what happened?' He gave her one long look of shock and disbelief and then his features seemed to crumble. He buried his face in his big hands and gave vent to racking sobs that shook him and the chair he sat in. Tears ran out through his fingers and pooled on the knees of his neatly pressed pants.

It was hard to watch, but Sarah never looked away. One of the worst cases she had ever worked involved an extended-care facility operated by a grandmotherly woman named Dolly Mulligan, who murdered a half-dozen elderly retirees and went on collecting their Medicare payments for several years. Sweet-faced in pastel dresses and pearls, Dolly told teary, sentimental stories about the happy times her aged clients had enjoyed in her house, while she led Sarah's team of gagging detectives to their burial sites in the yard.

So while Roger Henderson wept, Sarah Burke sat calmly across the table from him, waiting, her steel-blue eyes as still as a pond.

'Couple minutes under the shower'll do it,' Nino promised himself. The room swayed alarmingly around him when he stood up. He clutched the bedstead and plotted a careful course to the bathroom door.

The miserable lukewarm trickle in the shower got him just wet enough to be chilled, and the worn-out gray towel was sodden before he was dry. Living conditions above the theater were no worse than yesterday, but he felt the grubbiness more now because he was scared and sick and alone.

Or not quite alone, actually. The ghost of Pauly had begun to appear dimly from time to time, sitting cross-legged on the bed across the room, dripping blood from the front of its head.

'Why'd you have to go and shoot my face off like that?' it whispered. A few seconds later it added, improbably, 'Gimme a cigarette, willya?'

'I'm all out myself,' Nino said. Startled to hear himself talking out loud to a phantom, he whimpered in alarm.

He found jeans and a T-shirt, not too dirty, hanging from hooks in the closet. There was even a clean pair of socks in a dresser drawer. Probably Pauly's but – 'You already killed me, you silly shit,' the ghost on the bed whispered, 'you think I'm going to care if you swipe my socks?'

Don't listen to him. The black shoes he'd worn last night were under the bed. When he pulled them out, he saw a smear of something across the toe of the right one, some lint stuck to it and a pebble. He held it up and realized the shoe had dried blood on it – that's what the trash was sticking to.

'That's my blood,' the ghost whispered. Nino put it down fast.

There was a pair of old sneakers in the closet. They had holes, but . . . he put them on. They fit all right. The black shoes, though, he couldn't leave them here, could he? They might be . . . evidence. The word made his balls shrivel.

He was going to run. He always ran when there was trouble. If he could get out of town he might just be forgotten . . . he hadn't been around long, hardly anybody even knew who he was. Pauly was the only person in Tucson who'd cared about him, and now Pauly was sitting over there whispering out of a mouth he didn't have any more.

How was he going to get rid of the black shoes? A bag! There was a plastic bag under Pauly's bed, from the last six-pack they'd brought home. He gritted his teeth, reaching under the ghost, but it faded when he came near. Good, then, he wasn't really crazy. He was just freaked, and why wouldn't he be? He put the shoes in the bag. Now where was the nearest garbage container? God, he needed a beer. He began to search the room for money.

He remembered they'd spent almost all they had in the Spotted Pony Saturday night, telling each other there'd be food and some tips at the party Sunday, and the bartender at the Pony would let them run a tab for a few meals till payday. Still, there must be a little money around here some-where. In pockets?

No money in the jeans. He found the black pants he'd worn to the job yesterday. Nothing in those pockets either. Whatever he'd been carrying must have fallen out while he was lying on the floor by the . . . he kept wincing away from thoughts about the bodies. But he needed desperately to make sense of it – *Why can't I remember shooting that gun?* – but he couldn't. His memory went as far as the dancing, with nothing beyond that but a fluffy white cloud till Zack was shaking him awake.

He found one bent quarter under the cushion of their only chair. What good was that? He pocketed it anyway and tucked the plastic bagful of shoes under his left arm. Sweating with fear, he eased his door open and tiptoed down the stairs.

Felicity caught him on the third step from the bottom, swooping into the stairwell like a breathless swan. She posed there, tossing her hair back, turning her head a little to the right because she knew the left three-quarter view was best. 'Ah, good, here you are. Come on, time to boogie! Derek'll be here any minute with all those damn dancers in boots –' she laid the back of her narrow right hand against her forehead in a why-was-I-born gesture – 'and that ghastly green sofa is still on the stage!'

'I ain't moving any furniture,' Nino said, 'till I get me a beer.' He said it mostly to stall; he had no money for beer, and he had no plan. But instinct told him to find a way around her, so he said the first thing that occurred to him.

Felicity had instincts too, though, which evidently told her that if Nino had money for beer, he would have pushed past her by now and be sprinting for the corner. 'Help me move the sofa,' she said, suddenly flinty-eyed as a pit boss, 'and I'll get you a beer and a bacon cheeseburger while you sweep the floor.'

Nino's stomach growled at the mention of food and the stairwell swayed vertiginously before his eyes. Gripping the railing to stay upright, he waited a few seconds for the world to settle down, glowered down at her and said, 'Deal.'

The sofa was not as hard to move as it looked; an earlier crew member with back problems had fitted its legs with rollers. One grunting heave got it out of its caster cups, and they rolled it thunderously backstage. Felicity produced a push-broom from the shadows. 'Just set the small stuff out of the way and sweep the stage. I'll be right back with your food, and then I'll call for your ride.' Her long hair streamed out behind her as she pushed open the stage door and stepped out, into sunshine so brilliant it set off his nausea again.

Half his brain urged him to run away as soon as she was out of sight. But every molecule of his body was crying out for the food and beer she had promised him. He felt he might die without it. And what did she mean about calling his ride? Was she talking about Zack, had they made plans for getting him out of town? How could they when he didn't know yet where he was going? But she hadn't sounded threatening or anything, had she? His head hurt, it was hard to think.

He began sweeping trash off the stage randomly, pushing it under curtains and off into the dark. What the fuck, they could pick it up later. And suddenly Felicity was back, popping the top on a cold beer. He would have kissed her foot for it, but she handed it to him gracefully with a little smile. He dropped the broom and drank half the can in one long swallow. Then he lowered the can, belched, waited a couple of beats to make sure it was going to stay down, and said, 'What about my burger?'

'Zack's bringing it,' she said, 'and another beer. I found him in the Spotted Pony, wasn't that lucky? Let's see, what do we need first here? A couple of hay bales to start, I guess.'

A great many car doors slammed outside the stage door, and voices began calling to each other. Derek DeVoe, the bellowing stage manager, unlocked the stage door and strutted in, followed by a chattering horde of dancers and actors. The sight of Nino standing on the half-swept stage with an open beer can set him off at once. He began berating them both, calling the condition of the theater *absolutely unacceptable* and promising to have their jobs if they didn't hop to it *right this instant*. Nino and Felicity, in a rare moment of unanimity, met each other's eyes and muttered, 'Bullshit.' Stagehand jobs paid so miserably they attracted only drifters like Nino and Pauly, who, when they moved on to jobs in fast-food restaurants, considered it a step up. The theater was perpetually short-handed; nobody ever got fired.

Felicity took the broom from Nino's hands and pushed him to the door saying, 'I can handle the rest of this.' On the step, shouting above the chatter of many dancers, she told him Zack was waiting around the corner.

Getting away from the director's hectoring voice felt like a miraculous escape. Nearly blinded by the blazing sunshine after the dusk of the theater, Nino stumbled around the corner. And there, like some grubby dream come true, sat the catering van with Zack in the driver's seat.

'Strap in,' he said, as Nino climbed unsteadily on to the high seat. 'Your burger's in the sack, and there's plenty more beer in the cooler back there.'

Hardly able to believe his luck, Nino pawed open a white paper sack holding a juicy burger. There were fries, too, and plenty of salt and catsup. He was so hungry he ate the first half of the burger without pausing to breathe. He popped a second beer to wash it down and asked where they were going.

'Up north a ways, a few miles east of Globe.'

'What's there?'

'I've got a motor home parked at the Apache Gold Casino where you can stay the night. Nobody's going to look for you there.'

'Zack, I gotta get farther away than—'

'Oh, I know. Here, by the way, I paid you in cash for the last two parties you worked. Your share of the tip's in there, too. From the motorhome park you can get a free ride to Phoenix, the casino runs buses all the time.'

'Why would I want to go to Phoenix?'

'For the bus depot. So you can get a ticket to –' he waved a hand – 'wherever.'

Nino belched profoundly, waited while the world did its rocking and settling thing, and asked a thoughtful question. 'How come you're being so nice to me?'

'Hey, we pass it around, right?'

We do? Since when?

'You'd do the same for me.'

Nino could not remember ever feeling a single impulse to help Zack with anything. But the man was driving contentedly along North Oracle Road, apparently convinced they were old buds. The cold beer he had brought along was sliding in on top of that nice tasty burger like the right answer to all of life's questions. And maybe it was, because Nino's stomach was beginning to feel almost ready to get back in the game. The sun was warm through the window on his side of the van. Nino relaxed a little and let his eyelids droop.

'Gonna be a while,' Zack said, 'you want to put the seat back?'

In just under three minutes, Henderson began to make the snuffling, throat-clearing sounds of recovery. Without a word, Sarah pushed a box of tissues in front of him. Sheepishly,

he blew his nose and wiped his face. When his face was dry
he sat up straighter, looked at his watch and muttered, 'Sorry.'

'I understand,' she said. 'You've been through a very hard
time.' She let her sympathy hang in the air for a beat or two.
Then she opened a file folder, looked through a few pages,
closed it and said, 'Actually, we haven't identified the weapon
that killed them yet.'

The words 'weapon' and 'killed' were so brutal they usually
avoided them when they talked to family members of victims.
She used them advisedly now, to see what effect they had
on Henderson. He seemed to hear only 'haven't identified,'
and the words made him angry. His breathing grew ragged,
and his red eyes glared at her out of the swollen slits left
from his latest bout of weeping. His voice was like a rake
over gravel. 'So you were just fishing.'

She sat up straighter and recrossed her legs, feeling the
sting of his contempt.

'This is what you do, huh? Play tricks on people?'

'What's tricky about it?' *Never let them put you on the
defensive.* 'A shotgun killed your wife and your shotgun is
missing. So I'm asking, where is it?'

'I have no idea.'

'When did you see it last?'

'I don't remember.' He looked past her. Was he thinking
about it, or posing? 'I haven't been hunting at all this fall.
Let's see, last year? I'm not sure.' He shifted in his chair.
'It's an ordinary gun, I got it years ago from my father and
I hardly ever think about it. So . . . I don't know.'

'Where would it most likely be if it's not on the rack? Do
you leave it around the house someplace?'

'Absolutely not. Never. It should be unloaded, on the rack,
and the cupboard locked. How'd you get into it, by the
way?' He waited. Her shrug said, we're police. 'I better by
God not find any broken locks in my house when I get back
into it.'

'You won't. Or not broken by us, anyway. Do you belong
to a shooting club, could you have left your shotgun there?
No? Do you have a cabin in the mountains, a hunting lodge?'

'No. I never did hunt much, and these days I'm always
too busy to take long weekends.'

Give it up. 'OK. Let's get back to this weekend. When did the conference end?'

'Saturday night. That stupid banquet that I mostly skipped.'

'Why didn't you skip it entirely and drive home?'

'I considered that but I had some more . . . bankers I needed to see and I wanted to see that piece of land in daylight. So I stayed.'

'Oh? I thought you said driving out to look at that land was an impulse on Sunday morning.'

'No. I never said that.'

'Not too far out of your way, you said—'

'Well, I'm sorry if you got the wrong impression. It was no impulse, I'd been thinking about it for some time. I've had a couple of conversations with the owner—'

'You just said you wanted to see it before you talked to anybody.'

'I meant the county people, the boards and bureaus that have to nit-pick everything now. The rancher that's selling it, I've known him for years. We've agreed more than once that by the time he was ready to quit growing cotton, I'd be about ready to start building houses out there. And as soon as this slump's over I'll do it.'

'So you knew all along that you wouldn't be home for your daughter's birthday party, is that right?'

'No. I expected to be home for the party till I learned I had more work to do in Phoenix. Then I called my wife. She knew I wasn't going to make it.'

'And Patricia?'

'Well, no.' He went back into his personal cloud bank for twenty seconds or so, came back out and said, 'I meant to call her but I . . . things came up and I forgot.'

'Uh-*huh*.' Sarah decided to see if he even remembered what he'd missed. 'What time was the party?'

'I . . . some time in the afternoon. Kind of vague, I think. Like so many—' He stopped and went back in the cloud bank.

'So many what?'

'Hmm? Oh . . . my wife liked to do that – say, "Stop in around three," or, "Come over when you're free." Her parties often went on for hours. Where were we?'

'You were explaining that you had to go back to Phoenix and see another person. I still don't understand why you couldn't have made it home? It's only a two-hour drive.'

'Well, sometimes in Phoenix traffic, closer to three.' He lowered his head and glared around like a cornered bear. 'God, my wife is dead, why the hell are we arguing about a birthday party?'

He's using his wife's death to stonewall me. She wrote, 'Stalling,' on her pad, let a little time pass while she looked at it, put the pen down gently and asked him, 'Who's the man?'

'What ma— oh, you mean the man in the morgue?'

'The man in the morgue who was in the bed with your wife. Yes.'

'I have no idea.'

'Really? You don't know him?'

'To the best of my knowledge I never saw him before.'

'Did you know your wife was having an affair?'

'She wasn't having an affair!' He grew red again and bristled. 'Weezy didn't – it wasn't anything like that.'

'What do you want me to call it? When your wife—' There was a quick tap on the door. They both turned toward it as Delaney put his head in, said, 'Sarah?' and nodded toward the hall.

Getting up, she asked Roger Henderson, 'Can I bring you anything when I come back? Coffee, water?'

'No.' He stood up too. 'I really have to get going.'

Delaney raised a cautionary hand, blinking solemnly. 'Just have a seat, please, Mr Henderson. We won't be long.'

Challenge seemed to be Roger Henderson's Gatorade. Energy puffed him up at once; a muscle in his jaw jumped, his shoulder muscles bunched and he clenched his fists. 'Am I under arrest?'

'Not yet.' Delaney followed his laconic answer with a long moment of silence. He stood in the doorway like a sun-blistered sphinx and let the power of law and order pile up behind him. Sarah watched in wonder as Roger Henderson slowly sat back down, postponing a discussion of probable cause. 'We're just asking you to wait here while we check a couple things, hmm?'

Impressed, Sarah followed her boss into the hall. *How much of that gravitas*, she wondered, *depends on Delaney's size and deep voice?* And right away, *Better be thinking what to use instead.*

In his office he said, 'We found the car. Your hunch was good, it's got the same GPS device as the one out front. I sent a wrecker, it'll be down tonight. But you don't need to wait for the device itself, of course, what you need is access to the database. So go ahead and get your warrant.'

'Right, I will. Good!'

'How do you think he's looking?'

'Better and better. He's got guilt and anger coming out of his ears.'

'Yes. It's going to be awkward, though. Pinning a crime like this on one of the biggest players in town. We better be damn sure we're right.'

'We will be.'

'Good. And in the meantime, I'm thinking, why don't we let Henderson go?'

'Boss, I was just getting to the—'

'I know where you were getting, I was watching. You don't have enough to arrest him yet, though, do you?'

She frowned at the opposite wall. 'No.'

'So what I'm saying is, let's show a lot of compassion now for his tragic situation. You get your warrant and read his tracker, I'll have the lab check his car, and if you're still hot for him we'll arrest him when he least expects it.'

Which covers your butt with the powers that be in case Henderson comes up clean. 'OK. We can't let him back in his house yet, though.'

'Well, no.' He rattled the coins in his pocket, thinking. 'But he's easy to find whenever we want him. He owns Hen-Trax and a pile of other stuff, he's building eight hundred houses on the south-east side and bidding on another big project for Rio Nuevo, and he's got a GPS tracking unit in his car. Where's he gonna go?' Delaney stuck two fresh pieces of gum in his mouth and chewed them energetically. 'Does this case seem kind of like bad TV to you?'

'Opera, I was thinking.'

'I see what you mean. Crime in high places, lots of blood

and screaming.' He treated her to a rare smile. 'Proceed with care, huh?'

Better believe it.

She walked back in the interview room, thanked Roger Henderson for coming in and told him he was free to go. She gave him her card and told him to call if he thought of anything he wanted to ask, and then she led him down the hall to where Patricia sat across the table from Ray Menendez. They were talking quietly, like old friends. *You sure did a better job on the rapport than I did, Rye Moon Dough.* She watched them for a couple of heartbeats, thinking, *Of course you had the easy one, didn't you?*

Patricia Henderson was young and beautiful and rich and right now she was hurt and very vulnerable. Low-hanging fruit. *And even if he is a cop, Ray Menendez is still a twenty-something man. So let's be extra careful here.*

She watched Patricia march stone-faced out of the building beside her father. Then she hurried back to Menendez' cubicle, where he was typing his notes into his computer, and made sure he understood that Patricia's daddy had been escorted to the morgue a couple of hours earlier by an assistant county attorney.

Menendez rocked back in his chair and said, 'You don't say?'

'I do say. And not only is Patricia Henderson's father a mover and shaker, her mother was the daughter of—'

Menendez held up one hand like a crossing guard. 'Sarah, I know all about the Della Maggios, OK? My grandmother used to do housework for one of Patricia's great-aunts. You don't need to worry about me trying to pull a Roger Henderson.'

'I didn't mean—'

'Sure.' His ironic smirk turned quickly thoughtful. 'It's turned out pretty well for him, though, hasn't it?' Then he put the whole conversation behind him and got back to business. 'You want to hear the answers to all those questions you gave me?'

'Absolutely.' Chagrined, she sat down and turned a page. 'What have you got?'

'Number one, the man in the bed. She didn't want to talk

about him at first. Said, well, his face was gone and I certainly never saw any of the rest of him before, so . . . then she calmed down and said come to think of it, though, she *had* seen that stupid ring at the party, and she thought it was one of the caterers' helpers wearing it. And I'm inclined to believe her because it doesn't figure one of the guests would be wearing anything so tacky.'

'So Mama was sleeping with the help. Speaking of tacky.'

'Fairly shoddy, yeah. Then, let's see . . .' He was checking off a page of notes. 'Oh, yeah, number two, her mother usually didn't bother with a guest list, just asked everybody she could think of and told them to bring friends if they felt like it, come over whenever they could. Mom was a free spirit in more ways than one, I guess.'

'I wonder how she figured the supplies?'

'I asked that – aren't we practical types? Patricia said, "Mom always just told the caterers to bring plenty of everything." I guess if you're really rich you don't worry about getting overcharged.'

'Hey, the caterers.' She looked up, embarrassed. 'I haven't got anything on them.'

'I thought of that too. So I asked her who catered the party Sunday and she said she doesn't know the name of the company but one of the servers was an actress named Felicity, works at that community theater called Grand Street. It's in the book.'

'Leave me a note, will you? What else you got there?'

'Well, three, Patricia could always get a little extra money from her mother if her allowance ran short. But if she wants advice, which I gather she seldom does, Daddy's the Man.

'And four, her brother Adam's gone to eastern boarding schools since seventh grade. She thinks it started with some scrape he was in here in Tucson, but she was too young then to hear any of the details. Now she says he makes fun of dusty old Tucson and says he'll never come back here to live. As for five,' he looked uncharacteristically uncomfortable, 'I chickened out on the question of why nobody cares if Mom gets extra nookie – that's a hard question to ask a daughter, you know?'

'Rude. Yes. Seems kind of key, though.'

'You think?' He rolled his eyes up. 'What else?' He turned his handwritten notes sideways and read a scribble along the edge. 'Oh, yeah, six. The candy dish was Mom's. It was always filled with those wrapped candies and as long as Patricia can remember it's stood on that bedside table nearest the door.'

'Nearest the door. So Patricia's Mom was on the wrong side of the bed?'

'Uh . . . yes. Does that make this a cautionary tale?' They were suddenly grinning inanely at each other, remembering all the wrong-side-of-the-bed jokes they had ever heard. Then Menendez got serious and said, 'So . . . I guess this must have been their first time together.'

And Sarah, following his thought precisely, said, 'First time in that room, anyway.' *Always one of the first things settled between lovers, which side of the bed is mine? And I still don't know how we decide it.* Astonished to find herself trading intimacies about love-making with Menendez, she stood up and closed her notebook without quite meeting his eye.

This case had surprised her several times already and the first day wasn't over yet. Delaney wasn't going to have to tell her again to proceed with care.

Felicity Linderman had always known she was a star. She was Rita Mae Linderman's only child, conceived in her mother's fortieth year. Her father was a vague and distant figure, a blurry image in what Mommy said was their wedding photo. His absence never bothered Felicity much because it never seemed to matter to her mother. Rita Mae didn't need a husband. All her energy was absorbed by the need to make the world realize she had given birth to a multi-talented beauty, a prodigy born to thrill an audience.

Felicity's part of the job was to develop her amazing talents as fast as she could. You had to be ready when your big chance came.

In the beginning, her fees as an adorable child model paid for most of Felicity's lessons in dance, singing and acting. Rita Mae's function was to seek out the best teachers and get her daughter to the lessons.

At about age ten, though, most of the modeling jobs dried
up and the task changed for both of them. Rita Mae had to
come up with more of the money for training and Felicity
had to learn to work around her limitations. She was a fair
singer, not a great one, and a graceful dancer with ankles
too weak for ballet. What she was, she knew by her middle
teens, was a very good actress with the wrong face.

Alone on her most recent birthday (she no longer mentioned
birthdays to anybody else), Felicity had faced the terrifying
reality that she was *ohdeargod twenty-two years old already*.
With a portfolio that, after hundreds of hours of lessons, still
held only those three voice-overs on the exercise-machine
ads; the stills, admittedly lovely, from the underwear cata-
logue; and the tiny walk-on as a maid in the slasher movie.
Plus a long string of parts in regional theater, and letters of
high praise from third-rate directors out in the boonies, but
who gave a damn about those?

Her desperation had moderated last month when Madge,
looking for kicks he said, started hanging around the theater
and discovered her. Before long he was talking to her about
her 'prodigious talent,' the way her mom always did.

'Sweetie,' he said, 'you're so much better than anybody
else here that it's actually somewhat embarrassing. Why
aren't you in the big time?' All she needed, he said, answering
his own question, was a nose job and caps on her teeth.
'Remember what it did for Tom Cruise?'

She said she knew that but she'd never been able to afford
it. Money's just a detail, Madge said, waving it away – he
could always find money for friends in need. But . . . was
Felicity open to trading a few favors?

It was really just a series of small, harmless things he
needed her to do. A little play-acting, think of it that way.
Zack would explain the game as they went along; Madge
wasn't going to discuss this with her ever again. 'No, really,
sweetie, it's better this way, you'll do better if you're not
worrying about the small stuff.' Yes, he knew she was an
actress and he'd seen she could play any part, wasn't that
why they were talking? But this whole thing would work
better if she honestly didn't know what came next.

He gave her the first half of the money for the plastic

surgeon and her credit card covered the rest of the fee. The
surgery left some serious bruises, she played all the maid
and mother-in-law parts for a while. But it was almost healed
by the time Madge brought the boys to the theater. She helped
get them hired as she'd promised, guided them into the
catering job – Madge already had that set up with Zack –
and watched over them on the first party jobs so they didn't
totally screw up. Nothing hard about any of that, but she had
refused, Sunday night, to even talk about going upstairs.
When Zack came down and said he needed her help, she
shook her head, picked up a bus-box full of glasses and
headed for the back door. 'No way,' she said. 'You can't ask
me to do that.'

'I'm not asking, I'm telling. He's too heavy for me alone,
so you have to help me.'

'Get Madge—'

'Will you cut out the diva crap? You know Madge is gone.'

'I don't know anything, how could I? I've been out there
in the dark, breaking my back loading the van—'

'Yeah, yeah, you were outside so you don't know anything,
that's your story. I don't give a crap what you say later on,
but right now you gotta help me get this piece of dog shit
out of the house.'

'Forget it.' Felicity began to unbutton the frogs on her
white service jacket. 'I did all this clean-up by myself and
now it's done and I'm going—' She drew in a hoarse, shocked
breath as Zack reached across the two feet between them
and grabbed her almost-healed nose in a steel grip. Silently,
watching her through his mean little slits of eyes, he forced
her to her knees.

'Blease,' she blubbered in a panic, 'blease blease blease
don't hurd by dose.'

Because her new nose was the whole point of everything!
She'd never wanted any part of this cockamamie scheme,
whatever it was, for one second. But if it was the only way
to get the money for a nose job and caps on her teeth – and
there were just these few little things she had to do – then
why not go ahead and fulfill her destiny at last?

She'd never wanted to know any of the details. By the
time they finished whatever it was and went on to the next

whim, she would already have collected the rest of the money and paid off the card. And whatever happened she couldn't be expected to return it. You don't return a correction on a deviated septum.

By the day of the party she felt excited and happy, because the surgery was healing nicely. In her mind she was already on her way to Hollywood. Even if her legs were too short to be a top model and her dancing talent and singing voice were serviceable but not outstanding, she knew she was a very good actress now, and could be outstanding, maybe the best, with the right direction. But she was never going to get her chance in movies as long as she faced casting directors with a too-long, slightly crooked nose and an overbite. Her face had to be fixed! She didn't care what happened to Pauly and Nino, why would anybody? Louts, they were just louts.

'I know I have to suffer for my Art,' she'd told her mother on the phone, the day she showed the boys to their little room under the eaves. 'But really, some of the people I have to put up with in This Business.' They gave her the creeps, watching with dead eyes while she found sheets and towels for them in the prop room, scrounged soap and toilet paper from the actors' john. Then that pig Pauly asked, 'Ain't you even going to make up the beds?'

Her mother had put on her super-soother voice as usual, so familiar from the years of auditions, urging, 'Be patient, baby, your day is coming.' Her mother avid to hear every detail of the parts she was assigned at the theater, the only return she ever got on the long years of hauling Felicity to lessons and paying, paying. But then that's all she ever wanted. And God, who asked her to start the stage-mother stuff, anyway?

Not that Felicity would have changed the striving years if she could. What would life be worth without that extra heft, the zing that only achievement provided? The joy when you knew you nailed a part. To be in This Business, what else could possibly compare? But her mom put so much pressure on. Felicity dreamed of a short phone call in the future, her mother crooning with pleasure over her latest triumph, Felicity finally able to say, 'Gotta go, Mom, got all these people waiting . . .'

It would not be long now. As soon as the surgery healed she was going to take her newly beautiful face back out to LA and show everybody what she could do.

But first she had to stop this filthy pig of a caterer from wrecking everything, by breaking her nose all over again.

'Blease,' she begged him, 'led go of by dose and I'll do whadeber you zay.'

Naturally she had not been sincere about *that*. Being in the room with a slug like Zack was tantamount to being in the room alone, so why would you waste a moment being sincere with him? Felicity was going to say whatever she had to say to get him off her nose and then do what she had to do to get him out of her life.

As she rose from her knees and followed him up the deeply carpeted stairway she was already making plans not to remember any of this. She would focus on a bare white spot in the middle distance, the way she did when an actor in a love scene smelled bad or had a suspicious cough. She could always do that, focus on her part and delete the rest. Zack would fade and soon be erased entirely. His mean pig's eyes and crooked front teeth and his name that sounded like a grackle's cry, *Zack*, were only faintly in the room with her now and would soon be entirely gone.

When she began to feel somewhat faint, on her way out the door with the stinking weight of Nino crushing her right shoulder, on impulse she grabbed with her left hand for a few of the delicious-looking wrapped candies in the dish by the door. Zack felt her weight shift and growled, 'Hang on!' and she dropped the candies back in the dish, snatched the glass handle instead and brought the whole thing along. But outside by the fountain Nino began to mumble and pull away, and Felicity had to drop the dish and hang on to Nino with both hands. It took all the strength they had between them to get him into the back of the van, and the trip up the steep stairs at the theater was a sweaty nightmare that she was never quite able to disremember.

By the next afternoon, though, hugely relieved that her nose looked completely undamaged and was not even sore, Felicity watched the stage door close behind Nino and heaved a sigh of relief. He was out of her life and her money would be along soon. As she picked up the push-broom to finish sweeping the stage, she noticed the plastic sack he'd been carrying when he came downstairs. He'd forgotten it on the floor by a small table. *Should I try to catch him?*

She thought about it for one second and shrugged. Whatever it was, he wouldn't need it now. Would that braying jackass of a director never stop shouting? She broomed the bag offstage with the rest of the trash.

SIX

Giving in gladly to sleepiness, Nino reached for the lever to put his seat back. He could see that Zack was in the front rank of a cluster of traffic on North Oracle, heading for the light on Orange Grove. It was just turning green and he was holding his speed steady, expecting to sail on through. But just then the driver of an old Taurus heading east on Orange Grove convinced himself that the amber light he had been speeding toward was going to last for him. When it changed he apparently decided that red was a fine color too, and shot across the intersection immediately in front of Zack.

By hitting his brake hard, Zack managed to miss the rear bumper of the Taurus by a couple of inches. By about the same margin, the Hummer behind him somehow contrived to stay out of Party Down's rear cargo space. There was an electric moment when Zack's terrified eyes met the angry stare of the Hummer's driver in his rear-view mirror, and then Zack yelled, 'Asshole!' and leaned on his horn. The horns of the Hummer and the next two vehicles followed suit.

Nino had forgotten all about napping by then. He was watching his driver with growing alarm.

Working parties for Party Down, he had known Zack as an ugly, gloomy man who rarely spoke except to give orders. His directions were short and clear, though, and you could count on him to have everything he needed in the van. His events ran like clockwork and he paid what he'd promised on time. That was all Nino knew about him, all he'd ever wanted to know.

Now the grim but rational man of the party scenes was gone, replaced by a fuming nutcase. His face had turned purple with rage, his eyes were bloodshot and his snarling lips were drawn back in a fury over his crooked teeth. Once started, he could not seem to stop swearing. Curses poured

out of him. He sounded meaner than Nino's grandmother on
her worst day.

It didn't take a subtle thinker to recognize that this was
not the face of a man who'd go out of his way to help out a
part-time employee in a jam. Why, Nino began to ask himself,
did I let myself get suckered into a van with this person?

And how could I ever have believed he would take me to
his secret hideaway for the night and fix me up with a free
ride to the bus station tomorrow?

I mean, why not believe he was going to drive right up
to the North Pole and turn me over to Santa Claus?

He didn't think it through any more than that, he just got
ready to run the way he always did. But they were in the
middle of traffic on a busy six-lane highway and he had no
idea where to go. So he did the next thing his instincts told
him to do. He yelled, 'Oh shit, Zack, look out!' and pointed
across Zack's chest at the west side of the highway.

There was nothing over there; they were in the middle of
a block. But it was the side the Taurus had just come from
so it worked. Zack quit swearing and turned his head to look.
In that instant Nino unbuckled his seat belt, leaned across
Zack, and opened the driver's-side door.

Zack was looking into his left ear by now, yelling, 'What
the fuck?' Nino slid back quick as a snake, unbuckled Zack's
seat belt as he slid past it, braced his feet on the floor, and
pushed Zack out the door.

Zack hit the pavement with one foot, whirled helplessly
left with his arms out, and slammed into the car going by
him in the next lane. That car slowed, all the vehicles behind
it stopped, and most of the traffic in the nearest lanes got
stopped within a couple of car-lengths.

Zack was lying on the pavement by then, dazed and
bleeding from scrapes all over his body. He could see his
van far ahead, speeding toward the next intersection. Barely
able to hold his head up, he watched Nino maneuver into
the outside lane and turn right. The little shit was probably
headed back downtown, Zack thought. Then the world got
distant and blurry for a few minutes, and the next thing he
knew he was being helped into a squad by the patrolman
somebody had called.

They sat there for some time while the patrolman offered him water and then a ride to an emergency room. He took the water and refused the hospital, asking instead for a ride to his shop so he could get his other vehicle.

'I can do that,' the officer said, 'but don't you want to file a complaint against your passenger first?' He was watching his new victim curiously by now, so on the spot Zack invented a troubled nephew who needed help, not blame.

'I fired him today because he's no good on the job, but I certainly don't want to give my brother any more trouble than he's got already.' Stiffening up fast and still a little dazed, Zack was nevertheless clear on one point – the last thing he needed to do right now was fill out any damn police reports.

He persuaded the patrolman to give him a lift back to his shop so he could get his car.

'What about your van, though?' the officer said. 'Don't you want to report it stolen?'

'Nah,' Zack said. 'He'll go to one of his relatives and I know 'em all. I'll just drive around till I find it.'

'Well,' the officer said, 'if you're sure.'

'He can't seem to grow up,' Zack said. 'By now he's probably crying to his mama about his mean old uncle.' He shrugged and said, 'Families.'

'Yeah,' the patrolman said, 'ain't they the worst?'

Alone in her workspace, Sarah surveyed her littered desk and thought longingly, *Back in the day, I'd have stayed right here until midnight and cleaned up this mess.* She still sometimes yearned for the flat-out concentration of those first two kinetic years in Homicide, when her zeal to be the best female detective in the history of TPD kept her at her desk through many late nights. Secretly, she still believed she might have nailed the title if there'd been one.

'And all that cost you,' Andy Burke had pointed out near the end of that blurry work spasm, 'was our marriage.'

'Oh, right, and you jumping the bones of every waitress you could catch had nothing to do with it,' she'd yelled back, hurling a plate and two phone books at his head. Her aim and the strength of her pitching arm improved so much during that last disastrous year of marriage that on the final morning of white-hot rage she was able to heave most of his clothes and his Waterpik out the door before he got her stopped. Wherever the balance of blame lay between Andy's carousing and her drudgery, adding Homeric battles to the mix had made their home life too toxic to tolerate.

But now her divorce was yesterday's news, and the new priorities in her life demanded she get home for dinner if it was humanly possible. So she plunged headlong into the multitasking mode by which a Tucson homicide detective enabled a family life. Tobin called it 'Fun with both hands.'

Wearing her headset so she could talk on the phone while she sorted paper, she worked through several clusters of phone tag before she dug down to a memo in Menendez' hand-writing, 'One of the servers at the party was a girl named Felicity – actress at Grand Street theater,' and the number. She dialed and listened to the phone ring many times before somebody with a young androgynous voice picked it up and said, breathlessly, 'Grand Street Theater.'

Guessing that a theater group would be informal, Sarah took a chance and just asked for Felicity. The hurried person at the other end of the line shouted, without hesitation, into some echoing space, 'Anybody seen Felicity?' A distant answer floated back, filtered through the heavy breathing of the person on the phone. When the remote yelling stopped, the person on the phone said confidently, 'She's due to rehearse the next scene, so she'll be here soon.'

Sarah left her number, privately betting she'd leave it many more times before she got an answer. But five minutes later when she answered her ringing phone, 'Burke,' she heard a voice like a velvet mitten say, 'This is Felicity.' *I'm a kind, cultivated person*, the voice suggested, *and when you know me better you'll like me even more.*

'This is Detective Sarah Burke at the Tucson Police Department. I'm calling because I understand you were part of the catering crew that served the Henderson party Sunday, and I need to ask you a few questions.'

'Questions? I don't really . . . what did you say your name is? I'm sorry, there's a lot of noise in here.'

'Detective Sarah Burke, of the Tucson Police Department.'

She spoke louder and slower. 'I need to ask you about a party in El Encanto Estates, where two people were murdered sometime Sunday night.'

'I'm an actress, Ms Burko, I work here at the Grand Street Theater.'

'Burke. *Detective* Burke. You also sometimes serve parties, as a caterer, right? And you were on the crew at the Henderson house Sunday night.'

'Oh, ah . . . Henderson. I have worked there a couple of times, yes.'

'Including Sunday night?'

'Let's see, was that when . . . it was mostly in the afternoon, as I remember it. Cake and ice cream, a birthday party – for a daughter named, um, Patricia I think.'

The kind of thumps and crashes that in scripts are called 'noises off' had begun behind her. Felicity shouted, away from the phone, 'Oh, God, what did you do?' Into the phone she said, 'Could we talk about this later, please? I've got a mess on my hands here.'

There was one last crash and then a humming silence coming over her dead phone. Sarah listened for a moment before acknowledging to herself that this young woman had hung up on her. She said aloud, to her empty cubicle, 'What the hell?'

I'll catch her tomorrow, she decided, looking at her watch. She called her own house and asked her mother, 'Everything under control?'

'Pretty much.' At her house, the clattering noises meant Aggie Decker was unloading the dishwasher. 'Hold on a second.' The noise level changed, a door closed, and when Aggie spoke again a bird was singing nearby. 'Denny's got her nose out of joint about something, do you know what it is?'

'No. She was fine this morning. Did you just go outside?'

'Yeah, I'm on the back step. Denny came in from school looking like a storm in the desert, but when I asked her what was wrong she said, "Nothing." Changed her clothes and started on a big pile of homework, hasn't said a word to me since.'

'Huh. Better than having a tantrum, I guess. I'll see what

I can do tonight. But you know Denny, she marches to her own drummer. Anything else?'

'Will Dietz just parked his car at the curb. Were you expecting him for dinner?'

'More or less.' *As much as I ever know what to expect from him.* 'Have you got enough food or shall I—'

'We're fine. You on skej?'

'Yes, I'm just heading out. Do we need milk?'

'Tomorrow,' Aggie said, 'but I'll bring it with me when I come.'

'OK. Anything else?'

'No, we're good, just come on home.'

She punched END and stacked the last of tomorrow morning's work in the In basket, with the highest-priority stuff on top. One last check of her email, four more answers banged out in the semi-literate patois that was replacing decent English on electronic devices worldwide, 'c u 4 lunch thurs . . .' She shut the machine down, locked her desk, and grabbed her jacket in one fluid move, and trotted for the elevator.

Mount Lemmon turned purple and then slate as she zigzagged north-east on traffic-clogged streets. She swiveled her head to ease the tense muscles of her head and shoulders. *Relax* . . . but the thought came unbidden: *God, there's still dinner to get on the table and then dishes and help with homework, and after that whatever the hell is bothering Denny.* She had taken in her ten-year-old niece at the beginning of October, when her sister Janine took a powder. And in the same month, Will Dietz had landed in her life, tentative as a butterfly but with no apparent inclination to migrate further. He seemed to have two equally intense desires – to stay as close to her as she'd allow, and not to talk about his intentions, if any.

Not that Sarah was pressing him for declarations. Who had time to make big decisions? Just crowding her everyday life into her limited means felt like all she could possibly handle right now.

She knew Will Dietz was the man she should have been looking for if she'd believed he existed. But by the time he popped up on her radar screen she was dealing with a pothead

sister and a badly spooked niece. He had put aside his con-
valescence from recent life-threatening injuries, though, to
help her out during the disappearing-Janine crisis. Then he
had taken to turning up at her door, often unannounced but
timed so she'd know he researched her schedule. Meantime
he'd charmed her hard-edged mother off her feet by making
himself useful around the house. What could you do with a
man like that but take him in and feed him extra helpings?

As for the other unsettled factor in her life, she was fiercely
proud that Denice Lynch, a bright, tough kid who was
nobody's fool, wanted to stay with her in preference to other
relatives. But she was flying blind a lot of the time. There'd
been no trace of Janine since she disappeared leaving only
an enigmatic note. Forced to make decisions whether the
system said they could or not, Sarah and her mother had
switched Denny's school to one closer to Sarah, cleaned up
Janine's rental house, and turned in the keys. Sarah told
Denny, 'I'm trying to get appointed your legal guardian, but
I'd like to find your mother first so we don't have to sue her
in court, you understand?'

Denny dipped her head in the quick little nod that was
becoming her default response to the shame of abandon-
ment. Sarah wanted to make their relationship official and
see that look go away, but she was hoping to do it without
paying a lawyer, because she needed all her take-home pay.

Finding the hours and money for child care in the same
month she made space and time for a still-convalescing man
often felt like a bigger mountain than she could possibly
climb. She understood now why single mothers occasionally
wore the panicked expressions of horses running from burning
stables.

Aggie had promised, when Janine took off, to help care
for Denny. And she had been as good as her word, giving
up some of the fun and games in her retirement community
to come across town and cover the hours after school. She
did most of the cooking and laundry while she was there.
Dietz was picking up a lot of the slack too, doing grocery
runs and garbage and repair jobs. A sure-fire way to lose a
new boyfriend, Sarah thought, but once, when she started to
protest, he wagged his screwdriver at her and said, 'Sarah,

this is strictly business. Stay out of it.' He went back to resetting the hinge on a kitchen cupboard. 'Aggie traded me a mending job on my blue sweater for a fix on this door.'

Aggie made no secret of her opinion that Will Dietz walked on water. 'Anything is possible now,' she told Denny one day, ignoring Sarah who was standing right there. 'My daughter the cop has even landed a decent boyfriend.'

All she got back from her granddaughter was the look Sarah had begun to think of as the Denny Special, a smile so cool and polite it curdled milk. Denny Lynch had seen enough boyfriends come and go in her mother's turbulent household to convince her that the whole demographic ought to be driven off a cliff. Never exactly rude to Will Dietz, she treated him with stiff courtesy that carried its own indictment, and went out of her way to avoid being alone with him.

Dietz wasn't offended, or even surprised. 'Denny's been jerked around,' he said, when Sarah ventured an apology, 'give her time.' He and Sarah were alone that afternoon for once, in his Spartan casita on the east side, wrapped tightly around each other after one of their rare hours of lovemaking. Dietz's nondescript face settled into ironic folds beneath the diagonal scar that put a second part in his hair. 'The child can't possibly resist my charm forever.'

'Probably not,' Sarah nuzzled his neck. 'Although much of your charm is known only to a lucky few.' She caressed some of his hidden charm and Dietz chuckled low in his throat.

Inconvenient as their present living arrangements were, Denny's dubious nature wasn't all that kept Sarah from talking about moving in with Dietz. Her own house was too small to accommodate another tenant, and all Dietz had told her about his situation was, 'I'm too poor to seek help for my low self-esteem.' Even allowing for his quirky sense of humor, she could see that the thrift-shop decor in his apartment matched what she knew about him, that he'd had an accident-prone career in law enforcement and a divorce that dragged on for years.

'Will and I,' she told Aggie, 'have everything in common – unfortunately.' It was true, they were classic law-enforcement train wrecks. The crazy hours and emotional stress of their jobs put so much pressure on personal lives that the divorce rate in the department was an ongoing source of embarrassment. Not to mention the disastrously low survival stats during the first five years after retirement. Even a cockeyed optimist might suggest they take it slow.

But take it. Oh, yes. Locking her car in the carport, Sarah looked in through the narrow window by the door, marveling at the way her recently assembled family was adapting to her small spaces. Denny had set her placemat aside to do homework under the lamp at the round table where they would all presently eat dinner. Oblivious inside her self-made bubble of concentration, she was nibbling on her lower lip and her hair, as usual, was coming out of its braids.

Dietz had somehow created a small clearing at the end of the kitchen counter, where he chopped lettuce and tossed it into a salad bowl. He was sipping from a long-neck beer that he protected from spills by stashing it behind the knife-holder each time he set it down. The scar from his latest near-death experience shone pink under the overhead light.

Directly behind him at the stove, Aggie was being careful with her elbows, squinting through steam-clouded glasses at whatever she was stirring.

My funny valentines. Sarah walked into her house, and all three faces turned toward her, looking as if they thought she brought home answers. Happy against all odds, she smiled, and they all began to talk at once.

'I don't get this at all,' Denny said, pointing to her homework.

'Aggie says she can't stay for supper,' Dietz said. 'Tell the truth, am I eating her food? Because I don't have to stay—'

'I told you, I have to hurry home and get all gussied up.' Aggie was putting her coat on as Sarah took hers off. She pulled keys out of her purse, set them down and put her purse on top of them. 'Can you believe it? I finally talked ol' Sam into ballroom dancing. Now where'd my keys go?'

'Have fun,' Sarah said, fishing the keys out and handing them to her. 'Try not to wreck the car on the way home.'

'I'll be very careful.' She gave a great triumphant hoot of

laughter. 'I wouldn't miss tonight for anything! Sam's going to learn the samba!'

Sarah watched her mother out of the house, enjoying the reflected glow of her pleasure. When she turned back to the table she said, 'Denny? What were you saying to me before? When I came in,' she added, when Denny looked up at her blankly.

'Oh. I said I don't understand one of the questions in my social-studies workbook.'

'Ah. Let's tackle that after we eat. Will you set your books aside now and get ready for dinner?'

'OK.' Solemn and systematic, she stacked her homework in the space they had reserved for it on the buffet. In Sarah's house, spaces had to be reserved, or you might stand around holding something for a long time.

They ate quickly, with the ravenous appetites of hard-working people. Denny had been skinny and pale from an uncertain food supply when Sarah took her in, and it was a pleasure, now, to see her cheeks rounding out. She cleared the table while Sarah and Will had a coffee, then the two adults did dishes and Denny went back to her homework.

They'd established routines in the past month that jogged along without much discussion. And Denny was always quiet, so if Aggie hadn't warned her, Sarah might not have noticed how uneasy she was. But watching her covertly, she saw the child distractedly pulling hairs out of her head and scratching away at the skin on one thumb.

When Dietz put on his weapon and badge, ready to go to work, Sarah followed him out to his car. He turned at the curb, ready to give her a hug, but she held up both hands in a 'wait' signal and asked him, 'Any idea what's bothering Denny?'

'Little trouble with the lessons is all I know.'

'Something bigger. Ma saw it too. Well. Stay safe.' She hugged him briefly, gave him a just-barely kiss that was all he could afford to indulge in before ten hours on the griddle of Tucson after dark. She lifted a hand as he turned at the corner and he sent back a friendly little toot.

Homework problems were mercifully easy to solve that night. While Denny got her backpack ready for morning

Sarah started a couple of the perennial loads of laundry that she now thought of as growing like mushrooms in the house whenever the lights were turned off. By the time the washer and dryer were both whirring, Denny had her teeth brushed and was getting into bed. Sarah appreciated the fact that she never had to nag Denny over things like bedtimes, as she had heard so many mothers do. She sometimes reflected, though, that Denny's good behavior was a little unnatural. Maybe she still didn't feel sure enough of her welcome to misbehave.

Thinking about that, she went in and sat down beside the small solemn girl on the narrow iron bed – Aggie's child-hood bed that had served Sarah and Janine and now was Denny's. It was one of the few things they'd brought across town when they closed up the house on Lurline Street.

'We've got time for one chapter of *Tom Sawyer*, if you'd like.'

'OK.'

'Or is there something you'd like to talk about?' She picked up the hand with the tortured thumb. 'Did you have trouble at school today? You seem a little uneasy.'

'I'm OK,' Denny said quickly. Her voice broke when she said it, though, and then tears were running down her cheeks. Mortified, she pulled a sheet over her head. The sobs that came out from under it almost made Sarah's heart stop. Immediately, she began imploring Denny to stop. She knew it wasn't fair to ask a child to stop crying – but that was a rule for other people's children. This was Denny, whose suffering she found unendurable.

'Oh, honey, what? Tell me.' She gathered the pile of sheet-wrapped child in her arms and pleaded. 'Denny, please try to stop now and tell me what's wrong, so I can fix it.' The folly of promising to fix a problem without knowing what it was didn't even occur to her. Denny, who never cried, was crying. She had to fix it.

Denny heard her and believed – believed *something*, anyway, that was good enough to get her out from under the sheet.

A little bald spot was growing where she'd been pulling her hair out. Water in various stages of dilution was coming out of her eyes, nose and mouth. Too juicy to talk, she sucked air, uh uh uh. Sarah passed her a tissue and said, 'Blow,' and when that was done, 'Now tell me what's wrong,'

Denny hiccuped a couple of times and finally blurted, 'Why didn't you tell me Mom was coming back?'

'The police called me this afternoon,' Felicity said, speaking just above a whisper though she was alone in her casita with the windows closed.

'So?' That was standard Zack shtick. Always so superior and indifferent. You were supposed to just give up and slink away, ashamed of having, as he said, mistaken him for somebody who cared. *Not this time, mister.*

'Where have you been, anyway? I've been calling you for hours.'

'None of your business. The police called, so what?'

'The freaking Tucson police. How'd they get my name? You promised you'd keep me out of this.'

'You are out of it,' Zack said, 'unless you got yourself in. What did you say to them?'

'Nothing. I pushed over a couple of boxes of props and pretended we were having an accident at the theater so I could hang up the phone.'

'Oh, that's smart. Now they'll be sure to call you back.'

'And when they do I need to be gone! You hear me? You have to get me my money right away now so I can go to LA and change my name.'

'Change your name? Since when is that the plan? What about all those credits you keep bragging about?'

'The people who matter will write me a new blurb.' She hadn't thought of that before, but now that she said it she was sure it was true – the two directors who believed in her would understand a name change and write a new letter. New face, new name, why not? As for the catalogues, she had the pictures . . . Zack had just asked her something . . . 'What?'

'I said what about your job at the theater? You can't just walk out on Derek—'

'Who says? He's such a pig, he'll never give me a decent recommendation anyway. And nobody with any status cares what he thinks. All I need is the money and I'm gone.'

'Well, it's going to be a few more days yet.'

'Oh, Zack, honey, come on!' She uncorked her nuanced whine, practiced for years on her mother and perfected on a succession of boyfriends. 'I can't leave town without that money and I need to go right now! Haven't I' – she tried her Maggie voice from *Cat on a Hot Tin Roof* – 'been good to you? Well, then! Baby, you know I can't talk to the police, I'll get too scared!' She dragged it out over two syllables: scay-yered. A little fire, now: 'You better not let that happen!'

There was a silence, or almost a silence, a pause broken only by the rasp of a Zippo lighter wheel turning against flint. She heard him suck air as he lit one of his filthy Marlboros. He clicked the lid shut, blew smoke across the speaker of the phone, and said, 'Or what?'

She had been working hard to erase Zack from her memory since two nights ago on the stairway in the Henderson house. And she was making progress – most of the time he was just a blurry shape with fading colors. When stardom found her, as she knew it soon would, she was sure she would no longer remember him at all. In fact a Zack-free memory was one of the ways she would know when she had grabbed the brass ring, nailed the big part – made it.

But right now his image came up revoltingly clear in her mind's eye. He would be standing by the wall phone in the kitchen at Party Down. The front of the shop would be dark now and locked up, the harsh overhead kitchen light shining on the metal sinks and scrubbed butcher-block tables where she'd unloaded the remnants of so many celebrations. He'd have thrown his apron in the laundry hamper and hung his uniform jacket in the locker. His ropy white arms would show their garish tattoos below the sleeves of the sweaty white T-shirt he'd worn to work.

Of all the sacrifices she had made for her Art, none galled her as much as the fact that she had gone to bed with this man, in the dingy cheerless cave he occupied above the store. That was how she always thought of it, 'gone to bed,' never as 'fucked' and certainly not as 'slept with.' Fucking implied at least some stirrings of lust, an emotion she could not imagine feeling toward Zack, and sleep suggested a level of relaxation she would never be able to achieve in the same room with him, let alone the same bed.

She had endured his piggish rutting in order to secure her position as his Numero Uno, his Girl Friday, while still giving her job at the theater first priority. As long as she didn't charge him for sex and did the work of two people on the parties she worked, he accepted her frequent absences and late schedule changes, and gave her the lion's share of the tips. As much as anything else, it was the puniness of the rewards that put a halo of shame around the sacrifice of her beautiful body to this grubby man. But she did what she had to do for her Art. You had to find ways to keep yourself Out There, being seen and applauded by as many people as possible while you waited for your Big Break.

She had worked for Zack for nearly a year, adding steadily to her list of reasons to despise him. Aware from the beginning that he was a bully but believing her obvious superiority gave her the upper hand in the relationship, she had not begun to fear him until two nights ago when he grabbed her nose. Now she had been up the stairs at the Henderson house and down again, and understood how truly frightening he was. She longed to see the last of him, but at the same time she was desperate to hold his attention. She had to stay close by, tempting and goading him, so he would not try to cheat her out of her money.

Since the first time Madge had mentioned it, tossing off his casual offer and then waving away her thanks with a jolly shrug, she had hardly thought of anything else. And from that first moment she had called the money she was getting, 'My money.'

Madge had made it clear that he couldn't be involved directly and that the money would come from Zack. But it was Madge who had promised it, and while he was a relentlessly frivolous man he played, she noticed, mostly with rich people. There was a lot about him she hadn't figured out, but every word out of his mouth, his car and clothes and attitude, showed he didn't need to worry about money.

Why he hung around the theater where everybody did need to worry about it was one of the many mysteries about Madge. She had thought about becoming Madge's girl, had

trailed her coat a little, but while he slathered her with attention and extravagant compliments when there were people
around, he never made any moves on her when they were
alone. So was he gay? She couldn't tell. Anyway it wasn't
sex he was after with her. For all his light-hearted kidding,
Felicity thought she might have finally met a man who
appreciated her for her talent. It was a thrilling thought.

Felicity, all of her life, had been taught to think of herself
as being in the sweet spot, at the center, on top. The tough
things about show business, the fierce competition and people
who tried to take advantage, were temporary inconveniences.
Her mother had drilled it into her that she was special and
must always remember it, that positive thinking would carry
the day. Now that Madge had discovered her and she was
so close to achieving her goals, Felicity was becoming more
firmly positive every day.

So before she hung up she made it clear to Zack once
again that he positively had to bring her the rest of the money
right away. 'You don't want me to get trapped into talking
to the police, Zack. I might get rattled and say something
we would regret.'

Zack sat naked on the edge of his hard bed for some time
after Felicity hung up, smoking and drinking bourbon out
of the bottle on the floor. At intervals, in a rasping, barely
audible voice, he vented a string of profanity. Nino was a
treacherous snake, Felicity a cunt, and the army a whore's
nest of liars and thieves. His anger at the first two was just
a passing irritation compared to his mountainous ongoing
rage at the army, which had put him through ten years of
mostly hell and then robbed him of the rewards he had earned,
sending him home from Iraq with a dishonorable discharge
because he had done what everybody around him was doing,
but in front of a general with reporters nearby.

Now he was burning all over from road rash. A few pebbles
fell out of him every time he moved. He wanted to shower
but he knew it would hurt too much. He had a soothing oint-
ment he was rubbing on himself, and some gauze he was
going to wrap around his torn elbow as soon as the Tylenol
kicked in enough to mask the pain a little.

He had found his van just where he'd expected to find it, parked in the lot by the Greyhound bus depot. He had called an army buddy who left his auto-repair shop and brought a kid with him so there'd be enough drivers to make the shuttle. By the time all the vehicles and drivers were back where they belonged and he had bought the ultra-healing lotion at a drugstore and fetched the bottle of liquor out of the cupboard in the basement, he was almost too exhausted to climb the two sets of stairs to his room.

There was plenty of food in the coolers downstairs too, but he hadn't thought to bring any up when he came and now he was too tired to go after it. Anyway, he thought, if he kept on drinking on an empty stomach he would be drunk soon, and maybe he would pass out and stay unconscious till morning, which seemed like an excellent plan.

First thing in the morning, though, he had to figure out what to do about that fucking gun.

And then find Madge, and tell him to get his ass in gear and move the money, so they could get this squirrelly actress out of town. He had to have his warrior face on when he said it, too, because Madge had an uncanny antenna that would pick up the slightest twinge of uncertainty about the fact that he had let Nino get away.

But Nino would stay gone, he was sure of that. So Nino was just as good as dead.

Almost.

SEVEN

P ulling into traffic on her street Tuesday morning, Sarah glanced up and saw a contrail, high aloft in full sunshine, shining brilliantly white against a royal-blue sky.

Hey, too good a day to go inside, better call in sick. The antic thought came unbidden, a relic emotion from other glorious mornings like this one, shared with Janine years ago. They used to argue half-humorously, on the bus ride to town, about whether it would be a wretched waste of perfect weather to go in through the doors of the schools they were headed for. More and more often, as they got older, Sarah went in and Janine stayed out. Perversely, now, the memory made her both furious at her sister and longing to talk to her. To tell her, among many other things, that caring for her bright, interesting child wasn't getting any easier.

The half-hour after Denny's first crying fit had been loud and damp and confusing. The kid was so panicked by the prospect of having her life trashed again that she collapsed repeatedly into sobs. In the process of convincing her it wasn't going to happen, Sarah realized later, she had finally convinced herself.

Until she sat down on Denny's little iron bed and said it half a dozen times, she had not been so sure that she was anything more than she'd always been for Denny, the fall-back caretaker who took over whenever Janine melted down. But the more ways she said it, the truer it got – she was never again going to let Janine take Denny out of her house and put her through the jittery hell of living with an addict. Why had she ever even considered it?

'I'll nail the door shut before I let her take you away from me again,' she finally said, getting a laugh from Denny at last. But the child's emotions were so hair-trigger by then that the laugh turned into a hiccup that triggered a fresh burst of weeping.

'I think we need cocoa,' Sarah said. School night be damned, she had to find a way to shut the waterworks down.

They went back out to the kitchen, got out cups, warmed milk in a pan. 'You know, Denny,' Sarah said, as she poured two big cups of glorious-smelling hot chocolate and dumped a handful of marshmallows on top, 'when you were with me before, I wasn't sure . . . I thought maybe you'd rather be back with your mom. But this time . . . it feels like we've always lived together. I looked in through the window tonight when I came home, you and Aggie and Will Dietz in here, all so busy and peaceful, and I thought, Wow, it's neat to come home to a family.'

Probably the word family did it. Denice Lynch, for whom dubious reserve was the default expression, threw herself into Sarah's arms with a great cry that Sarah thought she would remember to her grave. 'Yes!' she wailed. 'Oh, yes, I like it too!'

Unfortunately that heart-warming moment upset the cup of hot chocolate that Sarah had just poured out in front of her, so they warmed up the dining table and Denny's night-gown and a big patch of rug. While they cleaned up the mess, Denny got the rest of the story out.

Janine had been standing by the row of yellow buses, 'smiling that creepy smile she gets from dope and beer,' when Denny came out of school. Making promises like, 'Soon we'll be together again,' she grappled Denny into a smelly hug, and held on so long Denny nearly missed her ride home.

'The last I saw of her,' Denny said, 'she was hanging on to a light post, waving at the wrong bus.' Halfway between laughing and crying, Sarah and Denny held each other while fresh cocoa warmed on the stove.

'So I figured, "Here we go again,"' Denny said. 'Just when I was getting my grades up, she comes back and it all starts over.' She looked sideways at her aunt. 'It *would* be better for you if I went back to living with mom, wouldn't it? I mean, you and Will . . .'

'Will Dietz doesn't change anything between you and me, Denny,' Sarah said, and got the Dubious-Denny look. 'No, listen, Will doesn't want to get between us and I wouldn't let him if he did. Whatever we decide to do about our . . . relationship' – she hated that word, but it would have to do for now – 'you still live with me. Period. Nothing's ever going to change that again.' They hugged some more, careful to turn the handle of the cocoa pan away first.

'Maybe this is opportunity knocking,' Sarah said when they were finally settled at the table. 'I'll try to find out where Janine is staying and get her to sign off on a . . . waiver . . . or whatever it is. Things are going to come up, decisions about schools and dentists and things like that. We need to make it official that I'm your guardian.' On that note, planning in a matter-of-fact way how to make Denny's situation more settled, Sarah finally got her calmed down enough to sleep.

Mornings, there was no time to talk. Denny stood patiently to get her hair braided. As she buckled on her loaded backpack Sarah said, for the umpteenth time, 'I'm afraid you're going to ruin your back with that thing,' and Denny rolled her eyes to the ceiling in the universal kid's expression that meant, fifth grade is all about homework, whaddya gonna do?

Now, in the car, Sarah told herself to put personal problems behind. She tried making phone calls to jump-start the day, but nobody else was at work yet. She called her mother, who amazingly was already out of the house. She left a message on the tape saying, 'Janine's back in town, call me if you can,' hating to do it but not wanting Aggie to get a phone call with no warning.

Press on. She left messages with Delaney and Judge Geisler, then gave up on the phone and drove to an automotive security store called The Specialists, where she picked up brochures and a contact number for the GPS tracker on Henderson's car. Feeling energized then by her early start, she sprinted for the elevator at 270 South Stone, hung her jacket on the back of her chair and grabbed the already-ringing phone.

'Judge Geisler is returning your call,' a clerk's voice said, 'hold on, please.'

Some thumping followed, and the end of a shouted greeting, before the judge rasped in her ear, 'If I have to talk to you every damn morning, Sarah, I'm afraid the magic may go out of our relationship.'

'Well, I'm sorry to take up your time before court, Judge, but I've got a question only you can answer.'

'My kind of a query,' he said, pleased. 'Shoot.' He made little humming, ruminative noises as she described what she wanted. Then he nit-picked her probable cause – going after the man's tracker looked suspiciously like a fishing expedition to him. 'All right, a crime was committed. But how does that get you to needing to know where he's been every minute? Out of town is out of town, isn't it?'

She went over the crime scene again, the rich wife murdered and the husband with the troubled business. He agreed, the crime was egregious, discretion appeared to have merit, delay was contraindicated. The judge enjoyed words like 'contraindicated.'

'I might be able to get what I need with just the warrant you already signed for me,' she said. 'That included all the cars. But I thought . . . in case I have trouble piercing the corporate shield at Accu-Trak . . .' The judge liked expressions like 'piercing the corporate shield,' too.

Finally he said, 'Yeah, you better have a separate instrument just for the tracker.' They agreed on the wording together and he authorized it over the phone as of a half-hour earlier, to keep it out of hours so she wouldn't have to come all the way to the courthouse for his signature.

''Preciate it, sir,' she said.

'My pleasure. Go fight crime, kid.' She hung up smiling, feeling the warmth of his approval. Geisler liked scrappers.

For once, being two time zones behind New York was an advantage. All the customer service phones at Accu-Trak were manned and eager to help. And, when they heard what she wanted, equally prepared to argue. An hour and fifteen minutes and several long phone conversations later, she blew hair out of her eyes, peered out into the support-staff area, and dialed an inside number.

The harmonically challenged voice that answered bristled with the disruptive energy of youth. Tracy Scott, working his way toward a degree in criminology at Pima Community College, rattled the walls of the second floor whenever he put in a shift on the support staff.

'Tracy, where are you?'

'In the bullpen with the rest of the sweated labor.' His voice tried hard for baritone these days and occasionally made it. 'Where else would I be?'

'Under your desk? I can't see you out there.'

'Oh, my desk got moved up in the north-east corner behind the file cabinet. The alien life form who runs this section has decided I'm too disruptive to be in the middle of the room.'

'What did you do?' The support-staff supervisor was an earnest perfect-margins striver named Elsie Dobbs. Sarah could well imagine the hopeless chasm of misunderstanding that must yawn between her and this relentlessly antic kid.

'I said something so brilliantly funny that even the janitor laughed. Witticisms are not allowed on Planet Dobbs. They cause too much noise.'

'I see. Well, if you tiptoed soberly across the room, do you think she'd let you come in here for a minute and help me?'

'And they said there was no God. I'll be there in a nanosecond.' His phone crashed into its cradle. Sarah was still massaging her ear when he appeared by her desk with all his acne scars aglow. 'Tell me you've got something hideously difficult that will take all day. I've been checking crime stats since shortly after the disappearance of the woolly mammoth.' Always somewhat theatrical, his speech became more grandiose when he talked to Sarah because she could not disguise how much she enjoyed it.

'Sit.' She hooked her spare chair with her foot and dragged it next to her desk 'You ready to live up to your hype? I'm going to give you a chance to justify some of those titles you keep awarding yourself.'

'Fear not, madam.' He stood up and raised an imaginary torch aloft. 'Genius Geek does not quail in the face of challenges. Where have I left my cape?'

'Tracy, sit.' Sometimes she sympathized with Elsie Dobbs. 'This brochure,' she laid a colorful folder on the desk between them, 'describes a GPS tracking system. It's used for—'

'I know what it's used for.' Tracy Scott's pale eyes, vaguely afloat behind Coke-bottle glasses, ogled the jolly looking little brochure the way a coyote eyes a rabbit. 'I've read all the ads.' Behind the covers of the department manuals he was supposed to be compiling, Tracy read the specs of high-end electronic devices as avidly as other young males read porn, apparently with equal titillation. 'You got a GPS tracker involved in this double murder down in El Encanto? That's what you're working on today, isn't it?' The metal braces on his teeth gleamed in the morning sun. 'You want me to tell you where the big-time rich husband's been all weekend?'

'What's this, a teenager who reads newspapers? Wonders never cease.'

'Newspapers? What are they? The blogosphere is alight with speculation.'

'You add one syllable to that speculation and you're outa here, you understand? I'm not really even at liberty to discuss this case with you. But – here's the short version of this part of the story. I wormed my way into the bowels of this company –' as often happened when she worked with Tracy Scott, she was beginning to talk like him – 'and found the number of the person who guards the database. One of his jobs is to keep me from getting the access code. I told him about the warrant just authorized by Judge Geisler that says he has to give it to me, told him I was faxing the warrant, gave him to understand that he had exactly a quarter-hour after the fax arrived in his office to send me the access code. Described all the dreadful things I could make happen if he tried to stall me—'

'Sarah.' Tracy took off his glasses, closed his eyes and pinched the bridge of his nose. 'I'm ready to stipulate that you're the staff specialist at mental waterboarding—'

'Actually I'm just blowing smoke while my throat muscles relax,' Sarah said, pushing her hair back. 'I wasn't sure I could make this work without bringing in bigger muscle, and I was trying to give Delaney a break for once. To my intense delight, the corporate geek believed me. Look, here's the access code by return fax.'

'Well done, O Mistress of the Brutality Squad! You mean we're now privy to the secrets of the Hen-Trax rolling stock?'

'More than you ever wanted to know. This will show you the movements of the entire fleet for the last thirty days. Don't bog down in it. All I care about is the vehicle checked

out to Roger Henderson. It went to Phoenix late Friday and
stayed there till Monday morning, when it was involved in
a collision on I-10, in the vicinity of Chandler.'

'You want me to pick out that one vehicle and follow it—'

'Wherever it takes you. Yes. As I understand it, this system
will give us the date, time, and distance for each mile driven
and every stop. But I expect it's going to report the locations in GPS points—'

'And you want them translated into street addresses, right?'

'If that's what they are. Or highway locations or . . . whatever.'

'No problem. Google Earth is my friend.'

'I expected no less. Are you pretty jammed up with those
crime stats? How soon can you get on this?'

'Never mind the dog work.' He waved crime stats into
insignificance. 'That's a whenever assignment, we fit it in.
I take it you want this quick and quiet, right? Or you'd have
asked the owner for the access code.'

Sarah smiled contentedly into the mottled face of the
support-staff clown who was always so much shrewder than
he looked. 'You know, Tracy, sometimes you're a real comfort
to have around.'

'Madam,' Tracy stood up again and bowed from the waist,
'Genius Geek's mandate is to serve the heroes. In return,'
he clutched the paperwork she had handed him and snapped
the rubber bands on his braces, 'you sleuths keep Genius
Geek from dying of boredom. Thank you, dear lady!' He
charged out, dodging through the doorway around Jason Peete
and Ray Menendez, who were walking in together.

'Sarah.' Peete planted himself firmly on both feet, thrust
his chin out and re-settled his collar. 'We got a proposition.'

'Which of course I'm impatient to hear. But first tell me,'
she plucked a printed sheet off the top of a pile and held it
up, 'where did you get this?'

'What? Oh, the inventory list? It was stapled to the inside
of the door in the gun cupboard.'

'The one in the den, where you said the top weapon's
missing?'

'Yes. I pried it loose ver-r-ry carefully and ran out to
Kinko's and copied it, and snuck the original back.' He

stroked the complex pattern of close-trimmed beard that now outlined his jaw and upper lip, and patted his soul patch. All the grooming time Jason Peete had recently saved himself by shaving his head had been redirected to his facial hair. 'That Henderson's a systems man, give him that. The numbers on that list correspond to numbered racks in the cupboard. Make and model of each weapon, date of purchase, maintenance record . . . very impressive.'

'And the one that's missing from the cupboard is a –' she looked at the list – 'Remington 870?'

'Exactly.'

'Well, *that* should be a snap to trace,' she said, making a sour face. 'Only eight or nine million of them around.'

'Most popular firearm in its class. Yes.'

'Swell. Chances are we won't find it anyway, of course. A killer with any savvy at all will bury it out in the desert someplace. But just in case we're dealing with a chuckle-head, I presume you reported it?'

'To NCIC. Sure.'

'OK. And who's reviewing pawnshop reports here these days?'

'Davies. I sent him the specs.' Peete stroked the corners of his mustache. 'What does Henderson say about the gun?'

'He didn't know it was gone. He doesn't know how long it's been missing. He can't remember when he used it last.'

'Uh-huh. And I am the Queen of Romania.'

'Right.' She drummed an absent-minded rhythm on her desk with a #2 pencil. 'The more I see of Roger Henderson the better I like him. What I can't figure out is why he's so defensive—'

'Well, why wouldn't he be, if—'

'No, I mean of *his wife*. I asked if he knew about her affair, and he jumped all over me. "My wife," he said, "did not have affairs."'

'What does he call it when his wife's in bed with another man?'

'I never got to ask him that. What about the fingerprint work on that second victim, Ray? Why is that taking so long?'

'I just turn 'em in, Sarah, I don't process 'em,' Menendez said reasonably.

'Why don't you ask, though? They should be done by now.'

'I can do that, I guess.' He dialed a number and sat through six rings. While Menendez waited, Jason Peete said, 'About my proposition?'

'Oh . . . yeah, what?'

'Ray's got a ton of reports to write up about yesterday, but I'm done – my only report was that weapons list.'

'They don't answer,' Menendez said. 'I'll go see about it.' He got up reluctantly and trudged away.

'So what I'm saying,' Peete said, 'is why don't you let me take the autopsies so he can get caught up with his record-keeping?'

'Um . . . you sure you have the time, you can give it all day?'

'You bet.'

'Well . . . OK, I guess. You need to get going pretty soon, then, don't you?'

'Right now.' He got up. 'I'm outa here.'

'OK. Thanks, Jason.' As he walked away, looking pleased with himself, she began twitching with suspicion. Why was Jason Peete, the most self-involved man in the squad, making helpful suggestions all of a sudden? On the other hand, what advantage could anybody possibly hope to gain from standing all day on a cold travertine floor, watching a forensic specialist dig shotgun pellets out of corpses?

Well, it's done now, live with it. As Peete left the floor, she watched Menendez stop in the break room to pour himself a coffee, and began twitching with impatience. Her annoyance brought back a memory of the anger-management techniques she'd had to learn to get through the year after her divorce, and she found herself grinning inanely at the memory of once trying to explain the Zen-like exercises to Will Dietz. 'But I found an even simpler thing that usually works for me,' she told him. 'I pick out some dumb piece of dog work and do it as well as it can possibly be done.'

Putting on his jacket, getting ready to go to work, Dietz burst out laughing – a rare thing for him. 'God, Sarah, maybe you could find a spot on a chain gang somewhere, huh? Break up all those rocks for everybody, manage the hell out of that anger.' He was still chuckling as he went out the door muttering, 'Anger management, Jesus.'

She thought of him now as she dug out a brown card-board folder and set up the Henderson case file. It was typical dog work, incredibly boring, invariably frustrating where the pieces didn't mesh, and she felt herself growing calm as she worked. What could go wrong while you were swamped in a task so mundane?

Her own notes were tidy enough, but fragmentary – yesterday had taken many unexpected turns. She finished transcribing her handwritten notes, printed a paper copy.

This was when you loved your computer. Sarah had not been a detective in the typewriter era, but some of the old reports gave her an idea of how cumbersome this part of the job used to be. *Carbons and white-out, argh.* Ollie's report was in her stack somewhere. She dug it out and read it as she attached it to hers. It was an unedited transcription off his digital recorder, obviously, and he had copied it off just as it happened.

Yvonne's memory had modified a little, by the time Ollie got there. She woke up, she said, because the phone was ringing. 'I sat up in bed and said, "Mike, the phone is ringing." But when I reached out to shake him he wasn't in the bed. Then I heard him talking, saying, "Yeah, I heard it, I already called the cops." And then I heard somebody yell something in the house across the street.'

'A scream after both the shots?' Ollie had asked her.

'I guess,' Yvonne said. 'I never heard any shots so it must have been after both. And all the dogs kept barking and barking. I said to Mike, "I'm going to lose my mind if they don't stop barking."'

'You always say you'll lose your mind,' Ortman said. 'I wonder if it was somebody in one of the other houses that yelled.'

'No. It came from across the street, at Henderson's.'

'You were still half asleep.'

'Have it your way,' Yvonne said, 'you always do. But I know what I heard with my own ears.'

Why didn't he get them apart? I suppose by then he figured they'd talked it all over a dozen times.

After that, it was all about the neighborhood, how 'this kind of stuff' just never happened here. They were all such nice people. 'We get along swell,' Ortman said. 'Play golf and tennis, the usual stuff.'

They buried him in golf chat.

Carrying his report, Sarah got up and wandered the section until she found Ollie Greenaway leaning against the door-jamb in Leo Tobin's workspace, deep in a discussion of the current season's university basketball team.

Sarah stopped rudely close to Greenaway and stood there, counting the stripes in his tie. He pointedly ignored her while the two men hurled a few more stats at each other. Ollie finally, reluctantly, turned toward Sarah, raised his eyebrows and asked, 'Something on your mind, Pilgrim?'

She held up his report. 'Why didn't Mrs Ortman like Mrs Henderson?'

'Whoa. Did I say that? I don't think so.'

'You didn't say much of anything. How come? Usually you dig right into people. Why couldn't you get the Ortmans to open up?'

'None of my interviews went very well yesterday, tell you the truth. Have you read the rest of them?'

'No.'

'When you do you'll see what I mean. Life is just a little slice of heaven in El Encanto Estates. Nobody has a bad word to say about anybody.'

'How about a good word?'

'Some, but they don't add up to much. The Hendersons are civic-minded. Eloise did things that make a difference. That's the big whoop in El Encanto, making a difference. And getting along. I think there must be a cheeriness clause written into the mortgage.'

'Oh, they're just protecting the value of their real estate. But there's always a snake in the cupboard somewhere. Were the women consistently more negative about Mrs Henderson than the men?'

'No. Well, maybe a little. One woman did say you couldn't have her on your committee, she was so unpredictable. She'd be all over you with plans one meeting, then the next one she wouldn't even show up.'

'Unpredictable,' Tobin said. 'God, I hope we're not going to start shooting people over that, my whole family could be wiped out. Why don't you both sit down?' He slid an extra chair into the space in front of his desk. 'Save me a crick in the neck.'

Sarah sat, absent-mindedly, on the edge of a chair. 'Didn't they even gossip about money?'

'Oh, sure. Henderson's a big mover and shaker. He's done several jobs in urban renewal. That everlasting Rio Nuevo thing. Turning old warehouses into loft apartments. Loft has become a holy word downtown, did you know that? Affordable housing, not so much. Although somebody said Hen-Trax is building a tract of reasonably priced bungalows out south-east.'

'Any trouble with it?'

'Not that I heard. Henderson makes buckets of money, everybody says so. "Wish I had his cash flow," I heard that more than once.'

'But these days,' Sarah was making notes in the margins of his notes, 'I keep reading stories about the housing bubble bursting, some big credit crunch.'

'Oh, he might be a little squeezed right now, all the builders are. But the Rio Nuevo projects have tax-increment financing, they're not going away.'

'Still . . . wasn't the Mrs inclined to be pretty spendy?'

'Big time. Beautiful clothes, big parties. But she had plenty of her own money, you know, she was a Della Maggio. You shouldn't leave your mouth open like that, Sarah, you'll catch flies.'

'Mrs Henderson was a Della Maggio? Of the department store Della Maggios?'

'And hotels and ranches. That was Mrs Henderson's grand-father, Vincente. The two sons got into banking and insurance, and kept getting richer. Mrs Henderson's dad was Fabian.'

'The Ortmans fed you all this local history?'

'Most of what I just told you I already knew. The Della Maggios are founding fathers. Some say the Sam Hughes neighborhood should have been the Vincente Della Maggio neighborhood, but it was too long for the sign and kept getting misspelled.'

'That first generation of merchants had it good,' Tobin said. 'There was a lot less competition and they had very few rules. Vincente Della Maggio made a ton of money in this town back when money was really worth something.'

'And Roger Henderson gets all of it, right?' Sarah said. 'Now that his wife is dead and the construction trades are, as you say, squeezed?'

'Oh, I assume so.' Ollie met Sarah's curious eyes and grew thoughtful. 'Might be good to find out, though, huh?'

Sarah said, 'Will you go to work on that?' She turned to Tobin, the wise old man of the section. 'We should be able to get a grand jury subpoena that will get us access to his bank accounts, shouldn't we?'

'Oh, yeah. You get a fair amount of circumstantial, you can get into the bank accounts all right. Accountants are going to stonewall you but you can compel them to testify once you've built your case.'

'I can get them after I don't need them any more?'

'That's about it. And you won't get a word out of lawyers even if Hell freezes over.'

Then Menendez walked back into the section, looking cheerful and waving a report. 'Hey, they should all be this easy.' He handed Sarah a copy of release records from Yuma.

'Paul Thomas Eckhardt,' Sarah read out loud. 'Three to ten for dealing. He didn't enjoy his parole for long, did he? A little over a month.'

'Better than average month for an ex-con, though, huh?' Leo Tobin had come around the desk and was reading over her shoulder. 'Five weeks out of the can and he hooks up with a high-dollar party-giver like Eloise Henderson?'

'Don't give him all the credit.' Ollie Greenaway winked at Sarah. 'Rumor has it Mrs Henderson had a fondness for bottom-fishing.'

Sarah said softly, 'So you did talk to Cifuentes.'

'Cifuentes? Does he know something too?' Ollie rolled his eyes to the ceiling in a ludicrous imitation of innocence. 'I heard she went for the lawn-care guy.'

'Oh? Fun in the compost heap, huh?' Sarah gave him her enraged-alligator face and he grinned happily. 'And this lawn-care guy will be ready to testify in court when the time comes?'

'Don't see why not,' Greenaway said, inspecting the point on his pencil. 'Should do wonders for his bottom line.'

Sarah made a hissing noise, stood up, shook her head, and sat back down. 'Seriously. Where did you say Delaney's keeping Cifuentes?'

'I didn't. But he's right over there in cold cases, they gave him a little table.' He got up and craned his neck. 'I don't see him right now. He must be in the records room, looking for something to work on.' He treated her to a cheerful leer. 'Bet if you took him a doughnut you could get him to talk all day.'

'I'll think about it.'

Tobin pulled his nose thoughtfully. 'There was something about the crime scene, though – in view of what everybody said about it – that bothered me.'

Sarah said, 'The screams.'

Tobin nodded. 'Exactly. All the stories about the screams match up pretty well, don't they?'

'Yes. They all said two screams and two shots.'

'Right. But Delaney gave the crime scene to me, remember? I had to sketch it, measure it, photograph it. I spent a lot of time in that room. Have you read my report yet?'

'Not all of it. I was just putting the file together.'

'Well, it includes a detailed description of the positions and appearances of the bodies. And I can tell you, it doesn't make sense that it happened the way they all said it did.'

'Show me.'

'Here's a photo of the crime scene from above the bed. I got on a ladder to take it. It shows the overspray of birdshot on the bed around Eloise Henderson. But here,' he shuffled pictures, 'this view's from the foot of the bed. Look at the overspray pattern on the headboard above the man.'

'Outline of a head and shoulders,' Sarah said. 'I noticed that at the time.'

'He sat up,' Ollie said.

'Damn right,' Tobin said. 'Now think about the screams.'

'She was shot first,' Sarah said, 'from above, while she was sleeping. The noise woke the man, and he sat up.'

'And took his shot right in the face, while he was upright,' Ollie said.

'That's how I see it too. So then,' Tobin looked from one to the other, 'who'd that second scream come from?'

'I met her in a bar out on East Broadway,' Cifuentes said, staring sulkily across Sarah's shoulder into the gloom. Even buried alive in the records room, he was maintaining most of his macho snap. His black hair curled crisply around his head, his slacks still held their knife-edge crease and his aftershave lotion almost prevailed over the miasma of moldering paper in the tiny room.

Delaney had given him a folding table in poor light outside one of the two cubicles assigned to cold-case detectives, and abandoned him. Given no choice but to treat his assignment seriously, he was standing under the harsh fluorescent ceiling light in a cupboard stacked with brown folders and cardboard boxes, comparing numbers against a printout list. He had legal tablets and a laptop on the table outside, and was working his way backward through unsolved cases, beginning with the previous three months. He didn't stop searching the shelves when Sarah walked in with her hands full – just looked up sullenly across the file he was holding.

Sarah stood holding two cups of fresh hot coffee and a basket of pastries, saying, 'Got a minute?'

He made a superbly ironic gesture toward the comfortless space around him and said, 'Mi casa, su casa.'

'Let's go back out to your table.' She pushed some records aside, put her pastries and coffee down, went into a corner, and brought back her own folding chair. This coffee was the first friendly gesture she'd offered him since the day he came on the crew, so he had a right to an attitude. But she didn't have time to indulge it now.

'This is good apple Danish, try some.' She shook out the chair and sat down. 'OK, you got a raw deal. You might as well just get over it, Oscar, because nobody on this crew is going out on a limb for you.'

'You come over here to gloat?'

'I might enjoy that a lot, but I don't have time. I'm stuck with this case that was supposed to be yours. Delaney's on my tail about it because it involves well-connected people

he can't afford to offend, and every place I try to grab it, it
slides away.'

'And I'm supposed to care about that because?'

'I came to trade.'

'You have something I want?'

'If you want to get out of this hole, yes.'

He gave a small shrug that indicated the answer to that
was too obvious to state.

She blew on her coffee and took a sip. 'I can tell you
where you should be looking.' His dubious little smile said
how unlikely he thought that was. She put down the cup
sharply and said, 'Oh, come off it!' The coffee slopped over
and scalded her hand. Mopping up the spill, her voice gritty
with pain, she asked him, 'How many other good offers have
you had this morning?'

She had been counting on his opportunism. It kicked in
now and goaded him to ask, 'And all you want for this so-
called favor is for me to disobey a direct order not to talk
about Eloise Henderson?'

'That's right.' A little edge of amusement showed around
his eyes – he'd expected her to temporize. 'You tell me everything you know about Eloise Henderson, I shut up about
where I heard it and steer you to the one case in that records
room that's guaranteed to get you off Delaney's shit list if
you crack it.'

It didn't take long after that. He even unbent and tried the
apple Danish. She sat quietly with dust motes from the files
in front of them tickling her sinuses, while he told her about
the night he met Eloise Henderson.

'The Claim Jumper, I think it's called. Funky place with
an ore car and a stone donkey out front? They serve burgers
and ribs at long tables, have this little stage in one corner
of the main bar. Live band on weekends, country music.
Seemed like it was more bikers than cowboys that night, and
rough and ready girls in jeans and big hair.

'And then all of a sudden, standing at the bar –' his voice
took on an edge of wonder as he remembered – 'this beautiful woman in hand-tailored pants and a beaded sweater,
carrying a Chanel bag that must have cost as much as everything on the back bar.' Seeing Sarah's surprised expression,

he said, 'My sister owns a little boutique. She wants me to buy in and help her expand. I'm learning about women's clothes.'

To add to the many things you already know about women.

He enjoyed a bite of pastry while he thought back. 'She wasn't lost, she hadn't just stopped in to ask directions. She was there with two friends – not as high-end as she was, executive types. They'd all had a fair amount to drink. They were talking about an awards banquet and then an after-party. Now they wanted to cut loose. They stood out so much in that crowd that the men around them were holding back a little, waiting for somebody else to make the first move. I sent them a drink and went over and asked Eloise to dance.

'I'm a good dancer and when I get the right partner I enjoy doing it well, but I figured this for a seduction scene, you know, two or three times around the floor and we're feeling each other up.' He shrugged. 'Eloise surprised me. As soon as she realized how good we could be together she said, "Oh, well now, isn't *this* fun!" and just went after it.'

The music in that place was pretty simple, Cifuentes said, but they started experimenting, trying out their good moves on each other, laughing when they tried something clever and it worked.

'We did every possible variation on the two-step, we boogied. That funny little band played a tango and we did one with so much sizzle it lit up the whole corner. People all around us had begun to watch, the band was playing whatever we asked for.

'Then her phone rang. She'd left that big expensive satchel on the bar, the bartender was watching it for her, and when her phone started to ring he got her friend Nancy to answer it. Nancy came teetering out on her stilettos on to the dance floor, giggling and carrying the phone, saying, "Your Prince is calling, Weezy." Eloise took the phone and stood there in front of the music saying, "Yes. Yes. Yes," with her eyes going dead. By the time she folded up the phone her face was white. She said, "I have to go," and walked away without a backward look.

'So I figured, of course, that was the end of it. She'd sneaked out to play, hubby jerked her chain, and back she

went. Classic. Too bad the sex part got interrupted, but
hell, I get plenty of sex.' He brushed a crumb off his lap
matter-of-factly. 'I did think, you know, that she wasn't
just a hot-to-trot housewife, she had class and she was fun.
But I didn't make any effort to find her, I don't need that
kind of trouble. I knew if I ran into her in a bar again I'd
ask her to dance, but that was it.

'A couple of weeks later, she called me at work.' He shook
his head ruefully. 'It was my second day in Homicide. At
first I couldn't remember who she was, I kept asking, "Who?"
She was quite pleased with the fact that she'd found out who
I was and where I worked. She said, "How's this for detective work?"'

She wanted him to come to a party at her house. A Thank
God It's Friday Party, everybody coming after work, he was
sure to know 'ever so many people.' She babbled gaily on
the phone, and left many sentences unfinished. It was like
talking to a teen.

'I had two people in front of my desk and calls waiting,
so I said yes and took down the address and time because I
had to get her off the phone. I mentioned it later when I was
having a drink with a buddy from Auto Theft – Artie Cruz,
you know him?'

'Oh, yes.' They exchanged, for the first time ever, understanding smiles.

'Artie said, "Ay Chihuahua, if you got a invite to a house
in El Encanto you be crazy not to go, amigo."' Cifuentes, it
turned out, could do a spot-on Artie Cruz. 'He said, "I worked
parties in that part of town when I was in school, horses'
doovers so good they make you cry."'

'Artie's a funny guy.'

'Good cop, too. So I went to the party and . . . well, you
know what her house looks like.'

'Beautiful.'

'Like her. The CA was there, several members of his staff,
enough lawyers to start a whole other county. A couple of
judges and several MEs. The ones who noticed me at all
looked at me like, "What the fuck are you doing here?"'
He scratched his ear thoughtfully. 'I had a little trouble
deciding on a stance.

'Cruz was right about the hors d'oeuvres, though. And after I'd eaten a few and had a couple of drinks my hostess asked me to dance. We didn't do so many fancy steps that night, and we certainly didn't snuggle. She danced me sedately around her piano and said, "We had fun that night in the bar, didn't we?" and after I agreed we did she said, "Let's do it again some time." I said, "Mrs Henderson, are you trying to have your way with me?" She smiled the sweetest smile you could possibly imagine and said, "I always try to have my way with everyone if I possibly can." Her eyes were telling me that if I had any balls at all I would go for it and I did.'

He was silent, thinking, for so long that Sarah finally said, 'You want some more coffee . . . ? I could—'

'No.' It came out muffled but then he sat up straighter in his chair, put his feet flat on the floor and his hands on the table in front of him like a good first-grader, and resumed his tale. 'At first she didn't want anything from me but a good time and I was happy to provide that. She was wonderful in bed, wanted everything, enjoyed it all. I said to her once, "If this is a dream I don't ever want to wake up." She laughed and said, "This is real. Everything else is made up." And for three or four weeks we stayed in that magic bubble, where nothing mattered but the time we were together.' He turned a little sideways in his chair, closed his eyes and pinched the bridge of his nose, turned back, and resumed his classroom posture. 'Then something changed. She wanted to *talk*, one afternoon when we met. I thought, Oh boy, here we go, because usually "We have to talk" means "I'm ready to start making demands." And I just don't *go* there. If I needed that I'd get married again.

'But she didn't want anything in particular, she was just on a talking jag. It wasn't original stuff, either – global warming, the importance of helping some Africans she'd seen on TV. Then she got passionate about carbon footprints. She'd read Kingsolver and had this great idea for tearing out her tennis court and planting vegetables.

'I quit even trying to follow, it was just ranting. After a few minutes I said, "You seem upset. Why don't we try this another time?" I stood up and pulled my keys out of my

pocket, and oh, my God, you would have thought I kicked
her pet cat. She started to cry, floods of tears, held on to me,
and kept wailing, "You mustn't leave me, I'm so lonely, I
need somebody to talk to."

'We were in a hotel room downtown, there were people
coming and going in the hall, I expected a knock on the door
any minute. I didn't know what to do, so I . . . sort of peeled
her off me and got out of there. I mean how would I give
aid and comfort to Eloise Henderson even if I wanted to? It
struck me like that Christmas question, what do you give a
woman who already has everything? Rich broad getting her
rocks off fucking a cop, what should I say to her? "I'm sorry
bottom-fishing is not enough?"'

But he felt bad about leaving her all strung out like that,
he said, she had her car but he didn't think she was in very
good shape to drive. He remembered the couple working
that party at her house. He thought they acted as if they
worked there full time. It was mid-afternoon, her husband
wasn't likely to be home, so he called her house, and a
woman's voice with a Sonoran accent answered.

'I said, "Mrs Henderson is in room so-and-so at the Four
Corners Sheraton, I think she might need help." She didn't
even ask me who I was. She just said, very calm, "OK. We
get her." She hung up and I hung up and that's the last I
ever heard of Eloise Henderson till the morning Homicide
got called to her house.'

'So she didn't seem surprised. The housekeeper.'

'Not a bit. Sounded like she knew just what to do.'

'So what did you think of that? I mean,' she said, into his
blank stare, 'how did you account for Eloise's behavior?'

'Why should I account for it? I'm a cop, not a psychia-
trist.'

'Don't give me that. You've seen just as many freak-outs
as I have. You walked away from a woman you intended to
go to bed with, you must have had some idea what you were
leaving behind you.'

He turned his hands up, thought a minute, and said, 'Off
her meds.'

'OK.' She checked her notes. 'Why didn't you tell Delaney
on the phone that you were going to have to recuse yourself?'

'I wasn't home when he called. I was . . . with a friend.'
He cleared his throat. *So busy and complex, the life of the
stud.* 'They paged me from downtown. When I recognized
the address I started calling Delaney. His phone was busy
for a solid half-hour. Finally I decided, I better get dressed
and go in, or he'll be on my tail about being slow to respond.
So I went to see him and he blew up in my face about
polluting his crime scene.'

'Boy, didn't he?' Sarah wiped up their crumbs and dumped
napkins and coffee cups in the wastebasket. 'Enough to make
you wonder if Homicide is really a step up from Auto Theft,
huh?'

'I've wondered that every day since I got there.'

'You serious?' Sarah had genuinely hated her time in Auto
Theft, which had felt to her like being trapped in a thug-
infested revolving door.

'I spent five happy years there and I'd go back in a heartbeat if I could. I *love* cars,' Cifuentes said, looking dreamy.
'I'm a stone expert, I can look at almost any car on the road
and tell you what's under the hood. And if you give me an
hour to poke around it I'll tell you exactly what's been done
to it since it rolled off the lot.'

'Have you asked to go back?'

Cifuentes shuddered delicately. 'TPD frowns on going
back.'

'That's true. Onward and upward, that's our motto. OK.'
She turned a page in her notebook. 'You ready for this?' She
read off a case number and he wrote it down. 'Let's find it
to make sure it's here.' They hunted along a shelf till they
found January, pulled down the box with the right case
number and carried it to the table.

'Verna Talbot.' Sarah lifted off the lid. Dust flew up
and she sneezed. 'Widowed, lived alone, kept a cat. Helped
out at the food bank, played the organ for the choir,
mentored slow readers in grade schools, did one afternoon a week at the wild-bird sanctuary. A helper bee.
Many friends, no enemies. Disappeared on a Tuesday,
found on Friday. She was upright behind the wheel of her
car in the parking lot at St Stephen's Methodist – not her
church, by the way – wearing a hat with a veil. Nobody

admits to knowing how long she'd been there. The weather was cold, below freezing at night, so the body was . . . well preserved. But a parishioner finally noticed this car that hadn't moved.

'You understand, we'd been looking for her, we thought everywhere, since the afternoon after she disappeared. She was due to drive a delivery for Meals on Wheels. When she didn't show up they phoned, then somebody went to see about her because she was never late. All her friends called each other, then they called 911. By the next day it was our case because – oh, you'll read it in there. The plants weren't watered, the cat wasn't fed, the garage door was left open. Four dozen or so of her closest friends called and insisted that you could set your clock by Verna, she would never let you down, she always did what she said . . . this department sounded like an answering service for a couple of days, all the phones were ringing.

'The morning we found her, the ME determined she'd been hit on the head with something heavy. He also thought, and the autopsy later confirmed, that she'd been asphyxiated. Smothered with a pillow or a plastic bag, something like that.

'Later the same day, the Burger King on North Oracle was robbed at gunpoint just as a Dodge van full of illegal immigrants was being chased north on I-10 by a carload of rival coyotes.'

'I remember that day.'

'We all do. Three people shot at the Burger King, one fatally. Eleven serious injuries when the van rolled over. Not to mention the mishaps caused by several foot chases, and one K-9 dog killed in traffic.

'We did the best we could, but it was a very cold trail by the time we got back to Verna Talbot. Her friends held a big memorial service with a lot of hugging and weeping. Two daughters came from out of town. Half the speeches mentioned "shoddy police work," and "miscarriage of justice." Delaney was mortified. He flogged this case for many months before he admitted it was a dead horse.'

'You got any ideas where I should start?'

Sarah drained the last of her coffee, leaned back in her

chair, and remembered. 'I never got a chance to prove this, but what I remember about this woman was that her house was full of very pretty things – porcelain figurines, several sets of china, elaborately decorated sterling table silver. It wasn't a big house, she wasn't rich and her friends weren't either, but she'd evidently spent a lifetime collecting and it was all in her house. Pretty clothes and jewelry, too, and she had lovely taste.

'The house was full of photographs, too, of her husbands and children and her, and what I noticed during the first half-day we spent there before we got called to the other crime scenes, and the one time I got back there before the daughters took over and dismantled it, was that in almost every picture she was wearing a four-strand pearl neck-lace – it was evidently one of her favorite things. But she wasn't wearing it when we found her and it wasn't in her jewelry box. I tried to ask about her jewelry when we got back to the case, but by then everything was scattered and her daughters didn't seem to remember her pearls or care about them.

'So . . . I know it isn't much to go on but I've always had the feeling somebody got to wanting some of Verna's nice things. There's a list in there somewhere of the items I wanted to chase down. But we're all so busy – other people got kidnapped and run over, and off we went.'

'Information on the daughters is in here?'

'Yes. And the telephone numbers of dozens of friends. Try the one named . . .' She drummed her fingers, thinking back. 'Brenda something. She'll talk your arm off, but she seemed to really care about Verna and know a lot about her.'

'Well, hey,' Cifuentes said, smiling, showing his charm. 'Muchas gracias.'

'De nada.' Sarah put her chair back on the stack in the corner. She reflected, as she walked away, that for a man whose stated avocation was cars, Cifuentes told a story very well.

EIGHT

After he parked the Party Down vehicle Nino scuttled, almost too scared to breathe, into the bus depot. Nobody grabbed him so he bought a ticket to Albuquerque. He had no reason to go there, but it was the next bus leaving, and the cost of the ticket left him enough for a few meals.

He hid out in the rest room for a while and then, as departure time neared, stood close to an exit and nervously scanned the room. He had no idea how badly Zack had been hurt by his fall on to the pavement. If he was in fair shape and able to get a ride he would surely think to look in the bus depot, so Nino knew he could be toast any minute. When the bus was announced he got into the last seat in back and crouched down, trembling with anxiety until they pulled away from the depot.

He was afraid to get off the bus in Willcox when they stopped there, so he waited till they reached the small town of Lordsburg, across the New Mexico border. When he came out of the men's room there, he stood in a line of men fishing coins out of pockets in front of the Coke machine. The man ahead of him looked part-Indian or Mexican, had a broad dark face and rough, hard-working hands. But his jeans were new and he had sturdy work gloves in his rear pocket, so when he turned holding his Coke, on an impulse Nino said, 'I'm looking for work. You know where the jobs are around here?'

'Oh,' the man said, slow and quiet, 'what kinda work you lookin' for?'

While his Coke rolled out of the machine Nino did his best to arrange his face in an imitation of Pauly's open, guileless expression. He told the man with the gloves he wasn't particular. He said he had been picking tomatoes back in Willcox and got laid off when one crop ended and another wasn't ripe yet. 'I live paycheck to paycheck,' he said, 'I can't afford to lay off.'

'Know what you mean, bro,' the dark man said. He took a long swig of Coke, belched thoughtfully, and finally said, 'You could get on out to Utley's if you don't object to some stoop labor. Mmm? Up near Hatch. There's work in the pepper fields there.' He looked at Nino, skinny in his ancient jeans. 'Ain't easy work, though.'

'Hey,' Nino said, 'what is?'

'Well, I'm going out there if you want a ride,' the man said, and Nino ran and got his nearly empty gym bag off the bus. Carlos, that was his name, said he was a crew boss at Utley's and had an open spot for Nino, 'if you can keep it moving, man, you know what I'm saying? I got quotas to fill.' He drove the big pickup fast along the Interstate to Deming, a little slower on the almost-empty two-lane to Hatch, where he stopped to pick up supplies. Waiting in the truck, Nino watched a brown-skinned man patching a tire in a garage, two others loading sacks of cement on to a flatbed. Down the quiet street, a woman with braids was selling strings of peppers out of a little stand. He liked the quiet way they talked to each other and the deliberate way they moved.

'The feds make me check this database here,' the foreman at the farm said, 'just hang on a sec.' Nino got ready to run. But he was not on a list of illegal aliens or wanted criminals, so they took his social-security number and assigned him a bunk in a long building under some trees.

By Tuesday night he was so tired his legs trembled as he walked to the tent where they were fed. There was chili with something in it he decided to believe was meat, plenty of rice and beans on the side, and heavy, crusty bread. Afterwards he sat on the long porch that fronted the bunkhouse, watching the stars come out. Listening to the slow-talking men around him, he nodded off sitting up.

Just before he went to sleep in his narrow bunk, in spite of his aching muscles he thought that this life might be OK for a while and even kind of fun if Pauly was here. Once again he felt a great surge of sorrow and asked himself, *Why'd I have to go and kill that silly little turd?*

Alone in her cubicle, Sarah pawed through the chaos of reports heaped on her desk, looking for Ollie's witness report, the next thing she wanted to put in the Henderson file.

'I was carrying it around, where did I put it?' She could hear Ollie on the phone in the next cubicle, talking to somebody about expediting a grand jury subpoena. Tobin had gone back to his work space to finish the rest of his crime-scene report – the expanded search of the house and grounds – and was making phone calls, on the hunt for the family of Paul Thomas Eckhardt. With a grunt of disgust, she pushed away from her desk, talking to herself. 'This desk is too crazy. I need another table so I can sort things out.'

She went out on the floor and found Elmer the Grump, the janitor/handyman. Before he even heard what she wanted, he began protesting that he was already overworked. 'They pile too much on me so's I can't do nothing right,' he said, leaning on his mop. Sarah surreptitiously timed his complaints: forty-eight seconds. When he paused for breath, she jumped in with her request for a folding table. 'Just the small size, nothing heavy.'

A few minutes later he stood at the door of her cubicle holding it, saying, 'Why'd you waste my time for? Ain't no way this thing's going to fit in there.'

'Just a minute, now,' she said, 'be patient.' While he ranted about the folly of wasting more of his time when he already had too much to do, she slid her desk closer to the file cabinet, and set her two extra chairs in the hall. 'Now,' she said.

'Still ain't gonna make it.'

'Try.'

He was right, sort of. The desk had to move a little more before the table came all the way in. But by the time Elmer had gimped away rubbing his back, Sarah had begun to transfer all the Henderson reports to the extra table. She found Ollie's witness report, uttered a triumphant cry and slid it behind her own in the folder.

I need a cup of coffee to help me finish this job. She walked out to the break room, poured a fresh cup, and came back savoring the good smell. Tracy Scott was peering in the door of her cubicle.

'Is that a clean desk?' he asked, when she walked up to

him. 'Zounds, I got here just in time! You mustn't let yourself get caught like that, Sarah. Sergeant Scrooge will pile
more work on you.'

'He'll do that anyway.' She sighed, eyeing his armful of
printouts. 'But you're going to beat him to it, aren't you?'

'This isn't work. This is truth. Take heart, Lady Crime-
Fighter!' He did some tricky imaginary-cape moves. 'Genius
Geek has come to lighten your load!'

He plopped the pile of paper in the middle of her desk
and began to spread it out sequentially. He used every inch
of space, moving her lamp and phone to the floor to make
room. When he'd covered her desk he moved to the top of
the file cabinet, displacing a potted plant and a row of books.
The last two printouts still wouldn't fit there, so he hung
them over the front edges of file drawers.

'For God's sake don't sneeze,' he said, as he moved back
to the starting point.

'Or laugh,' Sarah said, and then, like a child in church,
was overcome by perverse hilarity. Tracy Scott watched in
astonished horror as she quaked helplessly with a hand over
her mouth.

'Don't,' he begged her, and looked right into her eyes,
shaking his head, until she returned to sobriety, gave herself
a little shake and said, 'OK, let's go!' They sidled together,
intimate as dancers, along the gently fluttering pages of his
research.

'Here's the drive to Phoenix, Friday afternoon. Arrived at
the Airport Radisson at six thirty p.m., see? Long dry spell
here, that night and Saturday, when the car never moved – I
telescoped that. But now, here, at eight thirty Saturday night,
he's off across town to this address on North Fourth Street.'

'Who lives there?'

'An escort service named Frisky Ladies.'

'Oh, for God's sake.'

'Why are you surprised? Isn't that what husbands do when
they go to conventions?'

'I guess. Somehow I thought he had more class.'

'So few of us do,' Tracy Scott observed from the lofty
vantage point of his nineteen years. 'Looks like he enjoyed
himself, he stayed till after eleven.'

'Why would he stay there? An escort service is not a whorehouse.'

'You'll have to ask him that. He went straight back to the hotel from there. And stayed there till,' he pointed, 'right here, see? The car moved again at ten o'clock Sunday morning.

'Then for four hours he, or at least his car, drove all over this patch of, as far as I can see, empty desert. This whole segment across the middle of the desk here, he's on country roads south and west of Casa Grande.'

'Just as he said,' Sarah murmured, wondering about the mosaic of truth and falsehood in Roger Henderson's report of his weekend. *Although to be fair he didn't say he never left the hotel Saturday night.*

'Here's where it gets interesting. By four o'clock he was back on North Fourth Street—'

'What?'

'Back with the Frisky Ladies. Yup.'

'He went back to the escort service when he was expected at his daughter's birthday party?'

'Men are just no damn good, are they?' He scrutinized her face. 'Why aren't you pleased? Your chief suspect is behaving despicably.'

'It just doesn't fit with the image I have of him. He seems aggressive and hard, but not frivolous. But OK, work with what you've got – what next? How long before he finally did go home? No, wait a minute . . . I was there when he got home. Just after lunch on Monday. He must have found himself an unusually frisky lady.'

'Is this a monologue or can anybody join in?'

'Sorry, Tracy. It's just . . . go ahead, what else have you got?'

'Well, according to our faithful eyes in the sky, Henderson's car stayed on North Fourth Street till past midnight Sunday night.'

'But then he went back to the hotel?'

'Yes. At twenty-one minutes to one a.m. – see this right here? – he cranked 'er up and drove back to the Airport Radisson. Stayed there' – they were working across the bottom row on the top of the file cabinet now – 'till a few minutes before eight Monday morning, when he checked out and headed back to Tucson. But the story ends, of course, just south of the Sun Lakes interchange.'

'Where he had his accident.'

'Yes. So now, my pretty –' he favored her with his Johnny-Depp-as-Jack-Sparrow leer, and twirled imaginary mustaches – 'you like ze nize fresh dirt I dig up on High-Roller Henderson? Eh bien?'

'Well . . . sure.' Realizing Tracy looked crestfallen, she roused herself. He had worked hard and done everything she asked, and here she was frowning because the results didn't meet her expectations. 'Nice work, Tracy!' She gave him a high-five and two printouts flew off on the floor. They both bent to pick them up, and in the cramped space they bumped heads. 'OK, Genius Geek.' She stood up, flushed. 'You're terrific, now get out.'

'Don't you want me to help you put these back in—'

'No. There isn't room for two people to work in here. I need all my air to breathe while I decide what to do next.'

She was standing behind her reburied desk, pondering Henderson's incredible weekend, when six feet two inches and two-hundred-plus pounds of Ross Delaney bustled into her workspace and created a blizzard of brown-speckled pages.

'Oh, sorry – Sarah, my God, what are you doing in here?' He stared around the jam-packed workspace as the mini-whiteout settled to the floor.

'Setting up the Henderson report.' Sarah's voice came hollow and dry out of her stricken face.

'This is all that one report?'

'Yes. The Henderson case is beginning to make me feel like the sorcerer's apprentice.' She grabbed some paper out of the air. 'I've cleaned my workspace three times since it started, and now look at this mess.'

'Yeah, you better do something, we can't work in all this clutter.' Leering triumphantly, Delaney plucked a couple of sheets off his jacket, where they clung like baby birds. 'First answer a question, though. I've got a big high-powered attorney on the phone who wants to come down and talk to us.'

'Well, he can't come in here,' Sarah said. 'I've got all I—'
Something in his face stopped her. 'What's his name?'

'Devon Hartford the third. Of Hartford, Hartford and,
uh . . .' he read off a note, 'Zelnick. Roger Henderson's lawyer.'
He watched her neck start to get red. 'I told you it was going
to be this kind of a case.'

'You didn't say every day. What does he want?'

'To save us some time, he says.'

'Oh, sure.'

'Says he has information that will be very helpful.' He
pulled his nose. 'Maybe before I say yes or no we ought to
agree on what *you* want from *him*.'

'I want him to back off. Because all this paper you see
flying around here tells the story of Roger Henderson's
weekend, and you need to hear about it before you waste
any time listening to attorney bullshit.'

'Henderson's alibi's not holding up?'

'Henderson's alibi has more holes than a wheel of baby
Swiss. And Ollie's getting the low-down on the bank records,
and I need to go find that actress who served the party. She
doesn't want to talk to me, so I suspect she knows something about the shooting.'

'Ah. Well.' Delaney morphed into an inscrutable Irish
Buddha, blinking and thinking. In the deep silence, Sarah
stole covert glances at a drift of GPS information under her
desk, twitching to pick it up. When Delaney snapped out of
the zone he said, 'Why don't we ask the attorney to come
in tomorrow morning? And we'll keep what you got from
the tracker to ourselves till we hear what he has to say.'

'OK. While you were thinking I decided not to call before
I go see the actress.' Sarah stacked a few sheets of paper,
absently. 'I think she needs to be startled a little.'

The 'Closed' sign in the ticket window didn't mean
anything, the girl with the violin case said. She was sitting
on the bench by the sidewalk, looking adorable in hobo
costume and fake freckles, alongside a boy in a clown suit.
'Just go around to the side door and knock, somebody'll
let you in.'

'Down the alley there?' The girl nodded, bouncing all her

braids. 'OK, thanks,' Sarah said. 'You waiting to rehearse a play?'

'No, we're working a street fair today,' the clown said, bobbing his red nose precariously with every word. 'We're waiting for a couple of our friends to come out and go with us. They're in there auditioning. Singing that godawful music from *Phantom of the Opera*.'

'Ah. You know a girl named Felicity?'

'Sure,' the girl said. 'Everybody knows Felicity. I'm sure she's still in there. She won't leave as long as there's any chance for the lead.' They both laughed.

It took a lot of knocking. The kid who finally pushed open the door said, leaning on the panic hardware, 'Sorr-ee! Couldn't hear you over all the noise.' He let her walk right in – why did they even keep it locked? 'You here to audition? Follow me.'

She followed without comment, into a cavernous dusky space. Somewhere up ahead in the light, an exasperated voice was launched on a tirade. 'Now listen, people, we can't have all this noise and confusion! I want the actors waiting to audition standing in a straight line right *here*, and everybody else, get off the stage *right now*. Sit down and be *quiet* or I'm going to throw you out.'

Sarah grabbed the arm of the boy leading her, stood close to him beside an opening in the backstage curtain and whispered, 'Which one's Felicity?'

'Oh . . . by the piano. Holding the clipboard.'

He pointed to a thin, intense-looking girl, almost pretty, with a great fall of lovely dark auburn hair and bruised-looking eyes. Busily checking names off a list and grading performances, she remained so relentlessly self-aware that the hair she had tucked behind one ear stayed there while the hair on the other side fell straight and shining to her shoulder. Sarah made an 'OK' sign to her guide and picked her way carefully through shadowy backstage detritus to the other side. When she found the right spot she stepped through the curtain, cradled her badge discreetly in her left palm, and held it in front of Felicity while she whispered, 'Need to talk to you.'

The face that turned toward her showed shock and then terror for a couple of seconds. Felicity looked around for an escape route, disarranging the careful hair. But Sarah's right hand was clamped around her right shoulder and held her, locked in an odd, unstable embrace – Felicity in wriggling panic, Sarah firm as rock – while the baritone at the piano sang about love. Sarah said, just loud enough to carry into the ear two inches from her lips, 'I just have to ask a few questions.'

Despite her discreet murmur the director heard interference and turned to glare. In Sarah's sight-line, Felicity's startled eyes replaced her ear. She blinked once, set the clipboard on the piano with a decisive little click, and whispered, 'Follow me.'

Transformed in that instant into the leader, she stepped firmly around a bass drum and a stack of chairs, held aside a curtain and pulled Sarah after her down a short flight of steps and up a sloping aisle alongside empty seats. At the top of the slope she kicked up a doorstop and pushed out into the light. In the small hot foyer in front of the ticket booth she whirled to face Sarah. 'You can't come around here like this!' she hissed. 'What the fuck do you *want*?'

'I need to talk to you about the night you worked the party at Eloise Henderson's house. The night she was killed.'

'Why? I don't know anything *about* that.'

'How come? You were there, weren't you?'

'Earlier. For the birthday party. Me and a couple hundred other people.'

'So you can tell me the names of the guests?'

'No! Well, a few.'

'And the staff? You've worked with these people before, haven't you?'

'Some. Maria and Ramón, they're the couple that work there steady.'

'But the catering staff just comes in for parties?'

'Right.'

'What's the name of the company?'

'Oh . . .' She looked aside vaguely. 'I only work for them part-time.' Sarah waited. She finally said, 'Party something—'

Sarah tapped her foot. 'What's printed on their paychecks?'

'Oh, right. Let's see . . . Party Down, I think.'

'Thank you. Did the Hendersons always use that company?'

'Now why would I know that?'

'Would Ramón know? Or Maria?'

'I suppose. Ask them.'

'Who runs Party Down?'

'What?'

Is she a little deaf? 'The caterer, what's his name?'

'Oh . . . uh . . .' She stopped in the middle of tossing her hair back when she saw the way Sarah was looking at her. 'Zack.'

'What's his last name?'

Felicity appeared to think about it, shrugged, turned her hands up.

'He's the owner?'

'I guess.'

'Where's the shop?'

'Oh . . . somewhere on Speedway. I forget the street number . . .' She named some of the restaurants nearby.

'What's the phone number?'

Felicity looked vaguer still. 'They call me,' she said, looking into a corner.

'Never mind, I'll find it.' Sarah turned a page in her notebook. 'Will you clear something up for me? The night of the shooting, did you hear a scream before the first shot?'

'I don't know anything about the shooting,' Felicity said quickly. 'I was outside loading the van the whole time.' A second later, her horrified face showed she'd just realized that was not, after all, a great answer.

Panic hardware squealed metallically, and the director burst out of the darkened theater into the bright little foyer, saying, 'Felicity, for God's sake will you quit farting around out here and get back onstage and *help* me?'

'Felicity's not going to be able to do that,' Sarah said, tucking her notebook in the back of her slacks. 'She has to come downtown and help *me* for a while.'

I ought to figure it out some time, Zack thought. It had always puzzled him why so many senior women – Red Hats, book-club ladies, long-time office workers at retirement parties – drove out for lunch at the Desert Diamond Casino, which quite assertively aimed its advertising at a younger, livelier demographic. The restaurant served good food at an affordable price, maybe it was as simple as that. And it might be just about far enough out on Old Nogales Highway to seem like an outing. But his hunch was that the funky bleeps and wheezes of the slots and the occasional squeal of a small-time winner added a hint of adventurous sleaze they enjoyed.

He had often wondered, *If I figured out the right party room, back of the store, would they use it?* They weren't big tippers but they wouldn't be hard to satisfy, either, salad and soup, you could do it in your sleep. He had never wanted to bog down in the everyday food biz – why compete with the chains? But groups like these, especially the ones that met regularly, they'd fill in some of the slow times between the big parties, help him keep a stable staff.

There was a long table full of women in there now, a cake coming in with many candles lighted and two dozen terrible voices screeching, 'Happy Birthday.' As he watched them, his brain produced a rare treat for him – a happy thought. *If this deal with Madge works out, I won't have to worry about building up my crappy little business any more. My little party business will be just a cover for the blow.*

He pictured himself in the van with the clown and balloons on the back door, the multicolored confetti and signs painted on both sides, 'PARTY DOWN!' – the perfect front, silly and childish-looking, safe as a church. He could move a ton of product in that van, underneath the birthday cakes, and never give the narcs a reason to look at him twice. And launder the profits through a hundred fake orders for barbecues, crêpe paper, masks and boas and party tents. In fact one of the ironies he had already considered was that not all the orders would be fake, because his party business would actually need to grow so he had legitimate reasons for his vans to be anywhere in Tucson, at all hours.

He was already looking for one of those razor-sharp young saleswomen like the ones you saw around doctors' offices, selling the legal stuff Big Pharma was ruthlessly pushing on patients these days. A little downturn in that business – or maybe this soft spot in the real-estate market? – and he'd be able to afford one of those good-enough-to-lick chicks who had the knack of looking earnest in a mini-skirt. Put her out on the street selling parties and have half a dozen Felicity-types, actresses and students who needed irregular hours, doing the cooking and serving. Get them trained right, they'd keep the parties going with minimum supervision. And they were all so self-involved they wouldn't even notice the white powder he was moving under their noses.

Until Nino pushed him out of his own van, Zack was beginning to believe in his dream almost as fervently as Felicity believed in hers. He still thought he could salvage most of it, if he could get that nutcase actress out of town before she blew the whole thing to hell. Get Felicity on her way to LA, collect his own money from Madge and wave him off to wherever the hell he was going next, after that it wouldn't matter about Nino. *He shows his face in Tucson again, I'll whack him first and ask questions later.*

While the birthday ladies clapped and sang at the long table, he surveyed the room and saw that Madge wasn't there. But that was Madge's '62 Jaguar XKE out front, not likely there were two of those around with the original leather seats. So he was in here somewhere. Zack walked out to the gaming floor, the windowless cavern that created perpetual night so that blinking and slithering lights could brighten it up again.

The usual seniors, and service people with night shifts, were perched on stools in front of banks of slots all around the big room, feeding their hard-earned pay and social-security checks into the machines. ATM windows on all the walls made it easy to buy more of the coupons that had replaced quarters. In the inner circle next to where Zack was standing was the nearly empty pit for the twenty-one tables.

Madge was sitting at the long bar to Zack's right, chatting up the bartender. He must have been in the john before, when Zack walked in. Behind him, the early shift was breaking out fresh decks of cards and stacking chips at the twenty-one tables. The dealers wore clean shirts and bright-colored vests, had fresh haircuts and perfectly disciplined hands that seemed to move of their own volition. Madge was watching them covertly in the mirror behind the bar, his eyes luminous with the special longing of the addicted gambler.

Zack stepped back into the alcove in front of the rest rooms, opened his cell phone, and dialed. The room was so quiet at this hour, he could hear the pretentious ring tones – the opening bars of fucking Bach's Something in A Minor, as Madge loved to explain to the untutored millions who didn't give a shit. Madge answered, 'Yes?' in his snooty don't-bother-me voice, and Zack said, 'I'm parked around back by the storage units.'

He folded the phone, put it back in its holster, and stepped out of the shadows. Strolling back through the tables toward the slots, he never looked toward the bar, but he could feel the burn of Madge's angry eyes on his back.

Felicity's nerves went to pieces entirely when Sarah read the Miranda warning. She jumped up, venting a panicked scream, and wailed, 'Are you saying I'm under arrest?'

Sarah said, 'No. But I have to tell you what your rights are before I can even ask you any questions. I know it seems kind of backwards, but it's the rule.'

Something about the word 'rule' worked for Felicity. She said, 'Oh,' and sat down.

Sarah had phoned ahead, so Delaney had detectives looking for outstanding warrants, an arrest record, anything she could use to hold the girl if she needed some time to check her statements. He had one of the small interview rooms set up, too, and one glimpse of its bleak light on cold stone and tile – 'the entire spectrum from beige to taupe' was how Tobin described it – set Felicity stammering again. She fragmented further when she noticed the recording equipment beaming down from the ceiling. 'Don't worry about that – it's for *our* protection, quite frankly,' Sarah said, hoping to put her at ease with inside information. 'In case somebody decides to claim they've been mistreated in this building.'

'Have they?' Eyes darting. Spooked.

'Look at my hands,' Sarah said, holding out pristine nails. She sacrificed half an hour every week to the drudgery of keeping them manicured. 'Do they look like they've been beating on anybody?'

'Wow, nice,' Felicity said. 'Are they the glue-on kind or—'

'No. I take extra calcium and believe it or not I eat my

jell-o . . .' By the end of a painfully boring conversation about
nail care, Felicity seemed to be relaxing a little. The girl was
so afflicted by her deep need to be admired, Sarah realized,
that appearances took on life-or-death importance for her.
So work with that. Put her at the top of some heap.

Menendez was waiting to be her backup in the interview
room, and Tobin was watching the monitor outside. Delaney
had a strong belief in the truth that emerged in the interview
room, so he was standing by, waiting to watch as much as
he had time for.

'All right,' Sarah said when the three of them were settled,
as much as you could settle on those little round stools, 'let
me begin by saying I understand you were just there to serve
a party. You're a conscientious person, you were doing your
job, I get that part. But now, clear up this timeline, will
you? You didn't leave right after the birthday party, did
you?'

'Well . . .' Felicity helped herself to fresh tissues, dabbed
her eyes. 'No.'

'You had to stay and serve the rest of the party, right?
And that went on until . . . when?'

Felicity shrugged, thought, wriggled. 'Ten thirty. Maybe
eleven, by the time all the stragglers cleared out.'

'Eleven o'clock.' *Two and a half hours before the gunshots.
What were they doing all that time?* 'And then you still had
to clean up, I suppose?' She kept her voice sympathetic.
'There's a lot of that to do after a big party, I bet.'

'Well, sure. But it's an important part of the . . . part of
the service.'

'Naturally. Who else was there to help you? The couple
that work at the house regularly, did they work the party?'

'The first part.'

'But they didn't stay to clean up?'

'No. Seems like they have an understanding about night
work. They stayed to the end of the birthday party, cleaned
up the cake and ice cream, and disappeared.'

'I see. So you were doing the clean-up with, um, Paul
Eckhardt.'

'Who?'

'The victim. Isn't that his name, Paul Eckhardt?'

'Oh.' She shrugged. 'I always just called him Pauly because everybody else did.'

'OK. Who else was there?'

'Well, Nino, of course.'

'Why, of course? Did Nino go wherever Pauly went?'

'Seemed like it. Yes.'

'Pauly and Nino were friends?'

'Seemed to be. Room-mates, anyway.'

It took drudgery and patience, ten or twelve more careful questions to get what should have been easy information, that Pauly and Nino lived at the theater but were not actors, just muscle guys to move props and clean up. They had turned up at the theater more than a month ago, Felicity finally said. Madge brought them in and the director hired them.

'Who's Madge?'

'Just a guy who . . .' She had an odd habit of gently touching a spot under her left eye when they got close to a subject that made her nervous. It was faintly discolored, like the remnant of an old bruise. Had she been in a fight? Sarah wrote 'Madge' in her notebook and 'bruise.' Felicity said, 'A guy who's been hanging out at the theater lately.'

'That's an odd name for a man. Is it a nickname?'

'I suppose it must be. It's what everybody calls him.'

'He's an actor?'

'No. Just kind of a groupie, I guess. He goes to our bar sometimes, too.'

'You have your own bar?'

'Oh, you know what I mean, a place where everybody goes after the performance. The Spotted Pony. I think that's where Madge found Pauly and Nino.' After the boys got their job at the theater and their room in the loft, she said, pretty soon they began to help at parties, too. For Party Down, yes. Zack's catering service.

Why did that make you touch your eye?

'And Nino's still there?' Sarah waited through a kind of vibrating silence. She added helpfully, 'At the theater? I can talk to him?'

'No.' Felicity plucked a piece of lint off her sweater. 'He's not.'

'You mean he's gone?'

'Seems to be.'

'For good?'

'As far as I know.'

'When did he leave?'

'Oh, I . . . The day after the party, I think.'

'The day after the party.' Sarah felt her ears get hot as she calmly wrote the date in her book. 'That would be a few hours after the shootings, wouldn't it?'

'Well . . . yes, I suppose . . . yes.'

'Where did he go?'

'I have no idea.'

'Did he get fired? Is that why he left?'

'I really don't know. I suppose he might have.' She shrugged and added irritably, 'He's not a friend of mine, I don't have any reason to –' her eyes darted around the room – 'keep track of him.'

'I see. We're going to take a break now, Felicity, and check a couple of things,' Sarah said, getting up. 'When I come back, can I bring you anything? More soda?'

'Oh . . . no, thanks. Will this take much longer? Because I really should be getting back.' She slid a little sidewise peek at Sarah to see if that bluff had a prayer.

Sarah said, 'We're doing great here, Felicity. Detective Menendez and I need to check with our sergeant now, I think he had one or two questions. Hang on – we won't be long.' Afraid her cheeks were flaming – her face felt hot – she locked the door carefully and the two of them hurried down the hall to where Delaney stood by Tobin's shoulder, watching the scene on the screen.

He had seen the whole thing, had not been called away for other urgent business – were the planets lining up right for once? 'This actress,' Sarah said, walking into the equipment-packed space, 'is about as evasive as any suspect I've ever seen.'

'She's a suspect now?' Delaney cut to the chase. 'What, you're giving up on the husband?'

'No, no. But this girl knows *something*, boss. You agree, don't you, Ray?'

'Maybe everything,' Menendez said. 'And she's got a

couple of great ploys. Did you notice the extra-sincere look she gives you just before a non-answer?'

'Yes. She's trying to answer all my questions without telling me anything. What about outstanding warrants?' she asked Delaney. 'You find anything?'

'Not even a parking ticket. She just looks scared, to me. You really think she took part in the killing?'

'I don't think she fired the gun,' Sarah said. 'Ray?'

'I can't imagine her even holding a gun. But she acts like she knows who did.'

'But you're not sure?'

'I'm not, no.' Menendez looked at Sarah.

'At the theater,' Sarah said, 'before I brought her down here, she said, "I don't know anything about the shooting, I was outside loading the van." Something like that.'

'Well . . . outside, so what? All the neighbors heard the shots.'

'Exactly. But I don't think she realizes that yet. Also, the dead man had a buddy named Nino who was working there that night. Every time she mentions his name it's like a speed bump, did you notice that? She claims he left the next day and she hasn't seen him since. I'm wondering if he might be dead too.'

'She know his last name?'

'She says not. But Pauly and Nino arrived at the theater and lived there together, so we can get Nino's name from whoever pays the bills there. And then, since we know Pauly just got out of Yuma, why not see if Nino was in there too?'

'I'll get somebody working on that. What else?' Sarah asked for the full name of the catering company and the owner's name. 'You got it. Sarah, you can keep on with this for a while yet, but so far I'm not seeing anything here to charge her on.'

She walked back to the interview room, Sarah muttering, 'Why would she be so evasive if she doesn't know anything incriminating?'

'I've been thinking,' Menendez said. 'If you get the right opening with this girl, you want to ask her about the candy dish?'

Sarah chuckled. 'Ah, Rye Moon Dough, you'll get some-thing out of that candy dish yet. OK, we'll ask her. And you know what I've been thinking?'

'What?'

'According to Delaney, the motive always comes down to love or money.'

'So?'

'So I can't imagine anybody as self-involved as Felicity risking everything for love, can you?'

'Or even much of anything. Let's find out what she needs money for.'

'Working these parties, Felicity,' Sarah said, settling on her stool, pouring fresh sodas over ice cubes, 'I don't suppose you do it for the fun of it, hmmm? It's hard work, isn't it?'

'Keeps me slender. I try to think of it that way.'

'Not as much fun as dance aerobics, though, is it? What, the Grand Street theater doesn't pay enough to live on?'

'It's pitiful, I shouldn't have taken it. But . . . they got a grant a couple of years ago that allowed them to hire a couple of pros, and they had such wonderful plans to grow, I . . . took a chance.'

'They hired you and who else? The director?'

'Yes. The idea was to try to step up to a more . . . regional presence.'

'How's it going?'

Felicity shook her head sadly. 'Maybe if they'd found a better director . . . Derek is so very scattered. I've done my best to help him but . . . that place is just spinning its wheels. I'm ready to move on.'

'So the catering job is to get a little bankroll?'

'Mmm-yes.' She made that nervous gesture again, touching the pale yellow remnant of a bruise under her eyes. Sarah sat up straighter. *Why didn't I see it before?* 'And to pay for your nose job?'

The big changeable-colored eyes in their slightly swollen sockets opened wide for a second, then dropped demurely as she said, 'It's almost healed. Another week and you won't see it.'

'And it was very successful, wasn't it? You must be pleased. Wow, though, a lot of money, huh?'

Felicity licked her lips. 'Like everything worth wanting.'

Two lines from a Dorothy Parker poem came unbidden into Sarah's head. *And if that makes you happy, kid, You'll be the first it ever did.*

So the money was for the nose job. *Now let's find out who paid.* 'Were Mrs Henderson's big parties good for some decent tips?'

'Yes. She could afford to be generous, and she always was.'

'Was Sunday's party as big as usual?'

'Yes.'

'A hundred people?'

'At least. Maybe more, for a while.'

'Who else—' Her phone chirped and the text message said, 'got names.' Sarah said, 'Excuse me.' In the hall, Delaney said, 'Here's the name of your Party Down guy,' and handed her a slip of paper with a name, Zachariah Christou. 'And that second name, that's the other guy from the theater, the victim's room-mate. You were right, he got out of Yuma at the same time as the victim. Almost identical charge, small-time dealing.'

'Ah-hah. Thanks.' She went back in the room and said, 'So the ones who stayed late to clean up, that was you and Pauly and Nino?'

'Yes.'

'Anybody else?'

'Oh. Well. Zack, of course.'

'Zack always works his parties?'

'Usually. Starts them out and finishes up, anyway. Holds it all together.'

'And what did you say his last name is?'

'I didn't.' Her eyes wandered the room. 'I can't seem to . . . it's something Greek.'

'How about Zachariah Christou?'

'Yes! That's it! How did you—'

'And Pauly's friend at the theater, Nino? His full name is Anthony Giardelli, isn't it? Did you know that he and Pauly had been out of Yuma prison less than a month when they came to work at the theater?'

'No, I—' Felicity's mouth opened and closed a couple of

times before any more words came out of it. Her large eyes, which really were going to be fascinating as soon as all the swelling was gone, produced one fat tear apiece. As they rolled down in unison alongside her newly perfected nose, she said, 'Oh, God.'

She put her long white hand alongside her almost beautiful face, leaned her head carefully sideways, and closed her eyes as she said, with infinite sadness, 'If you know all that, you pretty much know the rest of it, don't you? You're just toying with me, aren't you? Like a cat with a mouse. And whenever you're tired of this cruel game, you'll swat me a good one and lock me up.'

Astounded to hear herself described in such powerful terms, Sarah thought, *Oh, Jesus, kid, if only.* She leaned toward the gently weeping actress and said urgently, 'Felicity, I'd like to help you get straight with this now, but you have to quit being evasive and tell me exactly what you know about the shooting after the party. Including the candy dish,' she added, in a flash of inspiration, rolling her eyes sideways to meet Menendez' delighted smirk, holding her breath for fear she might be wrong.

But the candy dish did it. That last random detail convinced Felicity Linderman that she was dealing with an investigator who knew her innermost secrets. Unable to resist any longer, she opened the floodgates and let the truth pour out. Abundant tears gushed out with it, some hand-wringing and several agonized howls. There was so much emotion in the small room that it raised the temperature. Menendez mopped his face.

Felicity described that terrible trip down the stairs with Zack, carrying the dead weight of Nino between them.

'Even though I told him no, I absolutely won't, but he's so – he doesn't listen, once he makes up his mind, it's just *over—*'

'You're talking about Zack now, right?'

'Of course Zack, who else? I said, "I won't go upstairs," but he said, "Nino's too heavy for me to carry alone and Madge is gone, so you have to help me." He said, "Nino shot Pauly and Mrs Henderson, and now we have to get him out of here before the cops come." He said, "You promised

to do whatever I asked if I gave you the money, and this is
what I'm asking." But I mean, really,' she clutched her hair
in aggravation, disarranging it briefly before she hurriedly
smoothed it again, 'naturally I thought when he said that –
wouldn't you? Wouldn't anybody? – that he meant anything
he asked in bed. Which, trust me, is not that much.' She got
a little of her own back for a few seconds with a mean little
sneer.

'But you managed to grab the candy dish as you went
by?'

'That probably sounds crazy to you, doesn't it? But you
know, stress gives me hypoglycemia, this awful empty-tank
feeling that makes me think I'm going to pass out. And when
I get that I need quick energy . . . usually I drink some orange
juice or eat a piece of fruit, but I saw that dishful of little
wrapped candies and I grabbed it.' She hid her face in her
cupped hands and wailed. 'But I know what you're thinking,
how déclassé can you get? The woman's lying there dead
and I stole her candy dish!'

'Not at all, Felicity, we understand that perfectly,' Sarah
said. 'Anyway, we rescued the dish' – Menendez was beaming
like a light – 'and when this is over we'll see it gets back
where it belongs.'

Felicity, once started, wanted to talk, explain what she'd
been going through, how hard she had 'tried to stay above
the fray.' But by then, Sarah and Ray had a whole other set
of priorities.

Arizona law said Felicity had to be charged with a crime
'within a reasonable time,' or released, and practice had
narrowed the reasonable-time window to something close to
two hours. 'Damn close,' as Delaney kept reminding them.
In a hurried conference with him, they decided on Arizona
Statute 13-2809, Tampering with Physical Evidence, a Class
6 felony. Once charged (and she needed to understand the
charge, and for that she had to be persuaded to shut up a
minute and listen), Felicity had to be transported to the Pima
County Adult Detention Facility on West Silverlake, where
she would stay overnight and could appear before a magistrate by closed-circuit TV tomorrow. That had to happen
sometime before 2 p.m., because Arizona law also required

that Felicity enter a plea before a judge within twenty-four hours of her arrest and have an opportunity to post bail and be released pending trial.

So time was the public enemy now. It kept scrolling away while they waited to be assigned a magistrate to hear the case in the morning and a public defender to represent the suspect, Felicity having tearfully pointed out once again that she had just spent her last nickel on a nose job.

'What are you thinking, chasing around after me like this?' Madge glared, sliding into the passenger seat. 'I told you we mustn't be seen together.'

'Well, we're not, are we? Is anybody seeing us?' Zack had the aluminum sun-shield in place on the front windshield, and he had pulled his car close up alongside the storage unit at the back of the employee parking lot. Their only exposure was on Zack's side, and an employee car was parked there.

'You never know.' Madge straightened his shirt. ('This classic Hawaiian print,' he would tell you if you let him get started. 'So retro and *fun*.') Zack knew all Madge's clothing spiels so well he could have recited them but would choke before he ever did.

Madge peered into the side mirror and patted his hair. Stroking himself was one of the ways he put distance between himself and anything he didn't want to face. 'I told you I'd come to the store tomorrow night after closing. What could possibly be so urgent it can't wait until then?'

'Felicity.'

'What about her?'

'The police called her and she freaked.'

'How on earth would the police know . . . Oh, I suppose Patricia remembered her name.'

'Whatever. Anyway they called her and now she's having a shit fit, says she has to get out of town right away.'

'Fine. Who's holding her? Not me.'

'Well, she wants her money.'

'Just like that, huh? Tell her she has to wait a while yet.'

'I did. But she's almost hysterical, Madge. Actresses can't have any dealings with the police, she says, it's death to the career.'

'Oh, the career. God, that girl talks such nonsense, doesn't she?'

'Well, sure, but—'

'What?'

'Well, the other thing she says is that if she does talk to the police, she's afraid she'll get too scared and spill the beans.'

'Oh, my, we're not too frail and hysterical to know how to aim a threat, are we? If she talks there's no longer any reason to pay her, is there? Did you tell her that?'

'No,' Zack said, sounding tired. He was beginning to see that the big step up he had been counting on might be turning into a big step down into a swamp he didn't want to navigate, and he was having trouble getting his breath. To cover his rising panic he said harshly, 'And I didn't tell her you're sitting out at the Indian Casino like a stupid jerk-off trying to lose all the money you're supposed to pay her.'

'Oh, don't be ridiculous. I'm not even playing,' Madge said, dismissive the way he always got when he lied. 'Just having a beer while I wait for Desmond. We're driving to Patagonia to look at a project he's interested in. This is my last play date for a while' – the little laugh, the jolly finger-wiggle – 'because Friday it all starts to come together. Tell Felicity, after Friday, it shouldn't be long.'

'Better not be. Because Felicity's right about one thing,' he said. 'She's too nervous to talk to cops.'

'Well, it's up to you to calm her down. Or if you really want her gone,' Madge said, drawling his words now, shrugging, looking out the window casually the way he did when he was about to suggest something outrageous, 'why don't you give her the money yourself?'

'Oh, no.' Zack bristled up like an angry dog. 'Put that thought right out of your mind. I did all the dirty work like I promised, now it's up to you to come up with the money like *you* promised.'

'Which I'll be doing soon.' The little hand-flip shooed away pesky difficulties. 'I'm just saying –' he yawned – 'it's only eight thousand she's waiting for. Surely you could put your hands on that much, couldn't you? Get her off our backs and we can add it to your share later on.'

'In your dreams,' Zack said. 'Every penny I've got is hard at work in the business. I told you that going in.'

'Fine, then tell Felicity her money's on the way and she should quit being a pain.'

'Easy for you to say,' Zack said. 'You're off cooing over dream houses with your fancy friends. I'm here cleaning up the mess as usual.'

'Oh, God, martyrdom is so boring.' Madge slid away across the bench seat and swung his feet out the door. Just before he dropped out Zack reached out his long right arm and seized his neck from behind. Madge cried out sharply as Zack pulled him back and clamped his left hand around his throat. Madge hung there off the edge of the seat, his immaculately clad feet kicking the air, while Zack leaned into his ear and rasped, 'You even think about cheating me and you're a dead man, capeesh?'

Without waiting for an answer he let go his hold and Madge slid out the door and fell on his knees on the dusty pea gravel. He got up slowly, bent over, gagging and gasping for air. Watching him, Zack put the car in reverse but did not release the brake. When Madge could breathe again he turned back to the car and screamed, 'You wrinkled my *shirt*, you *pig*!' He slammed the door as hard as he could. Zack flipped him the bird and backed away.

Giving vent to honest anger felt good for a couple of minutes. But as he drove away Zack realized he had jumped a wall he hadn't really wanted to get over. He had never before acknowledged, even to himself, his growing suspicion that instead of just being a self-indulgent wastrel with a gambling problem, a weakling who could be exploited, Madge might be a clear-eyed user who was close to getting what he wanted and was looking for a way to cut Zack out of the game.

Zack hadn't lost any sleep about what happened to Pauly and Nino. Couple of losers, they were going down anyway. As for Felicity, good luck to anybody who got ahead of her in the using game. Now, though, facing the possibility that he was next on the list to be discarded, he was beginning to see a red outline of rage around everything. *A ring of fire*, he thought, hearing the Johnny Cash song, *a ring of fire*.

The edge of adventure and gamesmanship that Madge had brought into his life was fading fast. He felt himself backsliding to the old ugly Zack, the one whose stepmother beat him, whose girlfriends left, who got a dishonorable discharge from the army after his squad wasted an entire family of Iraqis because somebody nearby had fired a gun. He was back to the life he had been trying to climb out of, and it was still the same old dirty, tiresome slog.

But at least, he reflected, Madge hadn't noticed any of his scrapes and bruises, hadn't asked if there'd been any trouble with Nino. And he probably wouldn't, either. Madge usually only noticed what he wanted to. And he was probably thinking that it was better for him, easier, if he could honestly say he had no idea where in the desert Nino was buried.

By ten minutes after six Sarah was coming out of her bedroom at home, comfortable in jeans and a shapeless shirt. The last hour at work had felt like the end of a marathon, but she had cooled out pretty well on the way home. She was good at leaving the job behind. She joined her mother at the stove, asking, 'Quick, tell me, how was ballroom dancing?'

'Sam says I should remember he's good with a hammer and saw,' Aggie said, 'and leave him alone about the cha-cha-cha.'

'But you can't shake your booty while he builds a cupboard, can you? Hey, this smells good enough to eat.' She peered into a bubbling pot.

'It's white clam sauce. I'm about ready to start the linguine, if . . . you want to make a little salad?' She peered over her glasses at Denny, who was drudging through a math assignment at the table. 'About five minutes, honey, before you clear that away and set the table.'

'OK,' Denny said, frowning as she erased a number. 'Why do I have to learn percents anyway? I'm going to use a computer for this for the rest of my life.'

'In case World War Three goes badly and we end up in caves, you'll be the one who can figure out what percent of the population is left to throw rocks.' She treated Denny to her evil-granny grin. 'Set for three.'

'I thought Will said he couldn't come.'

'He did, but I'm staying. I'm too tired to go home and cook another meal.'

Something in her mother's voice made Sarah stop chopping lettuce. 'You do look beat. How late did you dance?'

'Oh, we left early.' Aggie waved dismissively. 'Sam really hated it. But I had an early test this morning that I had to fast for, and it took so long I just got . . . kind of worn out with it.' She pulled out warm plates. 'Let's eat, that'll fix me up.'

Getting the food on, enjoying the tasty meal, they were quiet. When they finished, Sarah said, 'Sit still, I'll get the dishes. You stay too, Denny, I'd rather have you get through all that homework than help.'

'OK.' She brought her books back to the table and regarded Aggie with a cagey smile. 'And as long as you're sitting there so handy, may I extract information from your beautiful brain?' Denny had learned she could get almost anything from Aggie if she asked for it in an amusing way.

'The beauty of this brain is fading fast, child,' Aggie said, 'but go ahead, pull out what you can.' Watching her mother's tired face as she expounded on the value of percentages, Sarah thought, *I should caution Denny not to overdo it*. But the two of them got along so well, it seemed a pity to interfere. Anyway, Aggie had always been able to defend herself.

When the math lesson ended Aggie brought her coffee cup out for a refill and perched on a stool. 'Will said he had a briefing at five,' she said, 'but he'd have a couple of free hours later and he'll try to stop over.'

'Good.' She scrubbed the last trace of pasta off the colander. 'This test today, what was that all about?'

'Oh . . . little trouble controlling my blood pressure all of a sudden.'

'I thought you took pills for that.'

'I do. They've always worked before, now they don't.'

'So you saw a heart doctor?'

'Endovascular. They think I might have a blocked artery.'

'Oh, my. Then what?'

'There's a clever thing they can do with a probe on the end of a . . . something. Go in through the groin. Always wondered what a groin was for, now I know.'

'Not to mention it's where your legs hook on.'

'Oh, right, there's that. Anyway if they find a blockage they take it out and put in something called a stent. Little flexible gadget that holds the artery open. Marvelous.'

'You don't look like you think it's so marvelous. Is this operation dangerous?'

'Not very. Hardly at all.' She pushed her hair back. 'I'm not worried about the stent, I just look like this because I'm sixty-eight years old and had early tests.' She sipped coffee, and then said, so softly it was barely audible above the dishwasher, 'Also, Janine called.' She set her cup in the saucer with a firm little click and got up. 'I'm going home, I need to water my plants. Call me later if you have time.'

Denny finished her homework early enough to watch a game show and then went willingly to bed, yawning. Sarah started a load of laundry and phoned her mother. 'OK, tell me about it. Janine called you where?'

'Your house. About three thirty, just before Denny got home.'

'Ah.' She waited. 'What did she say?'

'She just wanted to say hello. She's staying with friends, but she's going to get her own place as soon as she starts her new job.'

'Which is what?'

'Something in an office. The more I asked, the more I realized there was no new job. Just an idea that one day soon she ought to get one.'

'Was she sober?'

'No. She's . . . more detached from reality than ever.'

'That's what Denny thought. Ma, you know, we've got to quit fooling around like this and get Janine to sign off on a . . . power of attorney, I think it is. I need to get Denny on my insurance, and for that I need legal custody.'

'Is she sick?'

'Not today, but what if she gets appendicitis, or breaks a leg? I can't even check her into an urgent-care unit without being able to prove I'm the person in charge, did you know that?'

'No. Who told you that? I could take care of that, surely? Her grandmother?'

'Don't kid yourself. I was only able to get her changed to Doolen Middle School because the social worker owed me a favor. Don't ever tell anybody I said that, by the way. See what I mean? This is crazy. I need to be Denny's legal guardian. This way, I'm responsible for her but I don't have the right to make any decisions. We can't go on like this.'

'I suppose you're right. I've been waiting for . . . I don't know. Just waiting. Because I hate to get tough with Janine, so I always hope that . . . you know. But the next time she calls I'll try to . . .' Her voice trailed off and Sarah realized she was crying. She said something that was too muffled by sobs to be intelligible.

'What?'

'I said I don't know what to do!' More stifled noises came over the phone, followed by a loud, metallic bang, some rolling-around noises, and a crash that hurt Sarah's ear. Aggie, who never swore, said, 'Shit!' in a loud, clear voice, from somewhere across the room.

'Mother?' Sarah waited.

When she was beginning to think about hanging up and driving to Marana, her mother came back on the phone and said, 'I'm sorry, sweetie, I knocked over a plant. May I call you back in a bit?'

She sounded so collected that Sarah said, 'Sure,' and hung up. As soon as she was off the phone, though, evil black birds seemed to swoop at her head from all corners of the room, screaming about wretched possibilities. What if Aggie were more worried about her health than she was letting on? Besides a traumatized niece and a crazy sister, would she need to help an ageing parent now? *Then I really will need a day-stretcher.*

She was folding towels, relieving her anxiety by snapping them into precise rectangles, when the phone rang.

'Well, of course it had to be my favorite plant in my best pot and it had to be the one I just watered, right? Water and dirt all over the floor, and I bet I'll be finding pieces of that pot for a week.'

'I'm so sorry. Are you OK?'

'Sure. Listen, sweetheart, forget the pot. And don't worry

about all that weeping and wailing before, you hear? I was just being a weenie.'

'Well—'

'I'm very sorry I made you listen to that. It's something your baby sister does to me that's really insane. I was always a sensible mother with you and Howard, but with Janine, even when I know she's playing me I can't seem to . . . never mind. I promised to help you take care of Denny and I meant what I said. We've got to save what can be saved, don't we?'

'That's what I think.'

'Me too. So here's what we need to do: you find your crazy sister and I'll drag her into my lawyer's office and get her to sign the whatever-it-is, the waiver, the power of attorney. Is that a deal?'

'OK.' She was afraid to say any more. Aggie still sounded a little shaky.

'You can do it, can't you? Find her?'

'I'm an investigator with the Tucson Police Department. If I can't find my own sister I'll have to turn in my badge. But – you really mean this now? You're ready to take custody away from Janine, you'll have a lawyer waiting with the papers ready?'

'I guarantee it. Pen in hand.'

'I don't have any money—'

'Never mind that. I've got enough.'

'OK. You know something, Ma, I think maybe this is a teaching moment.'

'A what?'

'I think from now on, when I'm trying to make a tough decision, I'm going to try knocking over a plant.'

NINE

Sometimes November mornings are so close to perfect they feel unreal, Sarah thought, driving to work Wednesday. Autumn sunlight blazed across the city's rooftops and turned the mountains golden umber in the high places, purple in the shadows. With temps in the low seventies and humidity too low to worry about, the air felt like a caress. NPR was reporting blizzard conditions in Montana and delays due to lake-effect snow at Chicago O'Hare. She smiled smugly at the red-tailed hawk drifting on a rising thermal across the shining face of Mount Lemmon.

As Sarah walked off the elevator on the second floor, the other elevator door opened and Ollie Greenaway walked out.

'Ah, Sarah,' he flashed his gap-toothed, Alfred E. Neuman smile, 'just the busybody I wanted to see.'

'What, you got something juicy from the bank?'

'Oozing, stinking wonderful.'

'Wow. I've got an appointment at nine.'

'This'll be short and sweet.'

'Lovely. Let me check my voicemail and I'll come find you.'

She scrolled through a number of messages that could wait. But the last one asked her to call Dr Moses Greenberg, at the medical examiner's office, ASAP. Concerned, she dialed the number. The Alpha-dog forensic scientist they all called 'Animal' came on and growled, 'Sarah? Hell you think you're doing, sending your trainee over here to my autopsy? I don't have time to dick around like this!'

'If you're talking about Jason Peete, Doctor, he's got eight years on the force and he's been a detective for three.'

'Three whole years, huh? In Vice, I bet, hassling the working girls up on Oracle.'

'Home Invasions, actually.' Sarah had been on the advisory committee that helped Delaney pick him for the Homicide squad in September, and had never heard anybody voice regret over the decision. Jason Peete was a quick study with an awesome memory. 'What's your problem, Doctor?'

'A detective who pukes on the floor of my lab and has to be helped into the rest room, that's my problem, dammit! I made him clean it up himself! Did you know this was his first autopsy, Sarah?'

'No,' she said, chagrined. Jason Peete had bluffed his way past the question with sheer bravado. She should have asked.

Delaney would have known. And she should have checked with him before she OK'd the change.

Damn. She walked toward Greenaway's workspace thinking, *That's one you owe me, buster. I'm going to make you pay for this.*

In Ollie's messy office, she stood by his extra chair while he cleared the seat, tossing a fleece jacket on to the floor in the corner and moving a stack of folders on to an already-teetering stack on the credenza. The mess in his workspace was easily equal to the one Delaney was giving her grief about in hers. Serves you right for usually being a neat-freak, Ollie would probably have said. He sat down cheerily in the middle of the random heaps, utterly pleased with himself.

'Early this year,' he looked at his notes, 'about a week after New Year's, Eloise Henderson's account at the bank was changed. Now her checks have to have her husband's signature as well as her own, and there's a monthly limit on the debit cards.'

'*What?*'

Greenaway grinned brightly, almost bouncing in his chair. 'No boolcheet, baby!' In antic moments he imitated Cheech and Chong.

'Well, but . . . it was all her own money, wasn't it?'

'Not all of it. It was a joint household account. They both made deposits and wrote checks on it. The account is balanced once a month at Hen-Trax. Eloise never bothered with trifles like totals, she just wrote checks and signed charge slips.'

'I don't suppose she was paying the routine stuff, was she? Power company, phone bills?'

'No, Hen-Trax does that. Eloise just paid for the whims – clothing store, beauty shop, gifts for her family and everybody else she knows – this woman had a real thing for gift-wrap. And lunch . . . lots of lunches. Her brokerage house put the most money in the account and she took the most out. Till last year, in the week before Christmas, when she overdrew the account by almost twenty-five thousand dollars.'

'That's a lot to me, but not so much for a rich lady, is it?'

'Henderson seems to have thought so. He transferred funds to cover the overdraft, and a couple of days later one of the vice-presidents of the bank witnessed a new signatory card for Eloise that requires both signatures.'

'My, my. Quite a slap on the wrist.'

'Well, see, twenty-five thousand was only the amount of the overdraft. Before she went on the spending spree, there was over fifty thousand in the account. And in the first week in January, another twenty . . . um . . . almost twenty-seven thousand in credit-card bills came in.'

'Ooh. Must have been some Christmas.'

'That's what I said to Akito.'

'Who's Akito?'

'My special buddy at the bank. Japanese exchange student who came to the U of A to get a degree in economics. He fell in love with the culture and never left town.'

'Is he fun?'

'A Japanese banker, are you kidding? He's so perfect, every time I look at him I tuck in my shirt. Anyway, when he told me about the big overdraft I said, "That must have bought some ho-ho-ho," and he kind of shushed me before he showed me it wasn't that simple. Eloise bought about her usual quota of Christmas presents, threw the usual big lavish party for the neighbors, but last year, in addition, she sent a check to her brother for fifty thousand dollars.'

'Theodore? Doesn't he have plenty of his own money?'

'Akito says, "So we are given to understand." He talks like that. But Theodore told Eloise he had some bad days at the track or something, now he was invited on a cruise over Christmas, he'd need nice presents for everybody. He was "temporarily embarrassed," Akito says.'

'Akito picks up jargon fast, huh?'

'It's kind of a pride thing around that bank. They talk about their rich clients in these hush-hush voices, like undertakers.

Especially when they mention large amounts. Around Hendersons' money they almost genuflect.'

'Lately I'm feeling pretty reverent about money myself,' Sarah said, 'especially in the grocery store.'

Greenaway rolled his eyes up and said, 'Try it with three kids.'

'But it was Eloise giving the money away to brother Teddy that got Roger to tighten up, huh?'

'Especially after he found out it wasn't the first time. In the course of this little tiff over Christmas, Eloise confessed that brother Teddy's been coming to the well every so often for the last couple of years. Akito says, the family legend is that he's always been careless, but lately it's getting worse.'

'Akito really opened up to you, huh?' She beamed at him. 'Nice going, Ollie.'

Greenaway flashed his open smile and said, 'We just kind of hit it off.'

'I don't quite understand the big alarm, though. I mean, Eloise never got anywhere near the end of the money supply, did she? How much is in the brokerage account, do you know?

'I haven't got exact figures yet, but I did some quick math based on the payments she's been getting, and it has to be close to ten million. That's not a huge fortune these days, Akito assures me, but it'll keep you in first-class seats if you exercise a little care. There's another account, too, though. I don't know how big that is yet. They call it the growth account, it's invested in long-term, high-yield instruments. That's what they call them, instruments. Like finely tuned violins or something.'

'You're kind of enjoying the bank, aren't you?'

'Whole different world. Makes you realize we're just spinning our wheels out here, paycheck to paycheck.'

'I kind of suspected that,' Sarah said.

'Me too, but I'm going to think about it some more. Anyway . . . I'll get the skinny on the growth account tomorrow, Sarah. I have to see a different vice-president for that.'

'But you're getting everything you ask for?'

'You bet. Eloise is deceased and this is her homicide we're

investigating, so they're not trying to keep any secrets about
her money. Hen-Trax, now, that's a different, as we say,
revenue stream.' Ollie raised his left hand, blew on his finger-
nails, and buffed them on his shirt.

'We don't get to go near the revenue stream?'

He nodded solemnly. 'Don't even think about dipping a
toe.'

'OK.' She thought about the amazing news. 'So this very
rich lady, since last January, has only been able to spend as
much of her own money as her husband would let her have?'

'Right. You think maybe that got kind of . . . annoying?'

'Would have been to me.'

'And yet,' Greenaway said softly, 'the husband's not the
one who ended up dead.'

'No. But the last thing she did on this earth was throw
one hell of a party and go to bed with one of the help.'

'I suppose that could be understood as an expression of
hostility.'

Nino's second day in the field was harder than the first
because his muscles were sore to begin with. And with one
day behind him, he knew how long days were.

They were picking tomatoes off staked-up vines. By the
end of the first hour, when he stretched up to reach the fruit
on top, his arms felt as if they weighed forty pounds apiece.
And when he bent to pick the low stuff his back hurt so
much he was sure he must have torn a muscle.

A couple of times during the morning he made up his
mind to quit. But a sinewy little Chicano guy working the
other side of the row with him, Juan he said his name was,
noticed he was in trouble and took pity on him. Using nudges
and nods since they had hardly any language in common,
Juan showed him how to hang the basket so it didn't hurt
his back so much. 'Así, OK?' Juan said, adjusting the straps.
Nino hefted the redistributed weight and said, 'Cool!' and
they high-fived.

A few minutes later Juan taught him another trick, to speed
up or slow down so they arrived at the end of the row when
the foreman was at the other end. That way they could take
turns sitting down for a minute when they grabbed a hose

for a drink of water, while the other stood in front for cover. Carlos didn't begrudge all the water they could drink – he knew they had to have it to work in the sun. But sitting down, he considered loafing, and he would roust them for that. It made all the difference, though – Nino's muscles didn't cramp so much if he could get off his feet now and then. Thinking about how good those few seconds of sitting were going to feel, timing his rows became almost like a game, and he made it through the morning.

He ate his noon meal as fast as he could so he could lie flat in the shade and snooze a few minutes before he went back to work. Juan said, 'Is bell. I call you,' and let him sleep till the last minute before they had to jump on the truck. Nino said, 'Gracias, amigo,' when they took their seats, and Juan grinned out of his little brown half-starved face and said, 'Cool, no?' He nudged Nino gently and said, 'Estados Unidos, no?' And when Nino looked puzzled he said, pointing, 'You. Me. Estados Unidos.'

'Oh, sí. Couple Estados Unidos guys, that's us,' and they high-fived again.

Having a new friend willing to help him got Nino thinking about Pauly again. He snickered, thinking about all the nudging and hand-signals they had used on that last day, at the party, so they could duck into the helps' bathroom with food and wine. Once that silly Pauly had come out of the lavatory looking pleased with himself, with chili sauce all over his cheek. Nino grabbed him, saying, 'Asshole,' softly but laughing too, and wiped it off before anybody else saw.

Thinking back over that day while he worked his rows, he forgot his sore back and the dirt and flies out there in the hot field. He had finally sweat all the drugs and alcohol out of his system, and was beginning to recover from the hysteria that had gripped him ever since he woke up in the terrible bedroom. Freed by the routine movements of his body, his mind drifted, and he had his first flashback. He saw himself smiling, watching Pauly dance the green-dress lady around the utility room, the two of them moving as if they were joined at the hip. He had been dancing too, he was reaching out with one arm around Felicity, interrupting their dance to take the drink Madge was handing him, Madge saying, 'Drink up, dear boy, the party's finally starting to fly.' And they all laughed, everybody laughed.

Pauly and me wasn't fighting. I wasn't mad at nobody.

He forgot all about grammar in the joy of that realization.

He wasn't drunk, either. He'd had some wine, sure, but he'd been working his ass off all afternoon and evening and then there was all this craziness with the dancing. He knew he could have passed a sobriety test at that moment, walked a line, touched his nose, whatever.

That last drink, though, must have had one helluva kick. The next thing he remembered was waking up on the floor upstairs with his head like a lead balloon. And there was this big heavy gun in his arms – hands? someplace there – Zack was lifting it off him, helping him up. Saying, 'Come on, for God's sake, we gotta get out of here.' And poor Pauly was on the bed with only blood where his face should have been.

I didn't do it, though, he told himself with sudden absolute certainty. *I wasn't mad, we didn't fight.*

Delirious with the joy of his discovery, he grabbed Juan and danced him down the row between the staked tomato vines. Workers all around them turned in alarm toward the noise, thinking they were watching a fight beginning. But Nino was laughing as he yelled happily into Juan's skinny little startled face, 'I didn't do it, amigo! I didn't kill that silly little turd!'

Sarah's phone chirped and she read a text message, 'Need 2 tlk, RD.' She called him and asked, 'The lawyer here already?'

'Be a few minutes. Couple things to tell you first.' Delaney had asked street patrolmen, as they'd agreed yesterday, to check Party Down. Zack was not there, and the shop was locked up. He had put out an APB for Nino, in Arizona and the surrounding four states. And Menendez was getting a warrant to search his room above the theater.

She told him about the money fight Ollie had uncovered at the bank, and the motivation it provided for Eloise to punish her husband with more philandering. 'Which in turn, of course,' she added, 'provided a good reason for Roger to kill her.'

'Except he wasn't there.'

'So it seems.'

'You still don't want to give him up, huh?'

'Well, he's just such a natural.'

'Except he wasn't there,' he said relentlessly. 'Hang on a sec.' He was gone a minute, came back, and said, 'Hartford's here. You ready?'

They walked down the hall together and paused outside the open door of the 'good' interview room, which still had grim overhead lighting and gray walls but at least afforded comfortable armchairs to sit in. Tobin was monitoring the video on the outside.

The steno brought in water and glasses and asked Devon Hartford III if she could bring him anything else. He assured her he was fine, thanks very much. She was solicitous. He was composed. Devon Hartford would no doubt be composed, Sarah decided, in a typhoon at sea. Assessing his neat close haircut, glinting rimless glasses, discreet tie, she muttered in Delaney's ear, 'This bird's not easy, is he?'

'Looks like he costs a lot and earns every penny.'

They walked in together. Delaney made introductions. Devon Hartford's handshake was firm, his just-barely smile serene. Delaney seemed equally relaxed, saying in his friendliest manner, 'Why don't you just go ahead and tell us what you think we need to know? Then if we have questions we'll ask them.'

'Very good.' Hartford tented his fingers, looked wise. 'Mr Henderson came to see me yesterday. Very upset, understandably. Told me how he came home and found his wife . . . ahem. Well. And he said, "As if that isn't bad enough, I get the feeling I'm a suspect." Of course I told him, "Oh, Roger, that's just standard operating procedure, the spouse always gets looked at first." But he was concerned that maybe Patricia would get the idea that . . . ahem.

He gets more out of clearing his throat than most people do out of speech.

'He said, "Bad enough she lost her mother like that. But then to be the first one there, she saw . . . " He was quite distraught about what she saw. He said, "And my God, Dev, think how terrible for her if she thought there was any chance

that I . . . "' Hartford's small firm mouth turned down just
enough at both ends to convey sadness. *Even his facial
muscles don't waste any effort.*

'So I told him, "Roger, you have so much to do. Let me
go down and visit with these folks. I'm sure I can clear up
any misapprehensions they might be having." ' His calm gray
gaze swept their faces, alert for signs of confusion.

Delaney, stoical as stone, asked, 'What is it you think we
don't understand?'

'Well, for example, you might be thinking Mr Henderson
stands to benefit financially from his wife's death.' *No throat-
clearing now.* 'And I want you to understand that actually
it's just the opposite. Roger signed a prenuptial agreement
stating that all the money that was settled on Eloise when
she married would remain hers if they divorced. In the event
of her death, if she had children they'd inherit, of course,
but until they were twenty-five the estate would be admin-
istered by surviving members of Eloise's family. And if she
had no issue surviving, the money would all revert to the
Della Maggios.'

'No settlement at all for the spouse? That's pretty restrictive for a prenup, isn't it?' Sarah said.

'Yes, I believe it is.' He gave a little satisfied nod. Evidently
restrictive arrangements were the most fun to make.

'So Patricia and her brother get all their mother's money?
And their father gets nothing?'

'That's right. Of course Roger Henderson isn't the penni-
less carpenter he was when they married. He's built up a
business with a very large cash flow of his own. I expect
you know about Hen-Trax, don't you? The company's been
in the news quite a bit lately.

'I should point out that Roger does lose some flexibility
from this. While his wife lived he was entitled to use as
much of the income from the estate as she cared to share
with him – all of it, in effect, because Eloise was the soul
of generosity. Particularly where Roger was concerned! But
now that she's dead the income from her estate is off limits
to him.'

'I see. Who'll administer the estate, then? Mrs Henderson's
parents?'

'No, sadly, both parents died in an automobile accident. Just last year, actually. So there's only Eloise's brother left. Teddy. Um, Theodore.'

'Oh? Nobody mentioned him before. Does he live in Tucson?'

'No. He visits here occasionally, but his residence is in Florence. Italy, not Arizona.'

'Indeed. But he's been notified? He's coming for the funeral?'

'Oh, I'm sure. As soon as they, um, find him. He travels a good deal – he seems to have a wide circle of, um,' a thoughtful pause, 'rather oddly assorted friends.' He shrugged minimally in a cleaned-up, lawyerly version of, 'Whaddya gonna do?'

The officers waited a few moments to hear more about the peripatetic habits of Patricia's uncle. When no more details were forthcoming, Delaney turned to look at Sarah. His red face inquired silently, *You still feel sure about the husband's guilt?*

Sarah watched her visitor turn a page in his notes. She was picking up a different vibe. 'Why do I get the feeling there's something more?'

'Well –' Hartford shifted in his chair – 'now I'm in the awkward position of divulging information to you that hasn't been made public yet. But I feel I owe it to you to share this now, so you'll understand Eloise's state of mind in the last weeks of her life. Because the circumstances of her death . . . ah . . . in view of, um, the way she was found.'

'In bed with another man, you mean,' Sarah said. Delaney looked at her in alarm, but she refused to meet his eye. Somebody had to say it, or they could sit here all day, clearing their throats and dancing around the truth.

An electric silence buzzed in the room while Hartford recrossed his legs. His chair creaked as he tented his hands again and looked at the ceiling. Sarah prodded again. 'Are you saying we shouldn't jump to the conclusion that the couple were estranged?'

'That's exactly what I'm saying, Detective.' He met her eyes and nodded approvingly. He seemed to be giving her points for clearing up confusion.

'All right,' Sarah said, feeling herself sink deeper in the weeds. 'How would you characterize their relationship?'

'They were a middle-aged couple working through some vexing problems. As so many couples do. And before I tell you what Eloise had decided to do about it, I must point out that until yesterday Roger knew nothing about her decision.'

'Her decision to what?'

'To cancel the prenup. She came to me about a month ago and said, "It's not right. I'm Roger's beneficiary but he's not mine." She said, "Daddy set it up when we married and I didn't object because I was just a girl, what did I know? But now Roger and I are equal partners – " she very much wanted to believe that, she said it several times – "Roger and I are equals and I want it fixed."'

'Why now?'

'I asked her that and she was quite evasive at first. But finally . . . she said she felt that they had been "growing apart." She talked like that sometimes, like the pop-psychology column in a women's magazine.' Hartford shuddered delicately. 'Poor Eloise had every advantage, in some ways, but her parents traveled a good deal when she was a child and took her along, so she never really got much education.' He cleared his throat again, deliberated, and finally said, 'Actually, there seems to have been a bit of a learning disability as well.'

Sarah, hearing her motive for murder come back, didn't really want to ask the next question. But Hartford had made the claim on which everything hinged and she knew she had to verify it now. 'You're sure she never told her husband?'

'Absolutely! She expressly forbade my saying a word to anyone. Their twentieth wedding anniversary was coming up soon, and she was determined this would be her surprise gift to him. And Roger . . . when I told him, yesterday, he was so touched . . . he all but broke down again.' Hartford's eyes took on a shine. 'Roger Henderson's an exceptionally fine man, as I suppose you've realized by now.'

Delaney murmured something vague. Sarah watched the lawyer, thinking, *And now he's your major client, isn't he?* 'How far did you get with changing the prenup?'

'It was all done but the signing. And we could have had

that out of the way if Eloise hadn't wanted to save it for their anniversary. It's no big deal to change a prenuptial agreement if both sides agree to it. Eloise's father was the only one who might have raised any objection, and he was gone.'

'The brother—'

'He got his initial share when he married . . . ahem . . . the first time. Five or six years before Eloise got hers. And the siblings split the balance of the estate, minus a few bequests, last year when their parents passed. He isn't entitled to any more.'

'But if the prenup hasn't been finalized, he'll be in charge of the money now, won't he?'

'Well. Yes and no. The deceased's intentions were perfectly clear, and since he's already been well taken care of there's no reason for him not to do the right thing and honor her last request.'

'Except people find reasons when money's involved.'

'Sad but true. But no, I can't believe . . . he's already been given plenty of money. No reason for Teddy to make any trouble.'

'Did you notify him of the change?'

'No. I'll have to when the time comes, since he's the other person affected, but for the present I'm sworn to secrecy. It probably doesn't matter . . . I have the feeling he only reads a fraction of what I send him anyway. I sent him a letter about some stock changes a couple of months ago, really quite important, but typically, he never answered.' A small, rueful grimace.

'He doesn't answer his mail?'

'His father used to say, "Teddy has no head for details, I'm afraid." Fabian Della Maggio was a paterfamilias of the old school, domineering and very protective. He worked himself and his employees hard, but he enjoyed indulging his wife and children.'

Sarah took another deep breath and asked him, 'Did you help Roger Henderson cut his wife off at the bank last January?'

'Well . . .' he recrossed his legs, looked at his hands a few seconds, 'yes. That is . . . we didn't cut her off. You don't cut a Della Maggio off from her own money, not in this town. But Roger and I persuaded her that she needed to control her overspending. And help with the fact that she could never deny her brother anything. So yes, I helped him get the bank to agree that her checks had to be signed by both of them, and the debit cards would have reasonable limits. I sympathized with his desire to save some of Eloise's money for their children.'

Delaney's cell phone vibrated. He looked, said, 'Excuse me,' and answered it. He listened briefly, raised his head and told the attorney, 'Well, here's a coincidence. The man on the door says Mr Henderson is downstairs and he's looking for you.'

'Why on earth would Roger . . . well, do you mind letting him come up? I'll just find out what he needs and then probably he'll be on his way.'

'No problem.' Delaney spoke into the phone and closed it.

Sarah asked him, 'You weren't expecting to see him today?'

'No. And I can't imagine why he'd come looking for me here.'

There was an abrupt little knock. The door opened halfway, and a handsome blond head, very young, appeared in the opening.

'Ah, there you are,' the boy said, speaking exclusively to Hartford, ignoring the two detectives. He came all the way in, looking pleased to have found his man, not concerned at all about whatever conversation he might be interrupting.

'Adam,' Hartford said, 'Roger said you weren't due until tomorrow.'

'Well, I've always said he doesn't know everything.'

His physical resemblance to his sister was striking. He had the same high blond coloring, Delft-blue eyes, and strong, confident bearing. He brought an entirely different vibe into the room, though. An extra touch of arrogance, Sarah thought, and a little tweak of – was it anxiety? Something goading him.

Then his eyes slid past her, just slightly out of focus and with that characteristic shine, and she knew what she was looking at. *Patricia Henderson on speed.*

'I called your office,' Adam told the lawyer. 'They said

you'd come down here and I thought, well, OK, I'll go there and get all the news at once.'

'Yes, um,' Hartford said. 'How'd you get here, Adam?'

Must be some kid. For the first time since she'd met him, Hartford looked uneasy.

'I flew. There's this device now, Devon, called an airplane . . .'

'I meant from the airport. Is Patricia with you, did she pick you up?'

'No. no, I rented a car.'

'Rented a . . . you have your license now?'

'Of course.' He pretended to be offended by the question, but his bright eyes slid away from Hartford in a way that made Sarah wish she could see the card.

'We could have sent someone to fetch you. Or Roger's secretary would have.'

'Have to have wheels anyway.' His impatient little shrug said, *Why are we discussing this?*

'Well. Um . . . Adam, this is Sergeant Delaney.'

Only half turned toward Delaney, he reached a hand out and they shook. Adam mumbled something that might have been, 'Pleasure.'

'And Detective Sarah Burke,' Hartford said. Adam nodded brightly at a point behind her shoulder. Practiced in the art of refusing to be blown off, Sarah gave him the small, correct smile of the officer on duty and extended her hand. He scrutinized it for two heartbeats as if it was some strange artifact of dubious interest before giving it the briefest possible shake – a touch, quickly withdrawn. His eyes grazed her left earlobe and returned to his attorney. 'How soon will you be done here? I need to talk to you.'

'Well. Ahem. Adam,' Hartford's gray eyes had clouded over, 'um, perhaps you could call my office and make an appointment? I can't, um, tell from here when I have an open time.'

'Well, Devvy, my God,' Adam raised his voice and set the tone at broad mockery, 'you mean you're not going to treat me like a rock star, take me to lunch? Come on, the prodigal son's returned, and now he's rich!' He turned back to Sarah, smiled at her cordially as if they were suddenly friends.

'Devvy's a Third, you know. Thirds are very upper-crusty, they have to be careful who they break bread with.' Hartford's rejection had set him on fire. His blue eyes blazed with barely controlled rage. 'He's always treated me like a dirty shirt in the past, but I was sure my coming into a pile of dough would soften him up. Because I've noticed over the years that ol' Devvy'll pretty much sit up and beg when he sees a stash of cash.' He did a quick imitation of a friendly canine lolling his tongue and wagging his tail, somehow retaining enough similarity to Hartford to be devastating. 'I guess Mommy's fortune must not be big enough after all. Damn! How much does it take these days, I wonder?'

'Well, now, Adam, we're glad to know your sense of humor is intact—'

'Oh, you bet! Still got my sense of humor and my dancing shoes and there's nothing wrong with my appetite, either, when I can get hold of anything fit for it to work on. But I've been locked inside a germ-infested airplane all morning and as Tom Wolfe would say, I'm starved to near perfection.' He turned his dazzling, overheated smile on Sarah again and asked her, 'Want to go to lunch, Ms Detective?'

'No thanks.' She stood up. 'Here's my card, though, in case you have any questions after you've eaten.'

'Questions. About the untimely demise of my crazy mom? Not likely. I bet *you'd* just *love* to talk about it, though, wouldn't you?'

There was a tiny moment of dead air, like the interval between lightning and thunder, before Hartford stood up and said, 'Your mother was always very kind to you, Adam. I think you ought to show a little respect.'

'Hey, I'll show you mine if you'll show me yours.' A hard little bark of laughter came out of him, and then he quit smiling and said, 'Fuck lunch, I want to go *home*. These people,' he indicated Delaney and Sarah with a tilt of his head, 'as I understand it, are somehow able to keep me out of my own house. Can you at least fix that, Mr Bigtime Lawyer the Third?'

'It's a crime scene, Adam,' Hartford said. He picked up his briefcase. His eyes had iced over completely. 'When they're done investigating it, they'll release it. To your father.

Talk to him about getting a key.' He walked around Adam without looking at him, and stepped into the hall.

'Don't you walk away from me, you prick!' Adam Henderson yelled at his back. 'I need to talk to you and I need it now!'

'Call my office,' Hartford's mild voice said, from somewhere near the elevator. 'Make an appointment.' The doors opened and closed and the car hummed downward.

Delaney's phone vibrated. He looked at the number, said, 'Excuse me,' and disappeared. Sarah was left in the small room with a young male person who looked as if he might be going to implode. *What do I do if he foams at the mouth?*

For a few seconds he did look as if he might go into spasm. His eyes rolled up and he turned white. But instead of slumping to the floor he turned all the way around, like a dog at bedtime, and by the end of that maneuver he was staging a comeback. He rattled coins in his pockets, frowned in a puzzled way, hummed a snatch of music, and abruptly began grinning at her brightly. 'Well, hey,' he said, 'at last we're alone, huh? Let's get better acquainted – what's your first name, Ms *Po*-lice?' That fierce bit of impudent humor snapped him out of his funk entirely. 'Hoo!' He clapped his hands over his head and rotated his pelvis in a prancing-stud move.

If I were still on the street I could take my baton to you, then we could both have fun. But she saw the sweat on his upper lip, and the jittery way his left hand kept tugging at the hem of his jacket. *Doesn't anybody care that this kid is a total train wreck?* A couple of years younger than Patricia and already well on the way to trashing himself. How long had he lived at boarding schools where nobody gave a damn about him? How many of those years had he been using?

'You can call me Detective,' she said. But she put a little glint in it.

'Because we're such special friends, huh?' Amusement perked him up a little, he backed off the crazy-loose-cannon anger trip. 'How soon do you think I can get back in my house, Detective?'

Wanting to get him out of the department, she said, 'Why

don't you come over to my desk for a minute? Maybe I can find out.'

He gave a big 'whatever' shrug. But he followed her.

She had forgotten the clutter in her office. They stood together in the doorway, looking in at the perfect storm of paper. Pointing at one of the chairs she'd put in the hall, she said, 'Have a seat here for a minute, will you?'

He flashed a mocking smile at her and sat down, saying, 'Tell you right now you're not getting your merit badge for housekeeping this month.'

She wagged a warning finger at him and went on to Tobin's space. He said he was done at the Henderson house, didn't know whether all the lab crews were out yet but would find out. While he was checking, she heard her phone ring, stepped back into her cubicle, and picked the phone up off the floor, trying not to make a breeze.

Delaney said, 'Have you still got that terrible brat there with you? Well, get rid of him as soon as you can because we need to talk. You got that list of weapons Peete found in the house?'

'Yes.'

'Bring it with you and come in my office. Is Tobin over there? Bring him along.'

When she turned away from the phone she found Tobin standing in the door of her workspace, looking around bemused. She said quickly, 'Don't come in.' She sidled into the hall. 'What?'

'Gloria over at the lab says she's finally done at the Henderson house and if she never sees another fingerprint it'll be too soon.' He was grinning. 'She says this time she means it, she's going over to Pima College tomorrow and sign up for courses in hotel management.'

'OK. And, uh,' Sarah leaned into Tobin's shoulder, gently nudging him toward his own workspace. Standing by his desk, at what she thought was a safe distance from Adam Henderson, she muttered, 'What about the rest of the crew?'

'What? Everybody's done,' Tobin said, in his normal voice, which suddenly sounded loud as a trumpet. He was thinking about his own work and hadn't even noticed her furtive behavior. 'The yard crew took the crime-scene tape down an hour ago. Gloria said she was the last one out so she locked all the doors and turned the crime-scene lock back to Delaney. What?' He finally noticed the distress on her face.

'Never mind.' Sarah stepped back out in the hall to tell Adam Henderson he could call his father and get a key. He was already walking away. She called after him, 'Your house is—'

Without turning, he called back, 'I heard,' and kept on walking.

In the hall, where the space opened out for standing room in front of the elevators, he passed Mary Waite, who was coming over from the support-staff bullpen with a couple of folders. She turned and watched him as the elevator door opened and he stepped inside.

'Whee,' she said, as the door closed, 'there goes a hottie.' She looked at Sarah. 'What, you don't think so?'

Sarah shook her head and hugged herself, rubbing her arms. 'Cold,' she said. 'Cold cold cold.'

Ray Menendez was sitting in front of Delaney's desk, looking pleased with himself, when Sarah and Leo walked in.

'Ray searched Nino's room this morning,' Delaney said, 'and found a twelve-gauge shotgun, broken down, on the shelf in the closet. Let me see that list, huh?' She handed it across the desk. 'Let's see, the Remington . . .' He compared it to a note on his blotter. 'Yes, by God,' he said. His eyes went back and forth, checking both lists. Finally he looked up, blinking. 'It's his gun. Can you believe this?'

'No,' Sarah said.

'No what?'

'No, I don't believe it.'

'Oh, now what? This evidence points to a shooter that yesterday's witness said was there, doesn't it? Said she helped carry him down the stairs after he passed out. But you're still holding out for the husband?'

'I'm not holding out for anything. I'm just saying, this feels pretty pat to me. What kind of an idiot flees the area but leaves the murder weapon behind in his room?'

'Well, pardon the hell out of me, Sarah, but that's where we found it.'

'Anyway, Sarah,' Menendez said, 'if bad guys never did anything stupid our clearance rate would be even worse than it is.'

'Which God forbid,' Delaney said.

'Well, granted. But this is so ridiculous it makes me wonder if something else is going on. Leo,' she turned to Tobin, 'you buy this scenario?'

'It seems incredibly stupid, but then how dumb do you have to be to kill somebody at a party with half a dozen witnesses? Anyway, I don't think ballistics is going to make this case for us.'

'You said that before, when we didn't have the gun,' Delaney said.

'So now you've got the gun and what have you got? OK, we can prove it's Henderson's. But we can't prove it's the gun that killed his wife, can we? Unless we found the cartridges, which we didn't.'

'They're testing it now,' Delaney said. 'By tomorrow we'll know if it's been fired recently.'

'And if it has, that's very strong circumstantial evidence but you're still not going to convict anybody with it.'

Delaney scratched his ear thoughtfully, blinked a while, and finally said, 'I guess you're right.'

'I know I'm right. All we've got in the bodies is buckshot that a first-year law student would tell a jury could have come from any shotgun. And even if we had the ammo we couldn't put Henderson there pulling the trigger, could we? Suppose the gun is covered with his prints and DNA, so what? It's his gun, why wouldn't it be? As for this Nino person, now . . .' He thought. 'If his DNA is on the gun, that might put him in prison. But it won't get us to murder one.'

'OK, Leo,' Sarah said. 'I promise not to rely on ballistics.'

Tobin shrugged. 'Just trying to save you some time.'

'Nothing so far on the APB on Anthony Giardelli,' Delaney said. 'And why aren't we finding this Zack person? He's right here in town.'

'Who says?' Sarah said. 'He's not in his shop, I've had patrolmen checking it every hour. The door is locked, the lights are out, and the van is gone.'

'Didn't Felicity say he's got a room above the shop? Maybe he's up there with the lights off, hiding.'

'I'll see if I can find out who owns the building,' Sarah said. 'Hate to break down a door if we don't have to.'

She was sitting at her computer, typing in the order for a Need to Locate on Nino, when a familiar shape scooted past her peripheral vision. She turned away from her screen and said, 'Jason Peete!'

He said, from somewhere in the hall, 'Yes?'

Two seconds later, Menendez popped out of his cubicle and stood in the hall outside Sarah's door, grinning, asking, 'Hey, Jason, my man! Come back here and tell us all, how'd the autopsy go?'

Hearing Menendez, Tobin came out in the hall, too, asking, 'You like the blood and guts, buddy?'

Ollie Greenaway called over the top of his half-wall, 'Did Animal let you hold the brain before he weighed it?'

Everybody on the whole flaming floor, evidently, except Sarah Burke had known this was Jason Peete's first autopsy. Did Elmer the Grump know it too? She actually opened her mouth to say how very helpful it might have been if any of them had seen fit to mention this well-known fact yesterday morning. But before she could say a word Jason Peete stepped into her doorway looking as if he might be getting sick again. And looking at his desperate face, she realized what he wanted to tell her: *the other detectives didn't know.*

Animal hadn't told any of them that Peete had hurled in the autopsy room, why would he? Animal didn't give a damn who took heat around here, he was a busy man. He'd only taken the time to call her, Sarah realized, for the sheer joy of dressing somebody down.

So now Jason Peete was standing in the doorway of her cubicle with *please please please* written all over his face.

She'd promised herself she'd get even for the sneaky way he'd finessed himself into the autopsy assignment. Now all she had to do was repeat what Animal had said, and the rest of the squad would punish Peete for her, for weeks, relentlessly.

But now she couldn't do it. The mocking faces of the three detectives in the hall took away her taste for revenge. Their days were tough enough in this department without playing any gotcha games.

So she ignored the taunting questions of the other detectives and asked Peete, 'How are you doing on that autopsy report?'

'Just, uh –' he swallowed hard – 'on my way to wrap it up?'

'Oh, good. Can you help me with something else this afternoon?'

'Sure,' he said. And then, trying hard not to look like a pitiful suck-up. 'You want to tell me about it now, or—?

'Might as well.' As the three detectives in the hall drifted away, she asked Jason Peete, 'I'm hoping you'll go on a little spying mission for me.'

Zack returned to his shop on East Broadway in mid-afternoon. He had not been hiding. He had not read the newspaper story about Felicity's arrest and had no idea he was being hunted. His army buddy's wife had taken a look at his scratches and persuaded him he'd heal faster if he let her help. Since then he had been lying on the couch in their condo, enjoying her cooling poultices and watching his scabs form.

Luckily, he had a couple of days with no parties scheduled. By Wednesday he was still stiff and sore all over, but a few tentative stretches and bends had convinced him he had no broken bones. Party Down was scheduled to do a big birthday party on Saturday, and he hadn't even staffed it yet, so as soon as he could move a little easier he went home.

He had no idea that a midtown patrolman, circling the block, would see the Party Down van parked by the front door and call for backup. When two officers in protective gear burst into his shop with guns drawn, they found him counting party hats. Recognizing overwhelming force when he saw it, he put up no resistance, which is not to say he went in willingly. He was prone to feelings of persecution at the best of times, and being marched out of his own shop in handcuffs, before the curious eyes of his neighbors in the antiques shop next door, blew the lid off his always simmering volcano of rage.

They put him on a hard little stool by a small gray table,

took off his left handcuff, fed it and a few inches of chain through the rope lead on the table, and clamped it back on his wrist. Being tethered to the furniture added a demeaning aspect to his arrest that fueled his outrage further. Bad enough to have been treated like shit by the United States Army, now he was getting more of the same from civilians.

Despite all the hard things he had to say about the army, Zack's years as an enlisted man had left him accustomed to hold civilians in contempt. Civilians hid behind the military but didn't give it the respect it deserved because that would mean admitting they didn't have What It Took to join up. Now he was in a room with two civilians who thought their guns and badges gave them the right to chain him to the table like a dog. He wanted to smash their faces.

When he demanded an attorney, the woman detective gave him her card and told him to have his attorney call her when he was ready to talk. She had already told him every move they made in here was being recorded. Now she made it clear that nobody was going to argue, and the two detectives excused themselves.

Pleased to see how quickly his resistance had fended off the detectives, Zack sat quietly, his eyes glittering bitterly in his white face, waiting for them to come back and release him. He thought if you declared you wouldn't talk without a lawyer they said, 'OK, then,' and turned you loose to go find one. Instead, this pair of dickheads came back and recited the charges against him, murder in the second degree plus a couple of other things about tampering with physical evidence and aiding in the commission of a felony. He didn't understand it all but what the hell, he was going to plead not guilty to whatever they said.

They detailed an agenda. He would be fingerprinted now, a sample of his blood would be drawn . . . they described his transport to adult detention, the phone and the list of bail-bondsmen that would be available to him there, the TV hook-up that would allow him to enter his plea before a judge in the morning. They were courteous and quiet and completely infuriating in their self-confidence.

By the time the two uniformed officers arrived to give him his ride, Zack knew that beating on the detectives would never be enough. To work off the venom that was churning his guts now, he would need to strangle them with his bare hands and then stomp and kick them, wearing heavy army boots that left the mark of treads on their faces. Like that houseful of ragheads in Baghdad.

Even when there was minimal conversation with the prisoner, Sarah fretted, it took all afternoon to observe the forms that finally got a prisoner locked up.

'It can't be four o'clock already. Can it?' she asked when it was.

'Nah. It's these damn digital watches, I knew they'd never work,' Tobin said. He derived endless free entertainment from Sarah's ongoing battles with the clock. 'Ready or not, though, I'm going to have to leave this party now. I gotta meet the second victim's mama at the morgue. What's his name?' He consulted his notes. 'Oh, yeah, Paul Eckhardt.' He made a sour face. 'So much fun, the mamas.' Then he was gone, and Sarah went back to swimming against the tide.

They had to decide on charges quickly, communicate them to a man who didn't want to listen to them, then coordinate with all the other people involved. Long before Zachariah Christou was on his way to jail, Sarah realized that the time eroding from under her feet at the station was carrying her household closer to the dinner hour. She called her mother and explained why she was probably going to be late. 'Tell you what, darlin',' Aggie said, 'I'll just go ahead and dish up, and save you a plate.'

An hour later, realizing the end was not yet in sight, she called again. 'Will's here, we're all keeping each other company, don't worry, we're fine,' her mother said. But Dietz took the phone and told her, 'Aggie's tired, she needs to go home. Denny says it'll be OK if she takes a book to bed and I stay out here and guard the door. I'm not due at work till ten, will that give you enough time?'

'Oh, plenty,' she said. It was, but not by a whole lot. Zack's ride was late, there was a wait for a cell, and getting an OK from a magistrate's clerk for a hearing before 4 p.m. tomorrow took three phone calls.

Driving home that night, gripping the wheel, Sarah pulled

her stomach muscles hard against her backbone and breathed deliberately. Hours of walking on mental eggshells with a hostile prisoner who was looking for any excuse to cry foul had left her strung out and depleted. Besides that, she had been nagged all afternoon by a persistent feeling that she was forgetting something. Working systematically through the routine of putting a prisoner away, trying to make the memory surface, she had not even known how tired she was until she walked out and started her car. The dashboard light came on and she said aloud, to the quiet street, 'God, it's almost eight o'clock.'

She parked under her carport vine in velvety darkness, thinking how comforting it was to come home to a lighted window.

Dietz kissed her quickly when she came in the door and said, 'Aggie left you some good stew, I'll warm it up.' He put a glass of wine on the table by her place. 'Denny would sure like to say good night before you settle down, though.'

She stood by the counter taking her gun and badge off, putting her keys away, so glad, suddenly, to be in this small orderly space with this decent capable man that she felt tears sting the back of her eyelids. To keep them from dropping she turned away quickly and walked across her bedroom and into Denny's bedroom niche, which still, alas, had a curtain but no door. Under the good reading light that Sarah had managed to squeak out of this month's grocery budget, Denny lay cradling a library book. Remembering the intense pleasure of childhood reading, Sarah felt a flash of envy. Then she noticed the handle of her one good French knife peeking out from under the pillow. *Looks like the onus isn't off Will Dietz quite yet. Oy vey, I better warn him not to make any sudden moves.*

When Sarah tapped on the molding Denny looked up and said, 'Hey, did you catch the bad guy, Aunt Sarah?'

'Sure did.' She bent for a kiss.

'My hero.' She gave Sarah a warm flannel hug. 'Bet you're tired.'

'Tired, hungry, glad to be home.' She stood up, holding the knife in her left hand, unobtrusively. 'You don't need this any more, do you?' she said, and without waiting for an answer added, 'Go to sleep soon, huh?'

'I will.' She had put the bookmark in place and turned out the light before Sarah had dropped the curtain. Sarah thought, walking away, that Denny was certainly clever enough to know she could have stretched the rules about bedtime a little tonight, if she was really enjoying that book. *She was making herself stay awake till I got here.* She was still afraid to be in a house alone with Will Dietz, but she had agreed to let Aggie go home. Because Aggie was tired, and Aunt Sarah needed to work, so Denny would look out for herself, and not be a bother.

Some days it's kind of tough to measure up to this kid.

She walked over to where Dietz was dishing up at the stove, slid the knife back in the holder, put her arms around his waist, and kissed his ear. While she was close, she murmured, 'Thanks for looking after Denny. I guess I better warn you she had that knife under her pillow.'

'I know,' he said. 'Don't worry. I can usually handle sixty-five-pound girls.' He kissed her and said, 'Sit. Take your shoes off. Eat.'

She sat at her place and took a sip of wine, sighed happily, tried one taste of Aggie's stew as soon as he set the plate down, and uncorked an appetite so ravenous she cleaned the plate before she said another word.

'There's a little more,' Dietz said, 'shall I—'

'No. Just right.' While she finished her wine she told him about the day's delicate business, tiptoeing around a hostile witness whose hatred was plain. She was comfortable and easy now, talking to Dietz who had been so often in the same situation, and understood the stress of such a day without explanation.

Then in the middle of a comfortable silence, she put both hands up to her face in distress and said softly, 'Omigod.'

'What?'

'I just remembered I never made one move today to do what I promised about Janine.'

'Aggie told me what the two of you decided. What were you supposed to do about it today?'

'Find her! She's back in town. Drifting around Tucson somewhere, having cannabis dreams about the great things she's going to do some day soon—'

Dietz stared at her for a few seconds. 'You know, you and your mother get exactly the same look on your face when you talk about Janine.'

'Oh? What look is that?'

'Unhinged. What is it about her that drives you both so nuts?'

'Well, she's out of control! You never know what she'll do next!'

'But isn't that typical addict behavior? Why do you let it upset you so much?'

'Because we always end up being responsible for something we can't control.'

'Like what, for instance?'

'Like Denny, for instance.'

'Denny's not out of control.'

'No, but her life is.' She told him about the scene at the bus after school, about Janine's crazy phone call to Aggie, and her own growing realization that she wasn't equipped to take proper care of Denny if she couldn't check her into urgent care, change her school, defend any decisions about care and feeding. 'I need to get Janine to give me legal custody. But I'm afraid . . .' Her voice trailed off and when she spoke again she put words to the terrible truth that Aggie had been trying to express when she broke the pot. 'I'm afraid if I persuade her to give up custody so Denny can have a life, Janine will have lost the only reason she has to sober up, and she'll be destroyed.'

She stared forlornly at Will Dietz, who shook his head in disbelief. 'You've been a Tucson cop for what? Twelve years?'

'Going on thirteen. So what?'

'And you still haven't learned that you can't fix everything?'

'Well, sure, in general, but this is my fam—'

'Sarah, nothing you've ever told me about Janine has surprised me. Everything she does is textbook addictive behavior. But you keep beating yourself up for it. Why?'

'Because she's my sister. Because I love the real Janine who's buried inside that nut case, and so does Denny.'

'Oh. Well. Love.' He sat back and rubbed his face. 'No

known cure for that, is there? Listen, I have to go to work, but – I know a couple of guys in Vice detail. You want me to ask them to look around for Janine?'

'Well . . . sure. If you . . . I mean . . . have you got time?'

'Time to help you when you need it? Yes, Sarah, I have time for that.' He did his I-can't-believe-you-said-that business with the eyebrows, added the ghost of a one-sided smile, kissed her quickly, and left.

One of the things she was getting used to, with Will Dietz, was that he hated lingering farewells and as often as not skipped saying goodbye entirely – when it was time to go, he got up and left. At first, she had perceived this as an odd streak of rudeness in an otherwise considerate man. Now as she locked her door after him she thought gratefully that his sensible habits had given her an extra five minutes to sleep.

TEN

Sarah got out of her car in the station lot Thursday morning and almost fell over Ray Menendez kissing a beautiful girl. Embarrassed, she tried to dodge past him, but he lifted his head and said, 'Hey, Sarah.' The girl in his arms smiled brightly, as if she thought making out in a police parking lot before eight in the morning was going to be the next big thing.

'Want you to meet my fiancée,' Menendez said. 'Her name is Maria. Isn't she beautiful?' They beamed at each other smugly, with the self-satisfied look young lovers get when they announce to a waiting world their new discovery: perfect love.

Sarah followed a still-glowing Menendez across the lobby and into an elevator. On the way up, she asked how long he'd been engaged.

'Three months,' he said. 'Since the day we decided to move in together and her father said if I didn't give her a ring first he'd shoot me.'

'That will move the jewelry, won't it?' She went on to her cubicle, thinking contentedly, *I guess I can quit worrying about him and Patricia.*

Tobin walked past her workspace, carrying his jacket. 'Pauly's mother,' she asked him, following him to his space, 'did she show up to ID the body?'

'Sure did.'

'What's she like?'

'Small tired-looking woman. Used to be pretty, I'd guess. She did some big-time screaming and crying when I explained why I couldn't show her his face. But . . . she's been through a lot, she didn't stay hysterical long.' He rubbed his face, looking weary. 'Families are the hard part of this job, aren't they? You never know what to expect. Soon as she quit crying over her son's mutilated body she started mooning over his tacky old ring. It was her father's, she said. She gave it to him on his thirteenth birthday. Couldn't afford to have the stone replaced, but she told him, "When you make it big you can have a ruby put in there."' Tobin rolled his eyes up. '"When you make it big." They always say that, don't they? The losers. She wants the ring back before he's cremated.'

'OK. Did she see anything else that looked familiar?'

'Yeah, she showed me his hammer toes, one on each foot, just like hers. And there's a crescent-shaped scar on his knee, from the time he fell off the roof when he was nine.' He shrugged. 'No problem with the ID, he's her son all right. But I think that one drug bust is all we're ever going to find on Paul Eckhardt. She calls him Pauly too, by the way, says she always did. He'd only been gone from home a few months more than he served in Yuma, and for at least the first three months after he left home she's sure he was washing dishes in a café in Benson. So I don't think he had time to get into much more than we know about, Sarah.'

'She know anything about the people he was hanging with here?'

'No – he never contacted her from Tucson. She cried some more when she found out he'd been right here for weeks before he died. "My second husband never liked him," she said, "but I could have figured out some way to see him."' Tobin sat down at his desk, looked at the ceiling and said, 'Twenty-seven years next month, I been listening to women cry over things I can't fix. I am so not going to miss it.'

'What, you're going to retire?'

'Well, not today. I can do my thirty like everybody else. But when I do move on, I promise you it's going to be to something that makes women smile.' He sat forward and fussed with his desk, straightened the desk blotter, and picked up some paper clips. 'I think Pauly Eckhardt was just in that house at the wrong time. I don't believe the shooter was after him.'

'I always do it the same way,' Arturo Espinosa said. The sheriff of Doña Ana County, New Mexico, must not be many generations removed from his homeland, Sarah thought. His Spanish vowels were still impeccable. The way he said Dough-nyah Ah-nah made her want to drive over to Hatch right away and take lessons. *Be worth the trip just to hear him roll his r's.*

'I tell my deputies, you find them wanted guys by being systematic. I look up that Need to Locate list every morning and check it against arrest notices and hospital admissions and welfare applications all over the state. If none of that pans out, I pull up the new hires from the employment offices. Lotta guys on the run, they get fake green cards and hide out in the fields a while. I got the best record in the state for nailin' them guys.' Sheriff Espinosa spoke the Spanish of kings and the English of roustabouts.

'That's how I found this Giardelli guy, on a list of new hires out at Utley's farm. They gotta send 'em in now for the Homeland Security.' He made a small whistling noise. 'Ain't that a rip?'

'You found him on a list? You haven't actually seen him yet?'

'Thought I'd check with you first, make sure you still want him before I drive all the way out there. You want him, I'll go get him.'

'Yes, please. And hey, I owe you one.'

'No problem. Tell you what, I was gonna run down to Lordsburg some time this week anyway. If I call you when I got this suspect in the car, you can send somebody to meet me there, OK?'

Nino's back was already killing him by ten o'clock in the morning. He wondered how long it would take to get himself toughened up like Juan, who looked stunted and starved but seemed to be able to drudge on hour after hour without complaint. Was he immune to the pain, Nino wondered, or had he just learned to ignore it like all the other things he couldn't change? Juan's default reaction to most of life seemed to be a shrug. *I don't know if I even want to get that tough.* Instinct told him the only way to get like Juan was to take a hell of a beating for a long time.

It was almost a relief, a few minutes later, to look up and see the sheriff's car parking on the dirt road beside the field. It was going to feel so damn good to throw that basket off his shoulder. And even though he was stiff he knew he could

outrun the fat man in the tan uniform who got out of the car
and stood talking to Carlos.

Nino began looking around for the best escape route.
Dodge through the tall vines to the far side of the field, he
decided. The man wouldn't fire his weapon into a field full
of workers. Then down into that little wash, probably, and
through the culvert. His eyes, scanning, met Juan's. His new
partner was watching him anxiously out of his bony brown
face.

'Que pasa, amigo?' he said.

'Looks like I'm gonna hafta run for it,' Nino said.

Juan, not understanding a word but liking Nino's confi-
dential tone, said, 'Estados Unidos, no?' and gave him a big,
conspiratorial smile.

And something about the way he said that, so happy and
friendly, and the fact that Nino had been feeling better about
himself ever since his flashback . . . he couldn't explain it
exactly, but he didn't want to run with Juan there watching.
Wait it out, he might be after somebody else. Then Carlos
walked over to his row and beckoned, and Nino decided,
What the hell, I didn't do it, there must be some way.

He turned to Juan and said, 'I didn't do it, amigo,' and
shook hands, and walked to the end of the row.

As he had expected, it felt very good to take the basket
off his shoulder.

Jason Peete toured the downtown lofts first, and by mid-
morning Thursday was idling his motor in front of a billboard
that read 'Quail Run,' at the entrance to a development in
suburban south-east Tucson. The sign featured a beaming
family in front of a house, with Day-Glo messages empha-
sizing family-friendly features: POOL! PLAYGROUND!
LOW DOWN-PAYMENT!

Beyond the entrance were newly paved streets fronting
single-family houses in various stages of construction. All
the streets meandered in a curving pattern that afforded
maximum privacy and many cul-de-sacs. They ended abruptly
in an empty field of dirt that had been ditched, heaped, raked,
and staked in preparation for the next batch of houses. An
earth-mover was working on the far side of the farthest

mound. Otherwise, work on this neighborhood seemed to be at a standstill.

Jason locked his car and wandered down a street of mostly finished houses, only two of which appeared to be occupied. He was peering in through a still-taped window into an empty living-and-kitchen space when a voice behind his left ear said, 'You looking for somebody, fella?'

Jason turned with his badge in his hand, said, 'Detective Peete,' and smiled. He had, when he wanted to have, an engaging smile and a firm baritone voice that usually kept him out of bar fights and angry confrontations with guys in hard hats.

This one hesitated two seconds before he stuck out his hand and said, 'Dan Bird.'

He was probably close to fifty, taut and wiry, with close-cut sandy hair sprinkled with grey. Clean-shaven except for an almost-white soul patch, he wore jeans and a T-shirt, sturdy boots, and tiny diamond earrings, an incongruous touch with his beginning dewlaps. *A hip grandpa. Pretty cool for a white guy.*

Bird cocked his head curiously and said, 'This an official enquiry or you thinking of taking advantage of our newly lowered price range?'

Jason debated going for the sleazy explanation Bird had just offered him. Pretend to be blowing off some city hours shopping for bargains, maybe he'd get the full tour. But he couldn't allow the implication that he might be malingering to pass unchallenged. Let Whitey get by with one of those attitudes, next he'd be asking if you wanted some watermelon.

'I work in the Homicide division,' he said. 'We're investigating the traumatic death of Mrs Henderson.'

'Uh-huh.' Bird did some thoughtful nodding. 'Sure is a sad thing.'

'Yes. We're all very sorry for Mr Henderson's loss.'

'Yeah. I still don't exactly see what it has to do with Hen-Trax houses.'

'At the beginning of a homicide investigation, we pretty much have to verify everything anybody says. Man says he's a builder, we gotta go see what he's building.' He looked straight at Bird without blinking, but he knew it sounded lame.

Bird gave a derisive snort. 'Not much doubt Hen-Trax is building houses, is there? We're one of the biggest developers in Pima County, getting bigger all the time . . . just finished that Rio Nuevo loft thing downtown, have you looked at that?'

'Swung by there, yes. Came out here to this one you're supervising . . . that's what you do, right? You're the supervisor?'

'Foreman's what they usually call me, but . . . you came out here why?'

'Because I know a few folks in the building trades and they all told me this is an excellent example of what Hen-Trax does best, affordable housing that delivers value.'

'Uh-*huh.*' His phone chirped and he answered, 'Bird,' listened a minute and said, 'I'm out there now. Got a detective here, says he's from Homicide.' His eyes were measuring Jason as he talked. *Five-eleven*, Jason wanted to tell him. *One eighty-five and I pump some iron.*

But Bird seemed to be getting friendlier. He folded his phone and said, 'The boss says show you around. Nothing secret about Quail Run, he says, which is sure as hell true. We got billboards up all over town, we're in the paper every Sunday—' His phone chirped again; he opened it, said, 'Bird,' listened a few seconds and said, 'No. No. Lock it up and leave it.' He folded the phone without saying goodbye.

'I'm not the salesman, you understand, I'm just out here to check a couple of things. You want to hop in my chariot, I'll show you around.' Jason climbed up on to the wide bench seat of his pickup.

'This front section here,' he waved his hand at one-story stucco houses with tile roofs, 'is almost built out.' He showed Jason three dozen houses, most of them sold and occupied. 'From here back,' he wheeled into a wide main thoroughfare that ran straight toward the Rincons, 'forty-eight homes, about sixty percent complete. Back of that,' he waved at a vast space, 'is ready to go when the demand is there.'

'Little dip in demand right now?'

'We hope it's little.'

'The houses in the second section, are they all sold?'

'Yyy . . . well.' Bird tapped the steering wheel with thin, freckled fingers, finally put the truck in reverse, and turned around. 'Hell, I might as well show you that, too.' He drove back almost to the entrance and wheeled into a side street. 'These houses are ready for the finishing touches – cabinets, doors, windows.

'Last June, we had firm orders for almost all of these, and the boss was going crazy trying to find more window-framers and another crew of painters, everything was go, go, go. Then in July, August, people started coming back to us saying, "We thought we had our loan but now the bank is saying they have to have more security." And these are working people that, you know, they've got their jobs and their cars, and that's about it. And they're saying, "Since when isn't that enough?" because that's what the subprime market was all about. You got a job? Sign here.' He shook his head and the earring nearest Jason caught the sun and twinkled.

'Last spring the boss was kicking himself when he lost a bid on another project just like this one but half again as big, on the other side of town.' Bird sniffed. 'Now when he thinks about that he says, "Thank you, Jesus."'

'I've read some of the stories in the paper,' Jason said. 'I still don't understand what happened.'

'You ask me,' Bird said, 'that's part of the problem, stories in the paper. "A crisis in the subprime lending market!" So everybody goes apeshit, starts yelling for more money down. It's the same world it was six months ago, only not. Whole housing economy drops dead because some wise-ass bunch of suits in Switzerland has a cow over a balance sheet? What kind of sense does that make?'

'Somebody told me it's some kind of bubble?'

'Makes as much sense as anything else they're saying. Anyway, long as I'm sharing our troubles with you I'll show you the part that really makes you want to kill somebody.' He stopped with a suddenly stricken expression. 'I didn't mean . . .'

'I understand,' Jason said. 'Just an expression.'

'Well, right. Although if I catch a couple of these little

rats I can't promise I won't put a bruise on 'em. Look at this.' He had stopped the truck in the middle of a section of oddly damaged houses – broken windows, a garage door hanging crooked.

'What happened?'

'Gangs of boys,' Bird said, 'roam through here at night, break windows and spray graffiti on walls and kick out door locks. For fun. Nothing personal, we don't even know them. Somebody ran a car into that garage door – see how it's hanging? Hundreds of dollars down the tube in the blink of an eye. Safe game for them because there's nobody around to call the police. Even if somebody did, the sheriff's deputies in this part of the county have more than they can do already.'

'Can't you put a guard on at night?'

'We did, we had to. The insurance company wouldn't cover us any more if we didn't. But the kids come in on bikes, or on foot . . . don't make any noise coming. You hear glass breaking, by the time you get there, they're gone.' He answered his chirping phone again. It was almost a fixture in his ear as he drove around. He answered each call, 'Bird,' without taking time to excuse himself, then with no apparent hesitation dealt with whatever poured out of its tiny speaker. 'Sweet,' he said once, in response to another damage report, and about a problem piece of equipment, 'Perfect.' He had a whole vocabulary of one- and two-word retorts. 'Keen. Hell *yeah*. Totally.'

'Well, you seem to be staying calm,' Jason said, as they drove back to the gate.

Dan Bird gave him the bare edge of an ironic half-smile. 'I'm not the one paying interest on several million dollars' worth of construction loans, Detective.'

'How's Roger Henderson taking it?'

Dan Bird gazed across his dusty domain, scratched his soul patch and sighed. 'Roger Henderson is a very smart guy. Hen-Trax will make it through this meltdown if anybody will. But . . . he's lowered the price on these houses twice, and we may end up selling some of them for less than they cost to build. Because as you can see here, letting them sit empty is not an option.'

'What about Rio Nuevo?' Jason said. 'I keep reading about all that tax increment money—'

'Beautiful green money, who wouldn't want it? Pays for the infrastructure and the low-interest loans . . . we've done a couple of those jobs already, and we're bidding on that big project at the foot of Sentinel Peak, the one they call Gray Hawk Terrace.'

'How's it looking?'

'Down to just us and that Ames Construction from Las Vegas. Should be out of committee any day now. We get Gray Hawk, that'll carry us till the rest of the business turns around.'

'What's left to do?'

'For us, nothing. Try not to die of impatience while the city fathers debate.' His smile added a few more creases to his face. 'The boss said the other day, "We get through this recession I'm never going to another city council meeting as long as I live." '

'How long have you worked for him?'

'Twelve years.'

'Guess you must like your job.'

'Oh, it has good days and bad.' The little bark of laughter again. 'Roger's a hard taskmaster, but he's not . . . tricky. Do your job right, you make out OK.' He stopped at the gate. As Jason got out he said, 'If you been thinking he killed his rich wife to get at her money, you can forget about that. Long as I've known him he's been working his butt off to show everybody he didn't need his wife's money.'

'Thanks for giving me the time,' Jason said, 'and the tour.'

'You're welcome,' Dan Bird said. 'Tell your friends we got some real bargains out here.' He winked, put the truck in reverse, and drove away toward the earth-mover.

Waiting for Nino, Sarah finally found a few minutes to put the Henderson file in order. With all that paper safely in one box, she got the extra table moved out, brought her chairs back in, and dusted her desk. Feeling like a mountain-moving winner, she brought in a fresh cup of coffee and read through the file.

Halfway through the Roger Henderson interview she looked up and told her desk lamp, 'I still haven't finished that!'

Tracy Scott had done all the work to expose Roger Henderson's leaky alibi for Sunday night, and she still hadn't followed through on it. If Nino proved to be the shooter, she had no idea what his motivation could be. Who was to say he wasn't working for Roger Henderson?

She checked the time; 11:30. *Even a Frisky Lady should be up by now.* She said it to herself, knowing probably none of the women who got their assignments there lived in that house, and then asked herself, *Why do I always feel compelled to make jokes about prostitution? It's the least funny subject I can think of.* She had never worked Vice, felt awkward about her lack of expertise. *But is anybody an expert in this subject?* She didn't know. *So I make these stupid jokes.*

So ask. She dialed the number. After three rings a light, pleasant voice with no accent said the number and waited. Having no name to ask for, Sarah said, 'This is Detective Burke at the Tucson Police Department. I need to talk to somebody who can verify a time and date for me.'

The person on the other end said, 'Hold on.'

In a few seconds a new voice, older and darker, a smoker's voice, said, 'This is Joyce, how may I help you?'

Like you're taking my order for blueberry pancakes.

She said her name and title again and then, 'Joyce, this is Frisky Ladies, right?'

'Yes it is.'

'Good. Will you verify that a person was at your establishment during certain hours Sunday night?'

'No, I can't do that.'

'Even when I get a subpoena?'

'Still won't be able to help you, Detective. We don't record the names of our clients.'

'You don't know who's coming tonight?'

'Who's coming tonight is some peaceful individuals with code names I've given them. They'll pick up their escorts, who have other code names. I have no idea where they will go together, and I certainly don't need to know their names.'

'OK. But I have information indicating that my person of interest stayed at your house for several hours, both Saturday and Sunday nights.'

'Then your information's wrong, Detective. This is an

escort service, not a whorehouse. Prostitution is illegal in Arizona.'

'But if I can prove that my person's vehicle was at your house during the hours I'm interested in, bearing in mind that you don't want to lie to the police, especially during a murder investigation, then we could have a conversation, right?'

'If you come to my house and show me your badge while you hand me the subpoena, then we could have a conversation in which I point out that I don't always know which vehicles are parked in front of my house. Yes.'

'Good system,' Sarah said. 'Talk to you later, Joyce.'

'Any time, honey,' Joyce said.

She wanted to talk to Delaney but he was on the phone, and then he had somebody in his office. Then his phone was busy a long time and finally he walked past her, talking on his cell. She wanted to ask him if he still thought they should keep the tracker information in-house. To her, it felt like time to go after Henderson with it, get the question of his whereabouts Sunday night settled once and for all, clear him or implicate him. But since they'd agreed on a policy about the tracker she didn't want to change it without Delaney's OK. And just then her phone rang and Arturo Espinosa said, 'I have your suspect in my car, Detective.' Together, they figured out the probable time he'd get to Lordsburg. By the time she had finished the second phone call that started a Highway Patrol car toward Lordsburg, it was well past noon.

She said, 'Oh, well . . .' took an energy bar out of her desk drawer, and walked out to the parking lot. In the back corner, she ate the bar and then sat on the wall for half an hour, staring at an imaginary blank spot three million miles away, while pure November sun scrubbed all but basic information out of her brain.

It was a meditation technique she had cobbled together from a couple of magazine articles and an improbable old TV show about a Chinese monk stranded in the desert. She knew she probably wasn't following the exact recipe, but since it refreshed her during the tired ends of tough weeks she did it every so often anyway and called it, if anybody asked, 'zoning out.'

A message light was blinking on her phone when she got back. When she pressed the button Menendez' voice said, 'Sarah, call me before you do one other thing.' The authoritarian manner was so unlike him that she obeyed at once. When he answered she said, 'Hey, whaddup?'

'Just got a call from that sweet pretty Henderson girl you told me not to mess with.' He sighed in mock distress. 'But what's a guy supposed to do when the chicks can't leave him alone?'

'Ray—'

He dropped his joking pose abruptly. 'She sounds really worried, Sarah. She said, "You told me if I ever needed help I could call you. Now I need help."'

'OK, so?'

'So will you help me talk to her?'

'Ray, Nino Giardelli's being brought over from Lordsburg right now. We need to get ready to interview him.'

'I know. This will only take a few minutes. I thought . . . you seemed to like her.'

'I do like her, but . . . when does she want to see you?'

'She's in the lobby now.'

'Oh. You think she has something new to say about the crime?'

'No, I think she wants to talk about her brother, the hard case. What do you think, shall I hold an interview room?'

'For sure. Member of the family, you never know what will come up. But who've we got to monitor the video? Anybody in here?' She stood up and peered around. 'I'll go get Mickey out of cold cases, she'll help us.'

Looking up with eyes that were miles away, deep in the case she was reading, Mickey marked the page carefully and came along. A striver and a learner, Mickey would soon, Sarah hoped, become the second female on the Homicide crew.

Patricia was a little put off that it wasn't going to be a tête-à-tête with Menendez, but he said, 'I asked Sarah to sit in on this because she's good at family stuff.' Sarah thought that was a stretch, but tried to look wise. Finally Patricia sat down on the round stool with that businesslike nod, so like her father, that seemed to be her default reaction in tight emotional corners.

The next hurdle was the recording equipment. She wanted it off, said she couldn't put this conversation on the record. But Menendez nudged her elbow and said, 'We have to do it, Patricia, so we can prove we aren't pouring water up your nose in here.' She looked into his face then and laughed charmingly and Sarah thought it was only natural that he flashed every dimple he owned.

Then Patricia turned abruptly grim, took a deep breath and said, 'OK, here goes. I feel rotten about narcing on my own brother, but I don't see anything else to do.

'Adam had a key stashed somewhere. As soon as he heard from you guys yesterday that you were done working at the house, he went home and took a bunch of stuff. Two or three pieces of Mom's jewelry and an inlaid chess set, I don't know yet what else. He helped himself to some money I had in a drawer, too, which is pretty spooky because it means he went through my room.

'He took the jewelry and stuff to a place he knows about, hocked it, and bought meth and dope and vodka. Maria called Dad to come home because of the noise. Dad found Adam up in his room, stoned out of his mind, with a rap station turned up as high as it would go.

'Then we had the calamitous family scene. Every time Adam comes home, you can count on at least one – this time it happened faster than usual and a little louder. Dad called me at school and told me to come home, made me listen while he recited the latest grievances and laid down the law.

'Dad took away the keys to the rental car, told Adam he was not allowed out of the house till after the funeral and then we'd see what comes next. But Adam – see, he's got this idea now that he's going to have a whole lot of his own money and he doesn't need to care what Dad thinks any more. It's made him just impossible. He keeps saying, "I'll do whatever I please, you don't control me any more!"

'It's total war in the house. Dad made me return Adam's rental car. He's gone through the house and sequestered all the keys and drugs and liquor. Even the medicine chests, God help anybody who gets a headache at our house this week. And he told Adam if he took one step out of the house before the funeral tomorrow he would have him arrested, and I honestly believe he's ready to do it.'

Sarah said, 'What's Adam doing now?'

'Sitting up in his room with a gooney grin on his face, reading some silly old Goth novel from seventh grade. Pretending to read – I hate to imagine what he's really thinking about. I tried to talk to him and he just . . . cut me off. "Don't worry about a thing, sweetheart," he says. He's got this new way of talking like Humphrey Bogart and calling everybody sweetheart. "As soon as tomorrow's over, sweetheart," he told me, "I know exactly what I'm going to do and there's not a damn thing he can do about it."

'Which of course is just plain crazy. He's only sixteen years old, no matter how much of Mother's money we're going to get eventually, nobody's going to deal with him as an adult this week, especially when he's acting so loony.'

'What do you think your dad will do?' Menendez asked her.

'What he's always done – keep the lid on, if he can. I feel so bad for them both. Until about three years ago, when Adam discovered the drug scene, he and Dad got along really well. I mean, Adam was always closer to Mom because she let him have his way all the time. But Dad really tried, they used to go fishing and watch sports together. Once Adam found dope and booze, though . . . it was, like, *at last, the right answer.*'

'The right answer to what?'

'Feeling like a dork, I guess. He always had a hard time in school. He hated having to have tutors and do summer school to get through. And when he got into controlled substances, he had his toking friends and he didn't have to try any more. In that group it's understood, trying is not cool. You stay a little high all the time, get really wasted on weekends, and you don't do squat.'

'How did your dad feel about that?'

'Enraged! But by then Dad was so busy building stuff, he was hardly home except to sleep. He kept telling Mom they had to do something. Mom just tried to talk Adam around and tempt him with a lot of new toys. Adam took the toys gladly but kept hitting the booze and junk too. Then one day

I came home from school and there was an angry couple in the house. Dad was home from work in the daytime and Mom was crying . . . it was something Adam had done. Nobody ever would tell me, exactly, but obviously it involved the daughter of the people who were there. She laughed at him about something and . . . one of my friends in school told me he tore off all her clothes. Dad did a lot of telephoning, and Adam went east to a special school. He's on about the third special school now and as you can see it's been a big success.

'After that . . . they both felt bad about Adam, but they showed it in different ways. Dad worked harder than ever, trying to build enough good stuff to make it right, I guess. And Mom . . .' Patricia's clear blue eyes met Sarah's and wavered. 'Mom was always kind of a ditz, you know. Couldn't balance a checkbook, forgot what she'd said she was going to do. But after Adam left she was all about anything that made her feel better. She'd been raised to be self-indulgent, and once Adam was out of the house she began to go seriously off the rails.'

'What happened?'

A helpless shrug. 'She'd always had mood swings and they got worse. One doctor said bipolar. They gave her medication but every time she felt better she'd stop taking it. When she was up, she gave big honking parties.'

'And when she was down? Did she take the bad moods out on your father?'

'Hey, we're a family, we all take everything out on each other! But Dad always kind of . . . looked after Mom, he felt responsible for her. Only . . . as she got more erratic . . . it was hard for him to exert control because the big money was hers. Big money,' Patricia said, thoughtfully, 'kind of has its own seat in the room, you know?'

Sarah saw Menendez' face reflect her own thought: *She's so young to know that.*

Sarah felt time scrolling away from her again and knew they'd have to talk to Nino soon. 'What kind of help do you want from us, Patricia?'

'Tell me what I can do for Adam. Dad's so angry, all he can think about right now is punishment. But if I found a good place I think he'd go for it.'

'Will Adam, though? Go for it?'

Patricia shook her head sadly. 'Adam's not interested in reform.'

Menendez said, 'All the treatment guys I ever met have told me the patient has to want it for the cure to work.'

'Before Adam wants a cure he'll be dead. Can't you steer me to a social worker who'll help me arrange for some tough love?'

Menendez, looking very dubious, turned and said, 'Sarah?'

'I can give you a name,' Sarah said. 'I can't promise what she'll do for you.' She went back to her cubicle, pulled up a screen, copied the email address and phone number of the last social worker who'd helped with Janine. Walking back into the interview room, handing it over, she said, 'I guess I'll share with you that this social worker helped me get my own sister into detox last year. So I can tell you she's very capable and she'll tell you the truth.' With Patricia's fingers already on the paper, she held it a moment longer and repeated Dietz's dictum. 'You can't fix everything.'

'I know. But I have to try.' She took the piece of paper Sarah handed her, said, 'Thank you very much,' and stood, folding it carefully into her wallet. She opened and closed her mouth a couple of times, and then said, in the rushed way that people say things they didn't intend to, 'My mother's being cremated this afternoon.'

The six terrible words seemed to suck up all the air in the little room. In the vacuum they left behind, for a long moment nobody moved. 'They're going to cook up what's left of my beautiful mother,' Patricia said at last, 'into a little heap of ashes that fits in an urn, and we're going to bury that tomorrow.' Her knees buckled and she sat down with a thump on the wretched little round stool.

ELEVEN

No two suspects are exactly alike, of course. But Nino Giardelli brought more mixed signals into the room than most. He was as dirty, weather-beaten, and ragged as the least-favored miscreants they got in inter-rogation, but he didn't give off the usual aura of hostility or evasion. He looked into her face searchingly, she thought, as if he wanted to talk and was hoping she would listen.

Espinosa had put him in full chains, and the patrolman who met him, rather than go to the trouble to take all that equipment off and gear up again, had simply traded out a set of restraints, escorted him as he hobbled past gaping customers to the restroom at the gas station, put him into the locked back seat of a patrol car, and sped home.

'Let's get him out of those chains,' Sarah said when he came clanking in, 'and give him a bathroom break right away.' They settled him in interrogation room #1 with cuffs only, brought him water, and read him his rights.

'I guess I might want a lawyer eventually,' Nino said at the end of the recitation, 'but I need to talk to you first.'

'Oh, all right,' Sarah said, not daring to look at Menendez. 'We can do that.' She turned to a fresh page in the legal tablet open in front of her. 'Where do you want to start?'

'With that night at the party, when Pauly got shot.'

'Good.' She held her pen poised above the paper, but kept her eyes on his face. He had a small, crooked mouth missing a couple of teeth, and watery, uncertain eyes. But his manner right now seemed straightforward, even purposeful. 'You were there?'

'Sure, we were the servers. Pauly and me and Felicity. Big mother of a party, went on for hours. And even when it ended it didn't end for us, because we had to clean it up.' He described the part of the evening Felicity hadn't wanted to talk about, the little group in the prep room cleaning up the messy leftovers of the huge party, working hard at first and then not so hard because of the music and wine and dope.

'Who put on the music?'

'Madge, I guess. This guy that got us our jobs at the theater? Everybody's pal, always the life of the party. He had the dope, too, got everybody all herbed up and dancing. And then that Mrs Henderson, man . . .' He looked from Sarah to Ray and back again, and gave a little puzzled shrug. 'I never seen . . . she started dancing with Pauly and pretty soon it was like she decided to keep him for a *pet*.'

'Was Zack there too?'

'Oh, sure, Zack was always there for the clean-up, to make certain all the supplies got back in the van. And you know, ordinarily, that Zack – he's not a mixer. Still keeping a tight hold on the first friendly thought he ever had. But that night, once the party was over, he was like, hey, let's have fun!' Nino made an almost-laugh sound, 'Ha!' and added, 'He even danced with Madge!

'This next part,' Nino said, suddenly quiet and thoughtful, 'is what I need to tell you about. And ask . . .' He leaned his work-scarred, grubby little hands on the table. The nails were all broken and filled with dirt, and there was a long deep scratch on the back of the right one that was healed over and crusty on top but looked puffy and feverish underneath. Absent-mindedly, he gently kneaded the cloth loop that fastened his manacled wrists to the table while he stared into their faces anxiously. 'I never been much good at holding my liquor, I know that. But that night . . . I'd been working all day and then dancing, and even though I'd had some wine I would have swore I was almost sober. But Madge handed me that last drink . . . I took a few sips and whirled Felicity around a couple times . . . and came back to the counter and took a couple more swallows, I think, and then I don't remember anything until Zack woke me up on the floor upstairs.'

He was quiet a few seconds and then asked, looking into their faces, 'Could that happen? You ever been fine one minute and the next you're passed out cold?'

He was sitting there waiting for their answer, apparently convinced they would be able and willing to settle this vexing question. Sarah remembered Leo Tobin saying, 'I think Pauly Eckhardt was just in that house at the wrong time . . . The kid was really small-time, Sarah.'

They were both just kids from small towns. She asked Nino to excuse them for a minute, went out, and found Delaney, standing mesmerized in front of the monitor.

'Are you seeing what I'm seeing, boss?'

'Yes. The real deal for once. We don't see this very often, do we?'

'You think he's telling the truth, too?'

'If he isn't, we should get him to run for President. He's the most convincing talker I've watched in a long time. This is an excellent interview, Sarah, the whole story's starting to open up and make sense. Keep going, get all you can.'

They went back inside and told Nino they would check 'with their lab people' for the answer to his question. Sarah was pretty sure he'd been subjected to some form of date-rape drug, but since there was no way to prove it now she saved the speculation for later and asked him to tell her the rest of the story.

Nino described the horror of being wakened by Zack, of seeing the bodies on the bed and recognizing Pauly's earring.

'Did you make any sound, do you remember?' Sarah asked him.

'Yeah, I hollered, "Pauly!"'

Sarah looked at Menendez, whose eyes said, *There's your second scream.*

'Zack put his hand over my mouth and said, "Shut up, we gotta get out of here."' Nino described the confusion, the gun that seemed to be in his hands and then not. 'And I kept fading in and out . . . so it's hard to know now what I remember from what I was told. When Zack said I killed them . . . it was like some terrible dream, but he was sober and I was drunk, so I believed him. Him and Felicity, man, they practically carried me to that theater and put me to bed. And when I woke up I was so hung over I wanted to die.'

He described the confusing combination of taunting and helpfulness with which Felicity helped him out of the theater next day. And the creepy unreality of Zack, who always seemed to begrudge everybody the air they breathed, suddenly acting as if they were buddies. 'But I was so sick . . . he said I was welcome to take a snooze, and I almost did.'

He told them about the car that ran the stop light on Orange Grove, and the sudden insight that told him to get out of Zack's vehicle. 'Or get *him* out, I thought, all of a sudden. So that's what I did. Is he hurt bad? From when I pushed him out?' He was watching their faces, getting disappointed. 'What, you haven't caught Zack yet?'

'We've talked to him,' Menendez said. 'He hasn't, um, said a whole lot.'

A funny little smile began to grow on Nino's face. 'Lawyered up, I bet. Sounds just like the sneaky sumbitch.'

'So if you'd like to get your story on the record first,' Sarah said, 'now's your chance. Tell us more about this man named Madge, what's his story?'

'Madge is just . . .' he shrugged, 'looking for a way to pass the time, I guess.' He described a man who seemed to be several steps up the social ladder and a lot better educated than himself, and she asked him, 'How'd you get to know him?'

During the whole interview, considering his limited vocabulary he had done a remarkably good job of describing the personalities at the Henderson house on Sunday. Now for the first time he became evasive, looking around the small room at nothing while he muttered something about a chance meeting in a bar. From his reaction, she guessed at a sexual connection he didn't want to talk about, and she didn't press it. She asked Menendez later and he said he had the same hunch. Ray figured with Nino it was more a way to earn the rent than a matter of desire.

What he wanted most to talk about was his flashback, the wonderful moment in the field at Hatch when he remembered how he had felt just before he passed out. 'Everybody dancing and laughing,' he said, 'watching old Pauly getting a hard on for that rich broad. I could remember just how I felt, having fun, not mad at nobody.'

'That made you feel good, when you remembered?' Menendez asked him.

'Like a million bucks!' Nino said, smiling his crooked smile. 'I mean I'm still sad he's dead, but at least . . . Pauly was the best friend I ever had. And all along I'd been asking myself, why did I go and kill that silly little turd?' He looked from one to the other, to see if they understood. 'When I remembered I wasn't mad at him, I knew I couldn't have killed him.' His eyes lingered on Sarah's face, which she was having a little trouble keeping neutral. 'You see what I mean? I feel like, for once I got a second chance.'

'Why'd you leave the gun in your room?' Sarah said.

'What?' He sat up straight and, for the first time, looked at her with suspicion. 'There ain't no gun in my room.' He looked around wildly. 'You guys trying to frame me for this?' His face got red and indignant. 'I told you the truth!'

'Nino, wait now, don't get excited. *Calm down.* Nobody's trying to frame you, we just want to get at the truth. You've been doing great in here, hasn't he, Ray?'

'Terrific. Yes. Just keep it up. Are you saying there wasn't any gun in your room when you left it?'

'Hell no, there wasn't. I told you, didn't I? Maybe I didn't. When they carried me back there that night, Zack said, "I'll take care of the gun," and that's the last time we ever mentioned it.' He looked from one to the other. 'You found the gun in our room? Then they was all in it together, wasn't they? Because for Zack to get the gun up there he must've had help from Felicity. Boy –' shackled in place on his stool, he still managed to turn his face to the wall for a long, sad moment of thinking – 'them guys was all out to hang it on me all along.' He looked really bowled over, as if for the first time he realized the depth of the evil he'd been playing with.

'He picked me out for this. At the Spotted Pony.' He was beginning to look a little sick. 'Here I am, thinking I'm so smart, coming back and telling Pauly, "I met this swishy guy in a bar and he took a liking to me right away, he's gonna find us a soft job with a room so you can quit this stupid burger joint." And all along that little dickhead of a Madge is figuring me for a patsy. Shit. And now poor Pauly's dead. Aw, Christ!' He buried his face in his hands.

Sarah and Ray, for a few minutes, found themselves in the unlikely position of consoling the prisoner. The game isn't over, they told him, we'll get Madge in here and get at the truth.

'You kidding?' he said. 'Madge never told anybody the truth in his whole life. He wouldn't know the truth if it jumped up and bit him!' He leaned his head against the cold gray wall beside him and said, mostly to himself, 'I need to grow up and quit being a fool.'

He was perfectly cheerful about going to jail while the crime got sorted out. He knew, he said, that he had made himself look guilty by running. 'It's just –' he ducked his head apologetically, looked into the corner – 'the only thing I know to do, I guess.'

For now, the detectives weren't pressing him on the subject of the other crimes he had run from. He had delivered for them wonderfully on the Henderson case. Sarah could see how tired he was, and suspected that a jail cell and three meals a day did not sound so bad after the pepper fields. While he waited for his transport, they were outside with Delaney, agreeing to re-interview Zack and Felicity, and to find Madge.

'But probably not tomorrow,' Sarah said.

'Why not tomorrow?' Delaney asked her.

'Tomorrow's Friday. Eloise's funeral. Ray and I want to go.'

Sarah had just emptied her In Basket and was shutting down her computer when the phone rang. It was two minutes after five and she considered not answering, then snatched it up and said, 'Burke.'

'This is Joyce Anders.'

She could almost place the voice. Searching her brain, she let a heartbeat pass. The voice said, 'Frisky Ladies?'

'Oh, yes. Of course, hello.' She was too surprised to sound any way but surprised, but her response was not a problem because Joyce Anders talked right on over the top of it.

As serenely as if they had been chatting every afternoon for years, she said in her Marlboro Girl contralto, 'I've been thinking, since you called. And it seems to me I could probably save you some time if we had a little talk.'

Twice in one week, a total stranger wants to save me some time. 'That sounds good.'

'Yes. And since I'll be in Tucson tomorrow on other business I thought I'd ask, what time would be good for you?'

'I can do nine o'clock, that's probably a little too early for you, isn't it? Or late afternoon, though that's a little iffier, it depends what happens.'

'Nine o'clock is fine,' Joyce Anders said. 'Thank you, Detective, I'll see you then.'

There was a distinct little click and Sarah sat listening to the hum of the dead phone in her hand thinking, *I hope she knows how many freeway exits are blocked off downtown.* Evidently Joyce Anders was too hip to ask about small things like street construction.

But now it was ten after five and she was really leaving, even though the phone was ringing again as she picked up her purse, found her keys. She walked away thinking, *Leave a message*, and as she approached the elevators her voice came on instructing the caller to leave a message. After the tone Janine's voice, high and uncertain, said, 'Sarah?' There was jukebox music playing behind her, bar noises on top of it.

Sarah sprinted for the phone, grabbed it up. 'Janine? Janine, are you there? Hello!'

The phone was dead again. She put it back on its cradle and said, to the top of it, 'Damn you to hell, Janine.'

Tobin, who had observed her mad dash past his cubicle, stood in his doorway putting on his jacket, saying, 'Usually that thing works better if you pick it up, Sarah.' He was smiling, but his eyes said he would listen if she needed to talk.

But now it was sixteen past five and she was going to make her mother late for Keno. She laughed, waved a hand, and said, 'Just cussing out my favorite sister again,' and ran back to the elevator.

Dusk was already purpling the mountains and there was a little hint of chill, just enough to make you think about Thanksgiving. Aggie had said she wanted to cook the feast at her house, have Sam there. She had already invited Will Dietz. Sarah was bringing salad. They both wanted it nice for Denny. Sarah didn't know whether to wish Janine could be there, or hope she'd stay away. *Of course it doesn't matter what I wish.* As usual, she had no power to control what Janine would do.

An ancient Nissan with bald tires pulled into her carport as she approached her house. A stranger who looked as if he might have slept in the vehicle got out of it, and wobbled up to her door. He must be lost, she thought, as she parked behind Dietz's car at the curb. Reaching for her purse and briefcase, she watched the stranger ring her bell. Denny opened the door, smiling, saying, 'Did you forget your—' and then, 'Oh.'

'Hi, there, honey,' the man said. 'You must be Denny.'

Speechless, Denny gave him one of her most dubious nods.

'I've got your mom out here in the car,' the man said, swaying gently, 'why don't you come out and say hello?' Sarah saw now that he was very drunk. He reached out toward Denny, saying, 'Come on, kid! We'll take a ride!'

Sarah was hurrying toward them, but Will Dietz was in the doorway now, asking quietly, 'What's up?'

'Hi, I'm Jack Smathers. A friend of Janine's?' He put out his hand. Dietz made no move to take it and he let it fall. 'We came to take her little girl for a ride,' he said.

Sarah saw Denny take a step back and Dietz move a little so he blocked the doorway. 'I don't think this is a very good time,' he said. 'Denny has to do her homework now.'

Sarah met Dietz's eyes from the sidewalk where she stood behind the stranger, who smelled really bad up close. She made a small gesture toward the car and he nodded, Go ahead. She turned and walked back to it, saw Janine sitting in the passenger seat. She walked around the back of the vehicle, pulled open the front door, and said, 'Hello, Janine.'

'Hey!' Janine gave her a supercharged but unfocused smile, aimed somewhere beyond her shoulder. 'How are you, Sissy?' She tried to get out, didn't quite make it and fell back, muttering, 'Damn seats are so low—'

Maybe if I'm very calm. 'I almost got your phone call at the station,' Sarah said, 'but you were too quick for me.'

'Oh, that's me,' Janine said, 'old quick-draw.'

'Yes. Where are you staying, Janine?'

'Oh . . . here and there.' She grabbed Sarah's hand and said, 'How's my Denny?'

'She's great. You can be again, too, Janine, if you'll let me help you.'

'Now, Sarah, don't start.'

'OK.' She held up a hand. 'OK! Do you want to come in now, say hello?'

'Well, I'm a little too . . . we were hoping to take her for a ride.'

'Denny can't leave right now. But will you come back to see her on Saturday? Please? That's the day after tomorrow,' she added helpfully.

She knew at once she had gone too far. Janine was never too addled to know when she was being treated like an idiot, and was instantly aflame with the anger that was always her favorite evasion tactic. 'I know what day it is, Sarah, fuck you,' she yelled. 'Always so damn superior!'

Leaning over, she blew the horn. It worked very well; the battery on this heap must be in better shape than the tires. She blew apart the quiet on the peaceful street, hitting the horn again and again and yelling at her messy lover, 'Come on! Let's go!'

And then, in a much quieter voice, 'Oh, shit.' Because her mother was parking her car behind Sarah's at the curb.

Aggie pulled a sack of groceries out with her as she got out, locked the car, and walked toward them, squinting. She looked across the car, saw Sarah standing there, and said, 'What's going on?'

Janine blew the horn again and her friend turned away from Dietz and staggered across the sidewalk, saying, 'Whaddya *want*, for Chrissake?' He almost bowled over Aggie, who dodged on to the gravel. She stood among the cactus in the yard and watched, astonished, as the foul-smelling stranger got into the Nissan, ground the motor a couple of times, and backed down the driveway. He turned a little too soon, demolished the cholla nearest the sidewalk, and missed the mailbox by a quarter-inch. A neighbor, coming home, just managed to stay out of his way at the corner.

'Sarah,' Aggie said, 'who on earth was that?'

'Janine's new friend,' Sarah said. 'Hang on a sec.' She had memorized the license number, out of habit, and now she speed-dialed the dispatch number and reported it, described the make and color of the car and the drunkenness of the

driver. 'There,' she said as she folded up the phone. She took
the grocery sack out of her mother's arms. 'You have to leave
right now if you want to play Keno.'

'Sarah, was Janine in that car?'

'Yes, she was, and yes, that'll probably get her arrested.'

'Honey, do you really want to—'

'No, but they didn't leave me any choice. We can talk
about it tomorrow. We've all had a hard enough day, why
let them take up the whole damn night too? Go and have
some fun, Mom. I have a feeling Janine is going to be all
too easy to find for a while.'

'You're right.' Aggie reached up and kissed her. 'Chili's
ready on the stove. French bread in the sack.' She waved to
Dietz in the doorway and hurried back to her car.

Sarah carried the groceries into the house, where Denny
was clearing away her homework. As Dietz put down three
water glasses, Denny looked sideways at him and said, 'We're
supposed to write a how-to paragraph for English class
tomorrow, about something we know how to do. You think
you could show me how to clean your gun?'

Dietz's startled eyes met Sarah's over Denny's head. Sarah
smiled back at him sweetly. Her eyes said, *Handle it.*

'Sure,' he said, 'be glad to.' He watched her stack her
homework on that one small spot on the buffet. 'I suppose
we might get some complaints from parents about what their
kids are learning in fifth grade, though. Why don't you write
a paragraph about how to take up the least possible space?
I notice you're good at that.'

'Who wants to know that?'

'Oh, I think that's going to be the next big thing,' Sarah
said, 'now that everybody's talking about how to leave a
smaller carbon footprint.'

'Oh.' Denny thought about it as she balanced her English
notebook on top of her math. She giggled. 'You mean like
keeping all your socks and underwear in two shoeboxes under
your bed?'

'Exactly,' Dietz said, 'and using the same table for homework and dinner and card games.'

She gave him the Dubious Denny look. 'What card games?'

'Well, if you can write that how-to paragraph fast enough,'

he said, 'I'll teach you how to play Texas hold-'em before bedtime.'

Joyce Anders managed the tricky traffic off the Interstate without mishap, apparently; on Friday morning, she walked into the station at nine o'clock precisely, wearing a perfectly fitted pale beige suit and stone-colored sling-back pumps. She had medium-length honey-colored hair that barely turned under at the ends, a discreet gleam of pearls at her throat and ears, and a slim alligator attaché case that quietly whispered, 'Money.' Her make-up appeared light to non-existent except for some cleverly composed magic that highlighted her topaz eyes.

Sarah had an interview room set up and a willing crew of monitors – Peete had traded Tobin unrevealed hours of dog work for one of the spots, and Menendez was in the other chair. He could ill afford the time, since he was going to the cemetery with Sarah in an hour, but he rationalized ignoring his voicemail, saying, 'After all, she says she's going to save us time later.'

The visitor turned down an offer of coffee, accepted water, and sat relaxed, in apparent comfort, on the small round stool. *A dozen years or so older than I am*, Sarah estimated, *but very much still in the game.*

'I know you're busy, Detective,' she said as soon as Sarah sat down, 'so I'll get right down to it.' She crossed her legs – a whisper of nylon, a whiff of sandalwood and spice. 'By now you've obviously figured out that Roger Henderson's car was at my house last weekend, and you'd like to know if he was there too.'

'Yes,' Sarah said. 'It would be very helpful if there were some way I could know that for sure.'

'Right. And since Roger and I are very old friends – and if you nosed around you'd no doubt find some people who've known us both since we were new friends – you probably wouldn't want to take my word for where he was, would you?'

'Not so much a matter of what I want, really,' Sarah said, 'as of what would hold up in court.' *I'll get right down to it, too.*

'Isn't that the truth? So what you'd need, I guess,' Joyce said, thoughtfully, 'is corroboration by a second person.'

'What his defense attorney would need, you mean,' Sarah said. 'I'm on the other side. What *I* need is enough incriminating evidence to give the county attorney so he can get somebody indicted for killing those two people in the Henderson house.'

'Uh-huh. And Roger's the husband of one of them, so he must be on the list of people you'd like to pin it on, isn't he?'

Sarah smiled and said, 'I can't discuss an ongoing investigation with you, Ms Anders, except to assure you we don't want to pin it on anybody but the culprit.'

Joyce Anders didn't smile back. The almost-yellow catlike eyes regarded Sarah solemnly. 'I'm not asking for your trade secrets, Detective. I'm trying to find out what would convince you that Roger Henderson was where his car was – at my house – Sunday night. How about corroboration by a second person, would that do it?'

'Well, yes. Probably. If the second person was, you know, not connected to you in any way. Not a relative or an employee.'

'Well, but everybody who saw him there works for me.'

'Pretty much destroys their credibility, doesn't it?'

Joyce Anders drummed a thoughtful march step on the table with her manicured nails. 'How about,' she said, and now Sarah thought maybe they really were going to get down to it, 'a document?'

'You have a document that proves Roger Henderson was at your house last weekend?'

'Yes.'

Resisting an impulse to ask her if she also had a wonderful bridge for sale, Sarah asked her, 'Did you both sign it?'

'Yes. And it's dated and timed, and witnessed by my attorney. And notarized.'

'Notarized, really? That seems . . . extremely convenient.'

'Yes. By a wonderful coincidence, it is.'

'How did you happen to be signing and notarizing this convenient piece of paper last Sunday night, Ms Anders?

'Oh, do call me Joyce. Everybody does.' A ghost of an

ironic smile flitted over her features as she recrossed her legs, and there was that wonderful faint essence of the orient again, so exotic in this grim little room. 'We signed this loan document Sunday night because we didn't get around to it Saturday night. By the time we'd figured out what we wanted to do, everybody we needed to help us with it had gone to bed. So he came back Sunday.'

Instead of going to his daughter's birthday party. What kind of a hold has this woman got on him? 'He came back Sunday night to lend you money? Why?'

Now her smile was brilliant. 'No, Detective. I'm not the one stuck with a lot of cookie-cutter houses I can't sell. He is.'

'*You* loaned *him* money?' Sarah seemed to hear little clicking noises as the facts of the Henderson case rearranged themselves around her. She asked again, 'Why?'

'I just told you. He needs a bridge loan until the credit market gets well.'

'I understand that part. I meant why would you put money into a troubled industry like the housing market?'

'We're friends.' Sarah tried to keep her face neutral, but knew a little doubt was leaking through. 'OK, a few details.' Her gaze was hooded now, looking across Sarah's shoulder at the featureless wall behind her. 'A long time ago, before he met the beautiful daughter of the Big Pooh-Bah of Tucson, Roger and I were more than friends. Then he got married and we didn't see each other for a long time. A few years ago we met again by accident and since then we've . . . kept in touch. Roger Henderson,' the artfully framed topaz eyes swung back to Sarah's face and stayed there, unwavering, 'is the best man I've ever known. He loved his wife and he tried hard to save her. He's stood between her and a lot of bullets. Now she managed to find one when he wasn't around to shield her, and left him with one more problem when he already had more than plenty. I'd like to help him with this one, if I can. He didn't kill his wife. He was in Phoenix, at my house, trying to scare up enough money to ride out the current liquidity crisis.'

'And you're prepared to show this document in court?'

'If I have to. Naturally I'm hoping that won't be necessary.'

'Naturally. I suppose it must have been rather a large amount?'

The shadow of a smile passed quickly over her face again. 'Small amounts don't do much for an operation the size of Hen-Trax.'

'It's a big risk to take for a friend.'

'Oh,' she shrugged comfortably, 'Roger will pay me back. I have no fear about that. But just to keep all the lawyers happy I now have a lien on one of his subsidiaries.' She chuckled. 'If Roger defaults I'll own a nice little machine-tool operation in Boise.'

TWELVE

'Ten o'clock mass at the cathedral,' Ray Menendez said. 'And a big crowd, it's going to take them a while to get away from there. So a few minutes after eleven by the time they're all in the cars, and then they have to drive to that new all-faiths cemetery on the east side, how long will that take?'

'Let's see, Avenida Los Reyes? Half an hour. A little more than that, for us. I'm going to make a couple phone calls and check on the status of our prisoners. Quarter of eleven, I'll be ready to go,' Sarah said.

Delaney didn't really see much merit in their going to the cemetery, but Menendez held out for it, saying they could learn a lot from seeing who showed up and how they behaved. Sarah agreed, but knew he also wanted them to be there to support Patricia. 'We asked her if there was anything we could do for her,' he told Sarah, 'and this was all she asked us for.'

'I know it's a lot to ask,' she'd said, mopping her eyes after her meltdown over her mother's cremation. 'But I feel like it would make all the difference if I could see a friendly face there tomorrow. And that sure as hell isn't going to be anybody from the Henderson clan.'

'Your father and brother still fighting?'

'Worst I've ever seen them. And to be fair, I understand why Dad's so angry. He needs to grieve for Mom and he feels like Adam has taken away all his time and space to do that. And Dad and I . . . ordinarily we're kind of partners, the two who keep things going. But I blamed him when he first got home Monday. I said if he'd been where he belonged it wouldn't have happened. I don't know how to take it back now, and he can't forget it.'

'Give it time, Patricia,' Ray Menendez said.

'And of course we'll try to come if you want us there,' Sarah said, 'if you don't think your father will object.'

'I don't care if he does,' Patricia said. 'I'm pretty sick of men and their objections. Why do they always have to run everything?' She looked at Menendez apologetically and added, 'No offense.'

'None taken,' Menendez said cheerfully. 'We're all crazy on testosterone is the problem, we just can't help ourselves.'

'As you can see he's disgustingly pleased about it,' Sarah said, and Patricia lost a little of her sad pallor as she rolled her eyes up and said, 'What can you do?'

Now Sarah checked the roster at County. Zack and Felicity had both pleaded not guilty at their preliminary hearing, and were being integrated into the system. Nino had not yet entered a plea. She phoned the Public Defenders' office to find out who was taking his case, was told all the lawyers were tied up with clients right now, but Carswell, their newest lawyer, had Nino Giardelli on his list. She wrote a note to remind herself to call him later, to suggest he come and view the interview they'd recorded yesterday. She already felt invested in Nino's defense.

'OK, you ready? Let's go,' Menendez said, a few minutes early. As much as anything, she thought, he was looking forward to getting outside on this glorious day. Tobin, coming in this morning, had said he was having trouble deciding how to feel. 'The weather's so perfect I can't concentrate on how terrible the news is.'

They were in plenty of time, she saw when they pulled into All-Faiths Memorial Park. They had the whole place to themselves. 'Look for the Garden of Saint Joseph,' Menendez said, 'that's the Catholic part.'

They pulled past the sign reading 'Please be on the lookout for snakes and scorpions' – the new cemetery was right on the edge of wild desert. Austere and impeccably tidy, every pebble raked severely within borders, it stood on a series of little rises overlooking a vast valley that sloped away to the east. Beyond the valley the purple masses of the Rincons rose into a clear sky, so blue it made Sarah's eyes water.

They wandered around the scant statuary and stone benches till Sarah said, 'Oh, there it is, the wall of crypts, see? Just ahead in the next section. Where the white statue is, in the

Garden of Saint Joseph.' They found the open niche with
Eloise Henderson's name on it.

'I wonder,' Sarah said, 'why Eloise isn't being buried in
the big Della Maggio plot up north on Oracle?'

'Patricia said the family offered, but her dad said he thought
the last few spaces there should be saved for older family
members. She thinks he wants to put as much distance
between himself and the Della Maggios as he can.'

When they saw the hearse coming, they stepped a few feet
back and stood under a palo verde, far enough away so Roger
and Adam needn't acknowledge their presence, near enough
so Patricia could see them if she looked.

The pall-bearers got out of the long black limousine behind
the hearse and the family out of the next one. Only a few
cars followed after them. Expensive vehicles had clogged
the streets around the cathedral, when they passed it – the
funeral was well attended. But the burial was for family and
close friends, and there didn't seem to be many of either. A
couple of elderly Della Maggio aunts toddled slowly toward
the wall, helped by younger cousins. There was not much
left of the clan in Tucson now, Patricia had told them, 'and
Dad comes from a small family in Texas that's never kept
in touch. His whole life has centered around taking care of
Mom and Adam and me. I kind of wonder what he'll do
now.' She gave a sad little shrug. 'Work, I guess.'

Roger Henderson, looking older and cramped in a black
suit, got out of the second limousine with his two children
following. Adam looked utterly wasted, his face the color of
chalk, his dark suit a little wrinkled and his tie askew. Patricia
was elegantly turned out in a black dress with a jacket and
a small pillbox hat with a veil. She was weeping, not making
any sound but occasionally wiping tears off her cheeks behind
the veil. She carried a small white missal, and four short-
stemmed red roses.

Another man in a dark suit got out of a car farther back
in the line, and walked up to join the family at the grave.
The cut of his elegant suit, his narrow shoes and longer
haircut said he was not from Tucson. Sarah felt a nudge on
her elbow. Menendez whispered, 'Who he?'

'Must be Uncle Theodore,' she whispered back. 'The

brother who lives in Italy.' She saw Roger glance at him once
and turn his face away. The man walked up behind Adam
and Patricia and touched their shoulders, then nudged into
a space they made between them. They each turned to him,
squeezed his hands. He bent his head and whispered something to Adam, who smiled at him out of his dead-white
face.

The priest was coming now, walking deliberately with a
Bible in his hands. Evidently not familiar with this family,
he gave them a formal nod and touched hands with Roger
before he took his place in front of the wall of crypts. At
the last moment Devon Hartford got out of still another car
at the end of the line and walked up to stand beside Roger,
on the side away from his children. Roger barely nudged his
elbow, but his body language said he was grateful to have
Hartford beside him.

The priest raised his Bible and began to read the graveside
prayers. A little breeze ruffled his white hair and lace-trimmed
vestment. It lifted Patricia's veil briefly and then dropped it
against her face, and Sarah could see tears glittering through
it. The priest paused in his solemn ritual and the pall-bearers
slid the ornate small urn containing Eloise's remains into the
niche in the wall. Patricia handed three of the red roses she
carried to the three men of the family and kept one. One after
another they stepped up to the wall, paused for a private
moment, and put the rose into the vase that had been affixed
in the door. Patricia said something, privately, to the contents
of the urn before she kissed the rose and slid it into the vase.
They all stepped back and the priest shook holy water from
a silver aspergillum on to the urn while he recited another
prayer.

Then it was over. Roger and Patricia turned from the
graveside to shake hands with the old Della Maggio aunts
and the cousins, and to thank the pall-bearers. Devon
Hartford walked to Sarah's side, looking curious, and said,
without preamble, 'Surprised to see you here, Detective.'

'Patricia asked us to come, so we did,' she said, and intro-
duced him to Menendez. 'I see Uncle Teddy made it from Italy.'

'Yes. And Adam got through the ceremony on his feet,
that's a blessing too.'

When Patricia finished hugging an ancient aunt who was wiping her face with a lace handkerchief, she turned and came toward them too, making no effort to hide the tears flowing freely down her face.

'That was nice, Patricia,' Sarah said, 'with the roses.'

'It seemed like something she'd do,' she said. 'It's hard to think what to do to make it as . . . loving . . . as she would have for one of us, you know? She always knew how to make me feel loved. So I told her "Bon voyage," when I put my rose in the vase. I said, "Don't you worry about a thing here, just enjoy the trip." Because that's what she'd have said to me, I think.' Tears were flowing freely off her chin.

'Good thing your uncle made it, huh?' Menendez said, in an agonized masculine effort to get her to stop crying.

'Actually, Madge has been around for a month or more, I think,' Patricia said. 'In and out of town, of course. Flying around as usual.'

'What?' Sarah stared at her and then at Menendez, who looked startled too. 'Uncle Teddy is Madge?'

'Yes, he's always had that nickname,' Patricia said, 'because the family name is . . . what's wrong?' She was speaking to their backs by now, because both detectives were walking away, muttering as they sidled through the stones together, moving toward Madge and the rumpled figure scuttling down the walk beside him.

'We're going to have to take him here,' Menendez said, 'like it or not.'

'I know. Damn, it's awkward. Why is he giving his keys to Adam, though?' Sarah said.

Adam had almost reached the absurdly stylish antique Jaguar hugging the curb now, and his uncle turned and began walking back toward the group by the grave. Deciding that this was no time to preserve decorum, Sarah asked Menendez, 'Can you take him by yourself?'

'Oh, hell yes,' he said, and trotted toward Madge.

Sarah ran past Menendez toward the mourners, calling out, 'Mr Henderson, Adam's not supposed to drive, is he?' She was pointing toward his son. He turned and saw the boy getting into the sleek roadster and ran toward him at once, without even a second's pause for thought. He was fast, for a big man, he still had some of his football player's muscles. He hit Madge's shoulder as he ran past him, and knocked him down.

'For God's sake, Roger,' Madge yelled after him, from the ground, 'what do you think you're doing?'

Roger had no time to answer. Adam had already closed the door and was putting the key in the ignition. But the top was down. Roger reached inside and lifted his son out of the car without even opening the door. He turned with the boy kicking and screaming in his arms, and carried him back toward Madge, who was still struggling to his feet.

'You get in that fancy car now and drive it out of here,' Roger said, 'and if I see it anywhere near my family again I'll set it on fire.'

Madge opened his mouth to protest, but saw Menendez coming, running, and Sarah beside him, holding up her badge, shouting, 'Wait!' He jumped in the Jaguar and started it, released the hand brake and rolled away as Sarah ran up yelling, 'Stop!'

'Too slow,' said Menendez, panting beside her. 'Sorry.'

'We'll get him,' Sarah said, 'the escort that came out with the funeral cortège is just down the road, come on!' Together, they ran to the squad car and jumped inside. 'Hey, Petey, stop that Jaguar that just went out the gate, will you?'

'That shouldn't be hard,' Officer Peterson said. 'Why's he driving so slow, something wrong with him?' He pulled through the cemetery gates and turned down the hill. The Jaguar was still only a block ahead.

Approaching the first intersection the Jaguar paused, cautiously, as if the driver couldn't decide which way to go. Then Peterson activated the siren and light bar on his vehicle, and Madge looked back in alarm. He accelerated suddenly, shot across the intersection, and headed down the twisting street at speed. The squad followed easily, still emitting both its 'Stop!' signals. When he saw himself ignored, Peterson activated the PA system on his mike and broadcast, in terrifying tones across the desert, 'Driver of the Jaguar, stop your vehicle at once!'

But Madge was surfing down the rolling hillocks of Avenida Los Reyes, evidently sure he could outrun Tucson's finest. There was something desperate, though, about the speed with which he approached the intersection at Twenty-Second Street, where plainly he would have to turn in order to avoid entrapment in the cul-de-sacs of the residential community just ahead.

'Why isn't he slowing down?' Peterson muttered. 'He can't make the turn at that speed.'

Madge was going to try it, though, they saw. The driver of the great little car apparently thought his skill and the fabled engineering that still made mechanics misty-eyed would be enough to carry the day.

But he was wrong. Tires shrieked on the asphalt as Madge tried to keep the Jaguar on the road through the sharp left turn. After a noisy skid, he crashed through mesquite and cactus into the sandy wash that bordered the road, and then into the brick wall that kept the wild denizens of the wash out of the yards above it.

They called 911 and the Fire Department and got plenty of prompt and skillful help, so Theodore Della Maggio was on his way to Carondolet Hospital in plenty of time to save, as Delaney later said, his drastically overvalued hide.

Menendez rode with the prisoner on his trip to the hospital, so that Sarah could stay with the Jaguar. She guarded its mangled remains as attentively as she had ever tended a wounded human suspect, making sure nobody touched it till she persuaded Delaney to send out the one person on the Homicide crew who could confirm her suspicions about the reason for the crash.

'I didn't realize what I was watching at the time,' she told Cifuentes when he got to Twenty-Second Street. 'But once he blew that turn – I think I figured it out.' She was sweating in the sandy wash, helping Cifuentes keep his rear end out of the cactus spines while he stuck his head under the wreck.

And she was mostly talking to herself, she began to realize. Because the other detective had fallen in love with the remains of an automobile almost twice his age.

'The Jaguar XKE,' Cifuentes said, 'is the car that changed everything.' Even indoors on a dark day in the dusty, crowded shop on Stone Avenue, Sarah could see his eyes shining. He had the poor bent wreck up on the hoist at the British Car Service, and had spent all day in the company of men who felt as he did about the importance of good workmanship. And Delaney, Ray, and Sarah were gathered around him now, waiting to see a display of his expertise. He was a happy man.

'After the war, this baby put the glamour back in the car biz. Six cylinders, and dual overhead cams, it could almost rip up the road. This one's still got the original brass fittings, see?'

'And the wooden steering wheel, look,' Tobin said.

'You were going to show us the brake system?' Sarah's interest in automotive engineering never extended much beyond, 'Does it run?' and, if answered in the negative, 'How soon can you fix it?' Also, she had signed statements on her desk from Felicity and Zack, both of whom had been more than willing to tell the truth in exchange for slightly reduced charges after they had watched the DVD of Nino's interview. The important thing was to nail Madge, the truly evil plotter of the plan, Delaney had agreed. Now she was anxious to wrap up this last bit of physical evidence and forget about the Henderson case until the trial.

'Yes. This happens to be the '62 model. The first year they went for a dual brake system, an extra safety measure that they were rightly proud of and bragged about plenty. Two cylinders here,' he pointed under the hood, 'and separate hydraulic lines for the front and back wheels. Our man put a pinhole opening in both lines, right here, close to the cylinders. Just a tiny hole in each line and he must have done it at the last minute, so he'd still have enough pressure on the brakes to drive it to the cemetery.'

'And there's no chance this happened in the accident?' Delaney asked.

'No,' Cifuentes said. 'You can see this portion of the firewall was untouched, though the front was crumpled. We believe we may have retrieved some DNA from this section around the holes that's cleaner than the rest, too – we're waiting on the lab for that. Either way, we'll remove this section of the lines, and the empty cylinders, to show the jury. But I wanted you to see them in place first, the way I did. In addition, we can point out the odd driving behavior that Sarah observed.'

'He was attempting to control his speed by downshifting,' Sarah said, 'and using the hand brake. He didn't dare tell Roger Henderson the car was disabled. So he thought he could just mosey away very slowly, but then Petey hit the siren and he panicked. When he tried to speed away, he lost it.'

'I have to say,' Cifuentes said, 'that was one damn smart call on your part, Sarah. Especially since –' he let his eyes play over the shop and yard where heaped car bodies and parts vied for space with workbenches and tools and catalogs, and happy men working patiently in the crowded aisles – 'you really don't give a damn about cars, do you?'

'Nope. Just people,' Sarah said, 'and I'm pleased to say I think we did some people a favor this time. When Patricia Henderson found out her old sweetie of an uncle was hatching a plot to kill her mother the whole time he was enjoying her generosity – and Adam realized his father saved his life pulling him out of that car – well, there's kind of a family reunion going on at the Henderson house this week.'

'So Adam's ready to be a good boy now?' Delaney's face said, Oh, please.

'Not yet. But getting ready to go into detox. Nearby, this time, so he gets visits. It *could* work,' she insisted, to the dubious faces around her.

'Sure,' Delaney said.

'Yeah, and both Henderson kids and half a dozen of their Della Maggio cousins have been calling me for two days,' Menendez said, 'asking me to find out if Madge killed his own parents last year the way he just tried to kill Adam.'

'What?' Delaney stared. 'No way in hell we're going to get any proof of that now.'

'Probably not,' Sarah said, 'But Devon Hartford says they all wondered at the time how a careful driver like Fabian Della Maggio could have hit that bridge abutment on a nice clear day. He's anxious to help if we decide to reopen the case. He feels bad because he . . . well,' she said, suddenly aware of how much space their four bodies were taking up in the tiny, crowded shop, 'I guess we better get out of the way here and let these people work.'

Later, when they were alone in the car on the way back to the station, Delaney said, 'I can't imagine Devon Hartford feeling bad about himself. Did he really say that?'

'Yes. He came to see me to confirm for himself that "brother Teddy," as he always calls him, has really been arrested and charged with his sister's murder. He feels a lot of responsibility for this tragedy, he says. "I'll do anything I can to help you put the ungrateful little whelp away," he told me.'

'Why would the lawyer feel responsible?'

'Remember when I asked him if he'd notified the brother about Eloise changing the prenup?'

'Yeah. He said he couldn't because it had to be a secret.'

'Yes. But he found out later that Eloise gave in to one of her impulses and told Teddy what she was planning. She said it was just too delicious to keep to herself any longer, she had to share it with someone. "But don't worry," she said. "Teddy won't tell."'

'I still don't see why Hartford would feel responsible.'

'He said he never thought to ask her if she told Teddy they'd also added a codicil to her will, since it was several months yet till the anniversary and she wanted to make certain. She said, "In case I step in front of a truck before then, I don't want anybody to be able to change it back." So in a funny way it seems as if she was really kind of on to how much her brother wanted her money to replace what he'd squandered, but he thinks she couldn't admit it to herself. Eloise was good at sweeping stuff under the rug, he said, she'd always had to be. Now he thinks, if he'd only sent that information to Theodore, Eloise could still be alive.'

'Wow. There's a dismal thought.'

'Yeah. I told him he should quit beating up on himself. Remember, I said, you told me yourself he hardly ever read your letters.'

'He did say that, didn't he? I believe it, too – brother Teddy's really a waste of skin. Speaking of families, was it you who steered Cifuentes to the Verna Talbot case?'

'Uh . . . yeah. I thought maybe . . . we were all so snowed under at the time—'

'Uh-huh. And you decided to give him a leg up out of the doghouse so he'd tell you about his dates with Eloise. Right?'

No way am I going to answer that. 'I didn't know at the time that he would turn out to be the resident local automotive expert,' Sarah said. 'But wasn't that lucky?'

'Uh-huh. He did a good job of chasing down that lead you gave him about the pearl necklace, too.'

'Oh?'

'The older daughter had it all along. She lied to Tobin when he asked her if she had touched anything in the house. She knew her sister would put up a fight for that necklace if she saw it, so she got it out of the house and told Tobin everything was just the way her mother left it.' He was getting pinker, remembering.

'She didn't kill Verna for it, though, did she?'

'No. She can prove she was home in Anacortes that whole week. I don't think we'll ever know who killed Verna.' He was scratching his ears now.

'Why'd she tell Cifuentes the truth?'

'You have to ask? Didn't he explain to you what a way he has with women?' Delaney looked as if he'd just stepped in something bad.

'And cars,' she said, 'he has a way with them too.' Because Cifuentes had done her two favors on this case and she didn't want to see him get marked down again.

'Well, yes,' Delaney said. 'The car thing, now that might come in handy.'